THE WEIGHT OF GLASS

ALSO BY TAMARA L. MILLER

Into the Fall

THE WEIGHT OF GLASS

A THRILLER

TAMARA L. MILLER

This is a work of fiction. Names, characters, organizations, places, events, and incidents are either products of the author's imagination or are used fictitiously. Otherwise, any resemblance to actual persons, living or dead, is purely coincidental.

Published by Thomas & Mercer, Seattle

www.apub.com

EU product safety contact:
Amazon Media EU S. à r.l.
38, avenue John F. Kennedy, L-1855 Luxembourg
amazonpublishing-gpsr@amazon.com

ISBN-13: 9781662526718 (paperback)
ISBN-13: 9781662526701 (digital)

Cover design by Lisa Amoroso
Cover images: © The Rauschen Collection / plainpicture; © Alex Dumitrescu / Getty; © Anna Sorokina / Stocksy

Printed in the United States of America

There is only so much a woman can do to help her children through the hard, dark, spinning sorrows of time and the world.

—Guy Gavriel Kay, *River of Stars*

Intro

The taste of metal and burnt flesh brought her to her senses. Cold, hard concrete kissed her cheek. Grit, like violent Pop Rocks, scraped the inside of her mouth, while a silent beat thudded inside her skull. Her eyes, still closed, filled with water behind the lids, but it did nothing to soothe the sting. Her palms throbbed, likely from the fall—hard—to the pavement. She smelled dust and rain and the iron tang of blood.

She remembered a whooshing sound, like a wingbeat. Her ears were numb now, unable to arrange the order of sound. A deafening ringing obliterated even the hammer of her own heart, which clawed against her chest like a wild creature desperate to be free.

She let her eyes flutter, slowly teasing the lashes apart until an image emerged, like an underexposed photograph. Black asphalt filled part of the frame. Beyond, raised gray pavement and an iron culvert, both at the wrong angle. She tried to move, but her limbs refused to obey. She willed her fingers to trace the edges of her existence.

She was on the ground, alive.

Reality hit like an anvil, robbing her of the next breath. An explosion. There had been an explosion. She had been running away from the car and was thrown to the ground. Someone had been in the driver's seat.

With effort, she pushed against the ground with her hands, bringing her torso to sitting. Her palms screamed at the pain. Her legs flopped into alignment, so that she sat like a rag doll, legs splayed and head bent over her chest. The world now righted, she raised her head.

Flames still licked at the car. The driver's door had been blown off. A chasm filled the space where the roof had once been. Around the gap, metal hung, like deranged icicles.

She stood. The world seemed to rock beneath her feet, and for a pulse beat, everything went black, before shape and color solidified. The broad outlines of squat buildings, the black road, power lines running like veins above the street. To her right and left, the street was calm, almost serene, under the sickly yellow light of streetlamps. Two men in security uniforms were running from the building across the street; one carried a fire extinguisher like a sword.

Blue and red lights shimmered from the far end of the street. She couldn't hear the sirens, but the colors moved toward her.

Leave, *her mind screamed.* Get away.

She turned her back on the approaching vehicles and disappeared into the night.

Chapter 1

Emma

Emma Meadows knew something was wrong with the kraft-paper-covered box. It stood out against the piles of bright gold and bellowing red beneath the Christmas tree like a blight. In the twenty years she'd been celebrating the holidays with her exuberant extended family, not once had she seen so little effort and style applied to a gift.

Then again, what was it they said about surprises in plain packages? Or was it small packages? Emma didn't have time to puzzle it out before her name was called from the kitchen. She threw on a plastic smile and resumed her hostess role, snatching up an empty tray of hors d'oeuvres and letting the brown package settle into the recesses of her mind, where it lay cantankerous and festering for the rest of the afternoon.

"Be there in a sec," Emma said reluctantly.

Mark, her husband, was one of four siblings in an Italian Canadian clan, all of whom were now in her house with their respective families, perched here and there, like turkey vultures at a roadside feast. Meadows family get-togethers—infused with loving arguments and habitual grudges—were more performances than actual gatherings, orchestrated and dramatized by all the affection and frustration of a close-knit family crammed into an enclosed space. This family was adoring, boisterous, and exhausting.

Emma often sought out quiet corners or lingered longer than needed in the bathroom to catch her breath.

In truth, she hadn't wanted to host the family for Christmas this year, but a burst pipe at her sister-in-law's house had left a vacuum. In the end, it was decided their rambling late nineteenth-century farmhouse had the space, including a dining room large enough to fit a children's table and the dogs that inevitably parked themselves beneath it.

Emma would have preferred a simple holiday with Mark; their daughter, Jaden—home from university for the holidays—and their golden retriever, Winnie. Before she could consider alternatives, however, her in-laws had descended with boxes of panettone and an army of casserole dishes. Now she had a full house, a burgeoning headache, and apprehension lodged in her gut, hard and jagged, like a sharp-edged stone.

Each time Emma returned to the living room, dropping off trays or topping up wineglasses, her eyes flitted to the dreary package under the tree. Fragments of words and shared laughter flowed over her like a warm wind, voices merging into a kaleidoscope of conversation.

"I said to the guy . . ."

"The doll was so expensive . . ."

She was sure the box hadn't been there before the onslaught of family had arrived. No one in Mark's family was subtle or reserved. Their tastes ran loud and proud, outdoing each other with style and garishness. She couldn't think who would have brought a plain brown package. Had no one else noticed? The box's presence jangled a cautionary nerve in Emma's brain; it didn't belong.

"Hey, does anyone know who brought that plain brown one?" Emma said. Her words barely pierced the cacophony of chatter around her.

"Which one?" Sheila, her sister-in-law, said as she came into the room with a tray of bloodred cranberry cocktails.

"The one without Christmas wrap," Emma said.

"Ugh. No idea," Sheila said, breezing past her, her Medusa-like curls piled high above her head. "It was on the front step when I got here. Someone must have dropped it on the way in. They're going to get a few choice words from me about effort, though, that's for sure. That wrapping is ugly."

Back in the kitchen, Emma poured herself a large glass of pinot grigio and stood by the sliding glass doors that looked out on the backyard. The wine helped dull a building edge along her spine but did nothing to loosen the knot sitting between her shoulder blades.

Pale afternoon light squeezed through gray clouds, smoothing out contours in the snow and flattening angles. She watched the gentle swirl of thick snowflakes with disdain. The holiday-card scene, with its light-footed squirrels and clinging icicles, seemed tailor made for Christmas Day, but Emma knew better. The universe never gave without taking its pound of flesh. A storm was forecast, fueled by a stream of arctic air and the north country's determination.

Emma had lived in White Falls for over twenty years and still hadn't made peace with the full force of the Canadian winters here. The unpredictability of the weather wasn't just vicious, it was vindictive. The town sat on the shores of Lake Superior, a capricious beast that took its role as the nastiest of the Great Lakes seriously. The few municipalities that dotted the northern shoreline were nestled into protective bays, and for good reason. Emma had learned early on, this part of the world could both seduce and kill you, depending on the day. From the first November snowfall to the breakup of the April ice, disquiet lived in her core. And this year, it fed on a new apprehension, one born of her own making. She found herself spinning within its clutches, like an insect trapped in a web.

You could leave. The pesky recurring thought flitted about in her head. It had been surfacing uncomfortably lately. A reminder that no choice or marriage or circumstance was ever permanent. Most lives are shaped by an endless litany of decisions and the inevitable fallout from each turning point. When to wake up? What to wear? Who to see? Whether to stay? Each answer shifted the path in front of us just enough that the outcome would always be fickle.

Emma batted aside the irksome thought as if it were a gnat, her decision rooting her to this place. At least for another day.

She had a house full of hungry people and a dinner to get on the table. Duty called. Yet still, she couldn't pull herself away from the window. She let her eyes relax, watched shapes emerge and recede in the shifting flurry, like a 3D picture. Snow accumulated on the windowsill. She imagined the bushes, the fence, and eventually the house itself disappearing beneath its crushing weight until even the memory of this place vanished.

A sideswiping gust sent a snowburst down from the cedar bushes that lined the edge of the yard. Squinting, Emma thought she glimpsed a hooded figure, moving behind the tree line. She stepped back, closing her eyes to readjust her depth of focus; when she opened them again, only the trembling cedars greeted her.

Not now, she thought. *Get a hold of yourself.*

A voice broke through Emma's morbid daydream. "The pot's bubbling over."

She looked across the kitchen to see Mark on the other side of the island, an empty tray in his hands and a curious expression on his face. From where she stood, Emma could see starchy water tumbling over the lip of a royal blue Le Creuset pot on the stove. She heard a hissing at the back of her brain without registering its meaning. She waited for her body to obey her mind's will.

"Oh, crap," she said finally.

"I got it," Mark said, his ever-present cowlick bouncing through the kitchen toward the stove. He lifted the pot effortlessly and dropped boiled potatoes into a waiting colander in the sink. Easy laughter escaped his lips as steam engulfed his face.

"Thanks," Emma said, coming back to herself. "Not sure where I went for a minute."

Mark looked at her thoughtfully, a question deepening between his brows. He opened his mouth, but the words were stalled by a burst of laughter from the other room. A reminder of what Emma had been doing before her wandering imagination had, yet again, pulled her away.

"Before I forget to say it," Mark said, the question on his face vanishing like lines on an Etch A Sketch. "Thanks for letting us host again this year. I know it was a lot to ask, especially at the last minute." He wrapped his arms around her waist, holding her in with a delicacy that betrayed his underlying concern.

"You OK?" he asked.

What could Emma say? That the laughter and joviality pulled her nerves so taut she thought her shoulders might snap? Should she admit she hadn't slept more than a few hours a night in the last two weeks? Not since she'd stumbled across an online article that mentioned a name, one she thought she'd buried long ago. Should she tell her husband that a past she'd never shared with him now had her imagining boogeymen in the backyard?

No. Bringing Mark into her mind right now would only hurt him. And she'd hurt too many people in her life already.

"Don't be silly. I'm happy to host. Besides, your family always brings enough food to feed a small village, so I only really need to worry about the turkey and potatoes," she said, gesturing to a mountain of casserole dishes and dessert pans teetering on the counter.

Guilt crawled up Emma's back, nestled into her brain, and settled in for a nap. She gave Mark's arm a small squeeze.

"How are charades going?" she said, eager to change the subject as she reluctantly drew herself away from him. She pulled heavy cream, butter, and chives out of the fridge for the potatoes.

"Actually, not so good. Mamma keeps asking people to speak up. Says she can't hear them," Mark said, his chuckle sinking into the lopsided grin that defined his face.

A sudden screech of laughter broke the conversation. Two young nieces tore through the kitchen, Winnie and a goldendoodle hot on their trail. Nails scrabbled at the hardwood floor as the dogs careened around the island, almost throwing Emma off balance.

Mark's full-throated laughter combined with the girls' wild giggles rose into a gleeful wall of sound.

The joy in the moment shattered Emma's heart. The past was too much with her, stealing moments of contentment and frivolity like a thief striking from the darkness in her head.

"I'm just going to take Winnie out for a pee, before she leaves a puddle of excitement behind her," Emma said, reaching for her coat and the leash that hung on a set of hooks by the back door. Winnie trotted over at the familiar rattle. "Can you find Jaden to take care of the potatoes? She said she'd help. I'll just spin around the block quickly. Be back before the turkey timer goes."

"Sure, we got this," Mark said.

Emma felt his eyes follow her to the door. She didn't look back.

As soon as the door slid open, the dog bounded over fresh snow in the backyard, leaping and snapping at thick, juicy flakes. Emma watched from the threshold. Would she sniff the hooded figure of Emma's imagination behind the cedars? Winnie just rolled in the backyard snow, her mouth dropping open into an anthropomorphized smile.

Emma shook her head at her own stupidity and followed Winnie out the door.

Their two-story colonial farmhouse stood out in the hastily built surrounding suburb. Somehow, their heritage home had survived the bulldozers and cookie-cutter homes. The contained order of the neighborhood, and White Falls itself, had always seemed an illusion to Emma. Deep, dense woods lay in wait just beyond the municipal lines, waiting for their chance to reclaim territory lost to concrete and human vanity, a forest that hemmed the town against the largest freshwater lake in the world. Everything about life here was defined by the elements and a coastline chiseled out of broad rock walls and choking wilderness. Existence here meant constantly recarving a place against Mother Nature's onslaught.

At Emma's whistle, Winnie trotted toward her and fell into step. They rounded the house. A few cars lined the street, but the neighbors were all tucked into their homes for the day. Through the front window,

Emma watched the family—her family—laughing and gesturing while her own pale reflection hovered on the glass. She knew their names and their faces, and shared bits of their lives, yet standing on the outside, she couldn't help but wonder how well you could truly know anyone. *Each of us has parts of ourselves we hide away,* she thought. The only question was how much and how deep.

A harsh west wind whipped at her face, sluicing away body heat. She tied her scarf a little tighter in defiance and headed for the road. As she walked, Emma's thoughts meandered to the chance encounter that had led her to this family and the life she now claimed as her own.

She'd been twenty-two and driving into an angry spring rain for hours when the revolving sign of the Half Moon Diner appeared out of the murk like an illusion or a pending mistake. With no destination in mind and no life ahead of her or behind, the restaurant had seemed as good a place as any to stop.

The smell of burnt toast and nostalgia had made her stomach churn when she walked through the door. Everything, including the walls, dripped in grease. She'd ordered a coffee and found a corner booth by the window. After a cursory nod, the waitress politely ignored the sad girl in the corner, preferring to chat with the cook while she filled saltshakers.

The jangle of a bell announced the arrival of the only other customer. Emma was vaguely aware of whistling and conversation but kept her head down, staring into her untouched coffee and batting away unbidden tears.

"You OK, Miss?" The voice was warm and genuine.

Emma nodded her head. Hoped he'd go away.

"I'm Mark," he said as he slid onto the bench across from her. "Mind if I join you?"

Emma looked up into eyes that were the pale-blue color of a dawn sky. A club sandwich and limp french fries sat on a plate in front of him.

"As you wish," she said, desperate for and terrified of company.

"Hey!" His eyes lit up. "Now I know I'm at the right table."

Emma smiled, despite herself.

"I hope you don't mind," he said, with that crooked smile. "You look like you could use a friend." Though she was a stranger to him, she felt his empathy and kindness like a familiar song on the radio.

That first meeting with Mark had been over twenty years ago, and now here Emma was: a wife, a mother, and a completely different person from the one who'd cried in front of a stranger in a dilapidated diner.

In another way, she was reinventing herself yet again now that Jaden, her only child, was out of the house. As Emma watched Jaden forge her own path into adulthood, memories of the young life Emma herself had left behind dribbled into her mind with more frequency, like a slow leak she couldn't trace. Still, she couldn't bring herself to tell Mark about the past she'd been trying to outrun.

Choices, Emma thought with a shake of her head and a small snort.

But what if that past had started to tap at her shoulder in unexpected ways? She thought again of the news article containing a name she never again wanted to utter. Its presence in her mind was making her paranoid. Then again, what was it they said about paranoia? Just because you have it doesn't mean someone isn't out to get you.

Maybe Emma was testing the Fates, and if so, she hoped they would fly right over the dense forest in which she had ensconced herself and leave her be with her secrets.

Chapter 2

EMMA

Lulling in an after-dinner inertia, Emma let herself sink into the deep L-shaped couch. The world outside had tipped into full night. The fluffy flakes from earlier in the day had morphed into a driving snow that slammed sideways against the windows, riding the wind.

Inside the Meadowses' mismatched living room—where family heirlooms shared space with dog-clawed leather armchairs and exposed wooden beams—soft table lights chased away the gloom. A distressed oriental rug in dark reds and blues held the space together, but no matter how hard Emma tried, the room always had a lived-in look. Never more so than now, with bodies sprawled on anything resembling a seat, including the floor, and empty dessert plates cluttering the coffee table. A sweet and sultry ice wine rolled over Emma's tongue, settling comfortably into her full belly. She'd read somewhere that wine and tea helped with digestion. She really hoped that was true.

The earlier disquiet and the oddity of the plain brown package had fled from her mind with the flurry of kids opening presents, followed by dinner, always an orchestration with this many people. Now, with a half a bottle of pinot grigio and a second glass of ice wine mollifying her head, both seemed less consequential. The package had clearly been opened in the tumult. A small kitchen crew of relatives tended to the remaining dishes, giving Emma her first opportunity to sit down since early this morning.

In the far corner, Jaden perched on an overstuffed armchair while she tuned a guitar. The settling of the notes brought down the volume in the room, and Emma felt herself lean into the comfort to be found as she watched her daughter's hand pluck lazily at the strings.

Though she still saw her little girl in Jaden's heart-shaped face and toothy grin, a self-assured young woman had somehow emerged over the last few years, one Emma encouraged but didn't always welcome. She noticed small changes every time Jaden came home. This time it was a handful of auburn highlights in her caramel brown hair, more angles to her face, and the condescending maturity of a not-quite-yet-grown adult who believed they understood the world. Her daughter was changing, leaning into a life that Emma would never have chosen for her but finding her purpose. It was all natural and needful, but Emma couldn't help pining for the toddler with the unfortunate bowl cut who would jump into her arms for an "uppa" not that long ago.

"Supposed to be about twenty centimeters before it stops," Finn, her brother-in-law, said, picking up his own guitar. His voice, laced with amusement, matched his arched eyebrow. "Forecasters keep waving their arms in panic."

"When are they gonna learn?" Mark said, mirroring his brother's tone.

"Steer into the slide." Several Meadows voices and glasses rose with the family joke.

The reference to driving in winter conditions—and turning the wheels toward the direction of the slide if the car starts to slip—was a de facto family motto. The Meadows siblings had all been born and raised in White Falls. Some had left, for college or work opportunities, but they all eventually came back home. They were as much a part of this place as the red maples and stubborn-rooted jack pines. And winter was their playground.

A few strums of guitar strings resonated against the chatter. When the second guitar joined, the room took a breath. Emma didn't need to guess what the first song would be. It was always the same.

The Gordon Lightfoot song about the *Edmund Fitzgerald*, the doomed freighter on Lake Superior, was an anthem along these shores. Laced with melancholy, the lyrics had their own beauty and wonder. Harmonies lifted to the rafters, pushing out against a cold night. Emma knew all the words, but she never sang along, fearful that joining in would court tragedy. Experience and superstition always stilled her lips.

She let her eyes travel around the living room, taking in the smiles and relaxed vibratos. Sheila caught her eye as her sister-in-law stepped into the room, a flash of recall brightening her face. She ducked out for a second and returned to hand Emma the plain brown paper package.

"I rescued this from the kids," Sheila said in a stage whisper beneath the music. "They were in a bit of a feeding frenzy, so I grabbed it when I saw your name on it."

Though the singing hadn't stopped, curious eyes turned toward Emma. She felt a flush spread through her body. Was it the booze or the attention?

Or something worse?

Emma turned the package over in her hand and froze.

For Emma, with grace was scrawled along the back in tight penciled script.

Nothing obvious suggested that menace lay beneath the brown paper, but Emma felt it. The apprehension that she'd tucked away exploded, a sour vinegar taste in her mouth. She swallowed, feeling the burn along her gullet.

Emma slipped a finger beneath the seam of the wrapping, splitting the tape with one smooth motion. The stiff, rough paper sprang open, relieved of the burden. A shock of smooth glass and tarnished brass lay like a flare. Her heart vaulted to her throat. She knew what this was. She'd seen it before. In another lifetime.

A glass music box, the size of an outstretched palm with metal piping along the edges and clusters of tiny flowers etched into the lid and sides, glared up at her. A warning and an accusation. The beveled edges captured sprigs of light in the dim room, drawing every eye toward it.

Emma hadn't noticed when the song ended or when the chatter had returned to the room as other song suggestions were bandied about. She heard none of the applause or encouraging laughter. Every sense she had was trained on the familiar box, a feral piece of history in cut glass and tarnished brass.

Maybe this is just a strange coincidence, she thought futilely.

Though she knew what to expect, Emma couldn't stop herself from opening the lid. In the pause before the family launched into the next song, small, tinny notes found their way to her ears.

Chance had no place in this.

Not wanting to draw attention to herself, Emma gently laid the music box on the coffee table. The singers started up again, but she didn't register their voices or the song they'd chosen. She ran her hand over the coarse paper on her lap, shaky fingers smoothing down the folds until she found what she was looking for.

Written on the inside of the paper in scratchy handwriting, not visible to anyone else in the room, but clear as ice to Emma, was a message.

I know it was you.

Chapter 3

Emma

Emma stood in the middle of the grocery aisle. In front of her, neat rows of cans stood at attention like miniature soldiers waiting for orders. She sighed. Struggled to remember why she'd even come here in the first place.

The house was teeming with leftovers from yesterday's Christmas dinner. The trip to the grocery store wasn't about food. It was about escape. Emma was finding it harder to keep her writhing anxiety at bay. Every time she opened her mouth, she felt it wriggle up her throat like live baitfish on a hook.

I know it was you rang like a demented mantra in Emma's head.

She hadn't slept much the night before, and when she had drifted off, she dreamed of the imaginary hooded figure moving between the cedars. Twice, she rose, softly so as not to disturb Mark, and stood at the window watching the dark, empty street.

All morning, she glimpsed the music box abandoned on the coffee table—a warning and a grief—grabbing for her attention like an unruly child. She almost told Mark about the box, convinced herself that releasing the truth would solve all her problems. Instead, she looked into his expectant eyes and swallowed it down, pushing it into the deep recesses where it had dwelled for over twenty years. Until last night.

By the time Jaden came into the kitchen at midday, wearing Hello Kitty pajama pants and a stained tank top, Emma felt her nerves strung taut as piano wire.

"Well, you're actually gracing us with your presence before noon," Emma said.

She pushed aside a quiver in her voice, aiming for a casualness that came out more as a scold. Mark, seated at the kitchen island, looked up from the crossword he'd been doing on an iPad. His gaze moved slowly between the women, a bystander to the lionesses' prowl.

A grunt rode out on a tiny nod from Jaden as she shuffled toward the fridge. She pulled out a slab of chocolate cake.

"That's a lot of fat and sugar first thing in the morning. Especially with nothing else in your stomach," Emma said.

What was she doing? All she wanted was calm. Yet worry and nagging had become the refuge for her anxiety. Jaden's response further shattered Emma's illusion of any sense of control.

Jaden rolled her eyes. "I'm good," she said. She grabbed a jug of milk from the fridge and sloshed a healthy portion into a glass.

As Jaden turned, Emma saw it.

"Is that a tattoo?" she said, managing to squint and raise an eyebrow at the same time.

"Fuhh—gsicle," Jaden said, her head rolling back and a sigh jumping from her mouth.

Jaden had been home for four days, and somehow Emma hadn't noticed the blooming cherry-tree branch creeping along her right shoulder and upper arm. The design wasn't finished but was clearly visible.

A slow drip of tension leaked into the room as Emma stepped closer to her daughter, her gaze flitting between Jaden's face and her arm, like a hummingbird looking for a place to land. Emma could feel Mark's eyes, annoying and vigilant, at her back.

"Did you know?" Emma said, turning a burgeoning wrath on her husband.

Not only was her baby changing, but now, she'd marred herself so that her very skin was unrecognizable to Emma. The kitchen spun around her, nausea and dread roiling in her belly. A litany of risks floated through her mind—disease, infection, regret—all coming for her little girl with the terrible choices she was making.

"Ya, she showed me last night. You like it?" Mark said, the forced nonchalance obvious.

"It's for Nonno," Jaden said, standing taller and challenging Emma to say more. An alliance between father and daughter. It had been the same about Jaden's decision to go to Toronto for university. Emma had been set against it, but the tag team—and Jaden's relentlessness—had worn her into acquiescence.

The pink-petaled flowers, it seemed, were a tribute to Jaden's late grandfather, one of the early casualties of the COVID pandemic. Mark's father had obsessively tended to his garden, gathering all the grandkids every fall to help make wild-cherry jelly. Jaden hadn't been able to go the last time. A regret she now carried like a scar.

Emma felt the anger dull just enough for the unsaid to remain on her lips. She held Jaden's eyes for a breath longer, recognized her child's unbending will, and turned away. Yet another buried argument lying between them.

Quiet descended. Mark returned to his crossword. Jaden pulled a long stainless steel knife from a wooden block. She spun to face the kitchen island and, with a flourish, lifted the cake bell. The smell of chocolate and orange extract made Emma's stomach turn. She was losing them. Bit by bit, the two people she trusted and clung to were stepping away from her. And if they learned the truth, they'd abandon her completely. Emma's dread was a silent scream. She moved around the kitchen, straightening the fruit bowl on the island and rearranging spoons in the drawer.

Jaden glided the knife through the spongy cake and aimed a large piece onto a waiting plate. She missed, hitting the counter instead.

Emma watched her daughter in profile, her face sitting atop the cherry branch like the angel on a Christmas tree. It was wrong. All of it was wrong.

Jaden scooped the piece of cake onto the plate.

"You might as well just throw that out. You can't possibly eat it now," Emma said. "It'll be crawling with bacteria." She moved around the island like an automaton, reaching for the cleaning solution and a roll of paper towels. She sprayed the counter in short, jerky motions.

"These counters are cleaner than a surgical table," Jaden said. "If anything's going to get me these days, it's going to be this hangover or a boomer-created catastrophe. Certainly not a bacterial infection from a piece of cake."

Emma scrubbed the counter as if she were trying to reach through the varnish to the ends of the earth. Jaden's words, while flippant, buried an incontrovertible truth. A mother's protection had limits. Especially if the very threat was Emma herself.

"You sure you don't want some?" Jaden said, her words stunted by the huge bite she'd just shoveled into her mouth.

Emma set down the sprayer and left the kitchen, her mind traveling a path she knew her body would soon have to follow.

"It's really good," Jaden had said to Emma's retreating back.

The grocery aisle in front of Emma blended like a watercolor painting left out in the rain. Fluorescent overhead lights obliterated shadows until shapes no longer held meaning.

"Excuse me," said a testy voice. A grocery cart brushed past Emma's hip.

A woman in a red ski jacket moved along the aisle, until she, too, disappeared into a blotch of color on the horizon. Emma stayed where she was, unmoving. Shoppers flowed around her. Some looked back; most steadfastly ignored the strange woman parked in the middle of the canned-vegetable aisle.

Images from Emma's past tumbled through her mind like water finding its way through stone. The music box had been the explosive and the carefully worded message written on the ugly brown paper the fuse.

I know it was you.

There were only two people in the world who could have known the significance of that music box. One was dead. The other, Emma had thought she'd left behind decades ago.

She'd worked hard—harder than most—to crush her past. She just hadn't been prepared for it to come pounding on her front door. For the first time since arriving in White Falls, Emma no longer felt she'd escaped the consequences of long-ignored mistakes.

Her legs wobbled. Looking down—though she knew it was impossible—she saw the lump of her heart hammering against her chest. Her hands shook. She gripped the grocery cart handle until nails pierced flesh. All she could think to do was get out.

She abandoned the empty cart and lurched out of the store. Muscles fought against her. Breath came in short, rickety strokes.

Loss had a cruel way of slithering into relationships, a creature tainting everything that came after by hiding in the darker corners of the mind. Mark was a good man, she knew that, and she believed he would always love her and provide for their family. But she didn't trust that either he or Jaden would stay if they learned the whole truth about her past.

She had to stop that from happening. She just didn't know how.

Cold hit Emma as soon as the electric doors swished open. The slap of air did nothing to stop the sweat pouring down her back. She shuffled to the curb, forcing passersby to step around her. Emma gazed out at the parking lot, willing herself to remember where she'd parked the car, but all she saw was a useless sea of vehicles. She used every ounce of energy she had to keep standing, keep breathing.

She shuffled a few feet away from the door, finally giving in to the will of her body by letting herself slide to the ground, her back against the cold, rough brick of the building. She propped her elbows on her knees and gulped at air with short, shallow breaths. The smells of exhaust and wet pavement were nauseating, but she kept downing air. Was she having a heart attack? Or a stroke? She needed to call someone. But how? She couldn't think. The edges of her vision blackened.

"Just breathe." A voice came to Emma as if through layers of fabric. "Slow, deep breaths of air through your nose."

Emma felt a gently firm hand on her shoulder and another on her wrist. She could vaguely see the outline of a person, head bowed over their watch.

"Do you have any pain or numbness?" the voice said.

Emma managed to shake her head.

"Can you tell me your name?"

"Emma. Emma Meadows."

"Hi, Emma. I know first aid. OK if I sit with you for a bit? I think you may be having a panic attack."

No, no, no, no, Emma's mind screamed. *I'm dying. I'm dying.* "OK," she said.

Emma felt something solid and warm drum on her hand.

"I'm tapping my fingers against your hand. Can you feel it?"

Emma nodded.

"Good, that's good. You're going to be OK. Just concentrate on your hand. Tune in to the feeling and listen for the sound my fingers are making."

Emma did. Her vision started to clear. She saw a woman's hand, dark with electric-blue nail polish. A crackle of lines, like dried earth over an abandoned field. Emma had no idea how long she watched the hand's slow, steady rhythm; it may have been a minute, it may have been twenty.

"Great. Now I want you to try to take a full breath through your nose and all the way to your belly."

Emma did as she was asked. The woman's voice, mellow and with a hint of a New York accent, felt like a balm on sun-scorched skin.

Emma lifted her head.

"Hey there, welcome back," said a middle-aged woman with easy laugh lines and a gap-toothed smile who crouched in front of her. She moved to sit on the ground beside Emma and stretched her legs out as if they were a couple of teenagers eating lunch by the school lockers.

Emma tried to smile back, wasn't sure she managed it. She had never felt more tired in her whole life. If it had been possible, she would have lain down on the ground and taken a long nap.

"How did you know?" Emma finally said, though the words were stilted and cracked.

"That you were having a panic attack?"

Emma nodded.

"Former military medic. Comes with the territory," the woman said with a shrug, though a sadness crept into her voice.

"Thank you," Emma said in a croak. She tried to get up. Wobbled.

"Whoa, whoa there. I wouldn't go anywhere just yet. Give yourself a few minutes. Is this your first?"

Emma sat back down, shaking her head. "No, but it's been a while."

In truth, it had been years since her last full-blown panic attack, so long that she'd forgotten how her body could betray her so thoroughly. The first time had been shortly after arriving in White Falls. She had been young and stupid and convinced she could outrun tragedy. She'd been wrong. It took a year of therapy and a lot of hard work, but with the help of a good psychologist, Emma had found a path to recovery. The nightmares had waned, until the debilitating anxiety was a memory among many from her past.

"Any new triggers?" the woman asked. Her tone was conversational, as if she'd asked Emma about the weather.

Emma looked into the woman's eyes. She saw concern and a hint of sageness. There was much she could lay in her compassionate hands: the fear drawing Emma's mind to horrible places, the untethered feeling of being watched, the conviction that the world was lovely, dark, and deep, and it could kill you.

Some beliefs, though, were too rooted to unearth. How could Emma explain everything that she held on to? The fears and threats clinging to her chest felt like a part of her. Letting them go would be akin to severing her own limb. Emma noticed the curious glances of passersby at the oddity of two middle-aged women sitting on the ground in front of a busy grocery store while the world went on around them.

The woman held the silence. She let Emma root around in her own thoughts, exploring the spaces between words. Could Emma tell her about the music box? How it had contained all the hopes and dreams of her youth, until a death had come as easily as pulling on a thread. How seeing it again was like throwing open a fear and a shame?

"My daughter's leaving again for school," Emma finally said, choosing another path. "It's . . . hard."

The woman looked skeptical, but she had the grace to keep it to herself.

"I get that," she said. "They drive us nuts when they're with us and fill us with dread when they go." The woman barked a laugh.

Emma found she could smile in response.

The woman stood and offered a hand, which Emma gratefully accepted. On her feet, her legs felt semisolid once again. She could see the woman watching, gauging whether Emma was all right. Apparently satisfied that the adrenaline surge had passed, the woman squeezed Emma's arm.

"Looks like another dump of snow is on the way tonight," the woman said as she flicked her nose to the sky. "Best we get home before it hits. Take care of yourself now."

"I will," Emma said. Though she wasn't sure if that was true.

Emma watched the woman disappear into the grocery store.

The theory of six degrees of separation—the notion that any one person on the planet could be connected to any other through a chain of acquaintances—was condensed in a small town on the shores of Lake Superior.

A legacy of settlement days, when survival had meant banding together against the onslaught of the elements, neighbors here sniffed out trouble, knew who belonged to whom, and generally looked out for one another.

If the woman who had helped Emma in the grocery-store parking lot had been from White Falls, she might have watched as Emma wandered the parking lot looking for her car. And if she'd been watching, she might have seen the shaky hand that fumbled for keys or heard the rattle as they dropped, twice, onto the pavement. She would have heard, perhaps, Emma's shuddery deep breath or seen the conviction on her face as she started the car.

Had the woman lived in White Falls, instead of being in town visiting her sister over the holidays, she might have recognized the wife of Mark Meadows, a town golden boy who'd been profiled in the local paper and who, as a real estate agent, had sold half the properties in the area. She might also have noticed as Emma turned left out of the parking lot, toward the main highway out of town—instead of right toward the warmth and safety of home—just as the first few flakes of the promised storm started to fall. The thread that connected people in a temperamental wilderness might have tugged, leading the woman to make a phone call to check up on the Meadows family and make sure Emma was doing all right.

As with so many things in life, much would have been different if the world had turned another way that day.

Verse

She sat in the back of the room, calculating.

It's what she did. Watch, listen, learn, compute. Some people called life an art; she considered it an endless barrage of proofs and refutations that needed to be added or subtracted according to a personal set of axioms. The trick was to balance the equation so that you owned it. Whatever the solution, you would come out ahead.

A yeasty smell, like sharp cheese and rotting leaves, slipped through open windows along the side wall. An October chill was helping to offset the heat in the room from too many bodies and poor ventilation. At the front, a group of overexcited organizers were trying to hype up the crowd.

She'd forgotten the name of the student group that was meeting. It didn't matter, really. All she needed was a cause, a way to pad the résumé and look engaged. Law school admissions officers liked that. Community engagement, they called it. Though really, all they cared about were undergraduate grades and LSAT scores. Still, she had a plan—an equation—and variables couldn't be denied.

The faces all around her had "lambs to the slaughter" expressions: wide eyes, darting heads, soft voices. When they did speak, their obsessions with pub crawls and Buffy the Vampire Slayer *irritated her, like an itch she couldn't reach. Americans would have called these first-year university students freshmen. She liked the sound of the word. Freshmen, fresh meat. Though they were her peers, she didn't feel herself one of them. These freshmen didn't understand the real world or the disappointments and horrors that fate could slap in front of you.*

Most of these students came from wealthy families. Privileged cherubs, fresh off graduation trips to Europe or silver spoon summer jobs. They didn't know the sting of having to scrape and cut and claw your way to achieve anything. It was all handed to them. And if they failed or fell, mommy and daddy swooped in, bought them a car, and sent them on their way.

None of them had lived her life—no family, no support, hardly any friends. No safe nest to go back to. She was alone, and nothing was going to change that. She didn't need a new family. What she needed was what they all took as their due: privilege, a leg up on an easy path toward the future. Well, if it wasn't going to be handed to her, she was going to wrestle it out of their hands through sweat and grit and blood, if necessary. Life had already tried to leave her behind; she couldn't let it outpace her entirely.

The dark-haired guy talking at the podium had a relaxed demeanor that she liked. He'd said his name, but she'd already forgotten it. Still, the warm and captivating timbre of his voice pleased her, like the perfect resonance of a tuning fork. He carried himself like someone who'd lived a more nuanced life. She saw an innate leadership and a je ne sais quoi that made him at ease commanding the room's attention.

He kept eye contact with his audience, drew them into his world effortlessly. She wasn't really listening to his words but was watching the reaction of others. She smiled when his eyes lingered on hers. The responsive flicker let her know he understood she was different than the other guppies swimming in the pool. She had substance and a plan. He could see. Perhaps he would be useful to her.

She watched the good-looking speaker leave with his arm around a pale brunette. Not a freshman. That was curious. Perhaps a problem. Not insurmountable, of course. She would put on the charm if she needed. Still, a girlfriend was an unpredictable variable.

The formula was still a work in progress but simple enough. School, profession, apartment, money, relationship: equaled happy life.

Chapter 4

Jaden

In Toronto, Jaden spent her days springing from place to place—school, library, work, out with friends—like a ping-pong ball stuck in the same volley. Now that she was home, familiar routines leeched at her energy, leaving only childhood habits and a mountain of shirked obligations. Mom was out. Dad had made his signature dish of spaghetti Bolognese for dinner, and an herb-and-garlic-rich aroma lingered in the wake, along with a synth-heavy eighties ballad.

When Uncle Finn's car pulled into the driveway, Jaden had been ignoring a book on her lap while floating in a Christmas-tree-lights-infused prenap state. She watched his arrival from the living room, not able to stir from her blanketed nest on the couch. Outside, snow was already filling in the tire tracks behind his car.

"Hello," Finn called as he strode through the front door. "Who's home?"

Finn was the youngest in the family and the closest thing to a brother Jaden would ever know. He had been in college when she was a tween, and she idolized him. All the more so when he'd confided to her once—on a particular deep freeze day—that he hated winter. His abhorrence of the season had seemed a titillating Meadowses' scandal to a thirteen-year-old.

Maybe the cold just got to you more as you got older, Jaden thought, listening to the stomp of Finn's feet as he shucked the snow off his boots.

The truth, though, was far more devastating.

"Talking to yourself again?" her dad said. Jaden watched him saunter through the hallway to greet his brother.

"Just commenting on your ugly face," Finn said.

Childhood habits, Jaden thought.

In the wide foyer of the old farmhouse, Finn pulled off his coat and hung it on the banister at the bottom of the stairs. Jaden could see the brothers, framed by the cased opening of the living room, as if they were living characters on a painter's canvas.

"Come on in," her dad said. "Just finishing dinner cleanup."

Jaden watched them pass. Neither noticed her curled up on the couch in the dark living room, a dim lump against oversize cushions. Their voices, though, trailed in from the kitchen, matching tenors still clear and warm.

"Ma insisted I come get her casserole dishes tonight," Finn said. "She was convinced you'd forget which ones were hers if I didn't."

"Beer in the fridge, if you want," her dad said.

Jaden heard the fridge door open, then the scrape of a counter stool against the floor. She should go say hello, she thought, but her eyes felt heavy. Her body melted deeper into the couch.

"Where're the girls?" Finn said.

"Jaden's upstairs, I think. And . . . uh, Emma's out," her dad said.

The slim stutter of uncertainty in her dad's voice was unmistakable above the clatter of a pot against the sink. Jaden's body instinctively shucked off a cloying sleepiness and leaned its attention toward the conversation.

"What's going on?" Finn said.

Another pause.

"I'm sure it's nothing," her dad said with a thin nonchalance. "She probably just lost track of time. Or maybe there was traffic with the snow?"

Jaden sat up, sleep sluicing away like rain from a downspout.

"She went out this afternoon, around five. Hasn't come back yet. I'm starting to get worried," her dad said.

We go through our days searching for answers that let us slot the world into the picture we've already formed in our heads. We think we want the truth, but what we truly want is a version of the truth that aligns with our preferred notions. Jaden had been out with friends most of the afternoon. She'd accepted her dad's bland explanation about her mom's whereabouts at dinner, had barely registered the answer, never mind the tentative timbre that must have been in his voice.

"She said she was going for groceries," her dad continued in the kitchen. "But she's not back yet. And she's not answering her phone either. I don't know why she even carries the thing. She never hears it. I don't know, maybe she decided to do a little Boxing Day shopping."

"It's almost nine," Finn said. "Stores must be closing soon."

White Falls, like most towns its size, had a collection of big-box chain stores hyping Boxing Day sales. Nothing, though, that would take four hours to peruse. You could visit every single one in under an hour, and her mom hated shopping. Jaden stood up.

"Have you tried tracking her phone?" Finn said.

"What do you mean *tracking*? She's not a deer."

Twelve years younger than her dad, Finn was more comfortable with technology and had even taught Jaden a thing or two about her iPhone. Her dad might have understood the basics, even been proud of his ability to use Google Maps, but he hadn't explored anything beyond the simplest functions.

"iPhones have a feature that allows them to locate each other using GPS. Assuming it's set up so that Em's phone is sharing its location with yours. Who set up the phones?"

"I did, of course," Jaden said, coming into the kitchen. "Hey, Uncle Finn."

She ruffled Finn's hair as she passed him, an old joke between them from when she was little and he'd have to bend down so she could reach the top of his head. Her dad's expression—a slight uptick of an eyebrow and deepened forehead wrinkles—was the standard Meadows look of concentration.

"We're trying to track your mom's phone," Finn said. "Did you set up Find My on your parents' phones?"

"What's that?" her dad said as he pulled his phone from his pocket.

He tapped at the screen.

"Here, let me, boomer," Jaden said. She held out her hand. "It'll take too long to explain."

Finn stood beside her and watched over her shoulder as she opened the app.

"Good girl, Jaden. She did set it up properly," Finn said to her dad.

A condensed map of White Falls popped up on the screen. "You just need to wait a second or two and voilà—" Tiny photos of Jaden and Emma popped up. Everyone in the exact same place.

"Shit!" Finn said.

"What? What's wrong?" her dad said, his eyes darting between Finn and Jaden.

"Mom didn't take her phone. It's here. In the house somewhere."

Jaden tapped at the screen, selected Mom's Phone from a list of devices in Find My. A staccato burst filled the kitchen.

Her dad followed the sound, nose raised as if following a scent. Finally, he opened a drawer in the kitchen island. The sound grew louder and more plaintive. Jaden pulled out her mom's phone and saw the notifications of missed texts and calls overlayed on a picture of Mark, Emma, and Jaden squinting into the sun with a summer lake behind them.

All three stared at the phone as if willing it to cough up answers. It stayed stubbornly mute.

"How long ago did you say she left?" Finn said into the quiet.

Two hours later, and six hours after her mom had left the house, Finn was still there, waiting.

Her mom hadn't yet turned up.

Outside, the snow continued relentlessly. Fifteen centimeters had fallen since late afternoon, and another twenty was predicted before night's end. It wasn't unusual for White Falls, but it was enough to cause problems. Accidents happened in these conditions. Deaths too.

Finn's straight-lipped frown sent a slurry through Jaden's blood. He was the family clown, quick with a joke and a laissez-faire attitude that made even her dad seem uptight. Silence from him meant something was very wrong. Finn had had firsthand experience with the madness of winter. Ten years ago, he'd been a volunteer with Ontario Search and Rescue.

For years, Jaden had been rapt by her uncle's stories of daring rescues on lonely highways and wild tromps through deep, uninhabited forests. He forded rivers, climbed mountains, and even rappelled off cliffs. Jaden had been in awe of him. And Finn had loved it. He'd taken every advanced course possible for a volunteer so that he was regularly called in to assist the Ontario Provincial Police with the more complicated cases.

Then one day, it all stopped. Without explaining to anyone, Finn hung up his climbing gear, retired his crampons, and quit search and rescue work for good. The family tried to get the story out of him, but Finn clammed up, refusing to explain or to talk about what had happened.

Jaden only found out the truth the summer after high school, when she'd gotten a job at the local Legion, tending the bar and listening to old-timers. The Legion pub was the watering hole of choice for the small police team in White Falls, along with the handful of search and rescue volunteers in the area. The job paid badly, but the tips were great, so she picked up all the shifts she could to make money for university in the fall. The basement bar served beer and hard liquor. Wine was for teetotalers, the regulars liked to say. The walls were plastered with photos of members past, and a large plaque on the wall bore the names of service members lost from the First World War to the present day. Too many names had been added after the COVID pandemic.

Jaden had been working when the search and rescue coordinator came in one night. The man's hands were crisscrossed by scars, while his face folded in on itself with age. He'd sat with a few of the new recruits, regaling them with stories of rescues gone wrong, heroic saves, and legendary screwups. After a few drinks, and the inevitable melancholy of a darkening night and too much rye, the recruits coaxed him to share the details of his worst call.

"Came in at the end of a long on-call week in the dead of winter. Finn Meadows and I were on duty that day," said the coordinator. "Ontario Provincial Police warned us it was a bad one. There was a kid."

Jaden's ear had been snagged by the mention of her uncle. She looked up from her end-of-night tally book and leaned against the bar.

"How old?" a recruit asked.

"Toddler."

The room was pin-drop quiet. Patrons and staff alike listened, helping carry the burden of a difficult story. Someone had turned down the music. Jaden stayed behind the bar as the man's voice moved through the room and through time.

"I just had a bad feeling, ya know," said the coordinator. "First time in my life, I wished I hadn't been on shift when a call came in."

They'd arrived on a clear blue morning at a lonely highway north of Lake Superior Provincial Park, he'd told them, stretching out the tale for a clearly rapt audience. The surrounding forest was dense and impenetrable, impossible to see into more than a few feet from the road. It was still early winter, so the woods weren't yet snowed under, though a recent dusting had coated the roads, making them deceptively slick.

"We got out of the truck on one of those perfectly serene stretches of road. I expected to see a mangled vehicle or destroyed guardrail. All we saw were trees and a ravine. And it was bloody cold. The mercury read minus twenty Celsius, without the wind. Thought my bones were gonna freeze in my skin.

"I asked about the wreck, and this stunned OPP kid pointed to the edge of the road, where a bridge piling marked the beginning of a ravine. Looking down, there was no trace of human existence. Only a thirty-foot drop to a thin line of a creek bed. I knew right away, ain't no way anyone survives something like that."

"Jesus," someone uttered. They'd all been to calls by then, seen the devastation that could start with a skid and end with mangled metal and broken bodies.

They'd needed to rappel into the ravine before they even saw the accident, the coordinator explained. A black pickup truck wedged so deep in a copse of trees that the foliage had swallowed it whole, making it invisible from above. The front of the truck had been crumpled like a paper fan, but the cab was remarkably intact.

"I get down there," said the coordinator, "and at first all I saw was a middle-aged white male in the front seat. Unbelievably, the guy was still alive, legs pinned in a bloody pulp beneath the steering wheel. He was fighting for his life, barely conscious. The truck had slid off the road two days earlier, hit a strip of black ice. Guess the tracks had been hidden by the little dusting, so it'd taken the OPP more time to find him, even though the truck's GPS was pinging. From the road, there was no sign the truck had ever existed."

Finn, it turned out, had been the rescuer directed to the back seat.

"That sight, man, it's gonna stay with me until I can't even recognize my own kids. Strawberry blond curls on a face as white as a winter witch."

The girl—maybe two or three years old—had been strapped into her car seat. Eyes closed, she was wrapped in a blue taffeta dress with a glittery plastic tiara on her head.

"She coulda been sleeping," said the coordinator, his voice breaking a little. "She was that peaceful."

While the others worked to free the driver in the front seat with the Jaws of Life, Finn's task had been to carry the girl to a waiting stretcher, as if hope remained.

"That boy cried the entire time. Wouldn't let anyone else touch her. Treated her like an angel, even kissed her forehead when he laid her on the stretcher. I heard he went to her funeral. That little girl was such an awful sight, it cost us a good man. Meadows never came back after that, so I'd say that was just about the worst I seen."

A tear slid down Jaden's cheek. She heard sniffles pepper the room, from the likes of the cocksure construction workers and seen-it-all veterans who frequented the Legion bar.

To Jaden's knowledge, Finn had never spoken of that call or that little girl to another living soul.

The memory of that search and rescue coordinator's raspy voice came back to Jaden as she sat at the kitchen island watching her dad pace. Her uncle, a steady presence in the room, had said very little in a couple of hours, but his body, straight and firm, was now telling them everything.

Finn knew. Of course he knew, with his years of experience dealing in tragedy and the heartlessness of the Canadian winter. Jaden saw it in the cool firmness of his eyes and the practiced blank expression now taking over his face. Her uncle was disappearing. In his place, the long-dormant rescuer was emerging, like a beautiful moth preparing for night.

"I think it's time to make some calls," Finn said.

He stood, ruffled Jaden's hair, and pulled out his phone.

Chapter 5

Jaden

Jaden didn't often understand the unspoken language that passed between her dad and his siblings. They communicated through silent messages and shared memories in a silent patois of smirks or raised eyebrows that could make her ache for a sibling of her own.

On the night her mom disappeared, she understood every nuance.

Standing in the kitchen watching her dad and Finn, she read their glances as if subtitles ran beneath their faces. Maybe she was learning. Or maybe the messages were so troubling, their meaning spilled out of the edges like water from an overfilled cup.

Her mom had left hours ago. Hadn't returned. And the snow was still falling.

"Start with family and friends?" Finn said.

The calls hadn't taken long. There was no family on her mom's side, and a group text to the extended Meadows clan was quickly answered. No one had seen or heard from Emma since Christmas Day.

The list of friends was even smaller. Her mom's social circle revolved around her job as an assistant director at the food bank. Over the years, she'd become friendly with a handful of people, most of whom were friends only for the period they worked together, their names drifting away as life brought them along a different stream. Some had moved on to other jobs; others had retired. The number of contacts in Emma Meadows's phone that mattered could be counted on a single hand.

While her dad made the calls, Jaden tried social media, but her mom didn't have any accounts. No Instagram or X or even Facebook. She tried googling her mom's name, hoping that a forgotten account might pop up or that a friend may have posted with a mention of her mom. She found pages of hits, but not one was her mother. Her name didn't even come up on the food bank website or community news. According to the internet, Emma Meadows in White Falls, Ontario, didn't exist.

With each failed attempt, Jaden felt a grimness shade her thoughts, sending her mind to dire places. Every few minutes, she wandered to the front window, expecting to see her mom's Subaru struggling through the deepening snow on the street. There had to be an explanation. Maybe she'd gotten stuck somewhere and was waiting for a tow? Or she'd stopped to help someone in distress? Or maybe she'd simply bumped into an acquaintance, gone for coffee, and forgotten the time? Each scenario Jaden concocted was more remote than the last. But what else did you do when your routine-obsessed home-bodied mom hadn't turned up as expected?

The snow finally stopped around midnight, leaving an undulating untouched blanket across the front yard. Jaden sat on the couch fending off sleep and watching the driveway. The perverse role reversal of waiting into the night for her mom to come home might have made her laugh if it weren't for the knot clutching at her stomach. She was losing hope of seeing her mom's car roll up the street; it was only a wish to which she clung.

A small army of Meadows family members—uncles and cousins—had fanned out across town, tracing her mom's probable route and checking back roads, where an accident may have been overlooked. It was like sending a message into a black hole, the darkness consuming light and sound.

Every time a phone rang, Jaden felt a futile hope. *Nothing yet, sorry, we'll keep looking* became a familiar refrain, a demented chorus that played over and over into the early hours of the morning.

At some point, the calls slowed. The only evidence of the search was trammeled snow in the driveway. The procession of relatives had come and gone, giving up until morning. Finn and her Aunt Sheila were staying for what was left of the night. Their presence felt even worse than the emptiness, an admission that something was terribly wrong.

Sometime before dawn, the words came out, sticky and horrible, like a betrayal of hope.

"I think you'll want to call the hospital now," Finn said quietly to her dad. She couldn't see them where they talked in hushed tones in the kitchen, but it was an old, echoey house. Sound, no matter how unwanted, traveled.

Her dad put the call on speaker. Jaden moved stealthily along the hallway, staying out of sight as the warbled ring echoed in the kitchen. With a quick peek around the corner, a new tableau seared into her mind; Finn and her dad hunched over the phone as if praying to a digital god.

"Emergency room," a woman's voice barked on the line.

White Falls Regional Hospital serviced the entirety of the region with a twenty-four-hour emergency room along with outpatient services. A rotating staff through the summer accommodated the ballooning population of cottagers that flocked to the area like a strange variety of migrating bird. Jaden had passed through the doors of the hospital only twice before: once to get stitches from opening a Swiss Army knife and once for a long-ago concussion after falling off a swing at the park. She'd never had to go for a true emergency.

"I'm looking for Emma Meadows," her dad said. The words sounded thick and gummy.

"Staff or patient?" the woman said. She spoke so fast, Jaden couldn't process the words.

"I don't know."

"What do you mean, sir? Either she works here or she doesn't." The voice wasn't rude, but it clung to the edges of impatience.

"No, she doesn't. Work there, I mean. But I don't know if she's there or not."

The woman let out a short, sharp breath. The phone was turned up loud enough that Jaden could hear background noise: a crying baby, the faint monotone of a loudspeaker announcement, and another line coming through. Trauma and pain filling in dead space like a baseline track.

Her dad tried again. "It's my wife. She hasn't come home, and I'm worried."

"Patient then." The steady click of a keyboard accompanied the woman's words. "That's Meadows, right? With an *s*?"

"Yes, exactly."

"No. I'm sorry, there's no one registered by that name."

It was a new lesson for Jaden that relief and disappointment could coexist in her chest, balanced like a tortured yin-yang circle.

"Have there been any Jane Does in the last few hours?" Finn said, his voice solid and professional.

"Not this evening, sir," said the nurse.

"I'm not sure what to do," her dad said. "She hasn't come home."

"Is your wife suffering from dementia or mental health issues?" There was a shift in the woman's tone, as if she'd turned on a recording of herself.

"What? No. Nothing like that," her dad said.

"Is she in danger of harming herself or others?"

Jaden felt a sharp pulse of anger against her chest. This stranger knew nothing about her mom. How could she suggest something so vile? As the idea sank in further, a sensation echoed in the pit of her stomach, like a stone dropped in a deep well. With a burning shame that quelched her paltry anger, Jaden realized she didn't know the answer. Maybe her mom had been depressed? Or dealing with issues? Jaden hadn't been home long enough over the past few years to notice or even ask. Her mom had never said anything, but then again, would she to Jaden?

"Of course not," her dad said. "She's fine."

"Then you have two choices. Wait for her to come home or call the police. I'm sorry, but I'm afraid that's all I can offer at this stage." The brusque words were softened by a sympathetic tone.

Her dad's perfunctory thank-you was iodine over a gushing wound. Why was he thanking her for nothing? Jaden felt a scream build in her throat, hard and pleading. She swallowed. It wouldn't help. In its place, tears of fatigue and frustration built behind her eyes. She blinked them away.

Jaden cursed herself for not being home enough and her mother for failing to come home at all.

Chapter 6

Jaden

Full consciousness came slowly. Jaden's eyes stayed closed while the edges of awareness confirmed she wasn't in her own bed. She stayed in the breath before waking, where life stands on a fulcrum. No past, no future, only existence in the moment. Clear thought was still evasive, like shadows moving around an unseen corner. For a heartbeat, she was awake without memory.

"We'll be here," she heard her dad say.

The faint crackle of the steam radiator and her dad's deep murmur pulled her forward. His words threw Jaden into a sickening vortex as the last twelve hours came hurtling at her. The sun had risen and crawled along the horizon, and her mom still wasn't home.

"Jaden, honey."

She felt gentle pressure on her arm. Her eyes opened to see her dad's five-o'clock shadow and tight smile. "Malcolm's on his way over. He wants to ask us a few questions," he said.

The morning was bright and blue and felt like a slap. Jaden had fallen asleep on the couch sometime after 4:00 a.m. Her dad had encouraged her to head up to bed, try to get some sleep, but she'd refused, preferring to stay with him in the living room until sleep snuck up and claimed her, despite her best efforts.

For hours the night before, Jaden had replayed every exchange she'd had with her mom since coming home, a wild-goose chase for a thread that might offer clues to her whereabouts. The one thing that kept resurfacing—though Jaden didn't understand her mind's fixation—was the music box and her mom's odd behavior right after opening it. Just before falling asleep, she'd argued it away as her mind's desperate attempt to cling to reason, however faulty.

Still, it was the first thing that came to her mind as her eyes adjusted to the sunlight streaming through the window.

"What time is it?" Jaden said.

"A little after nine. Malcolm said he'd be here in about half an hour. I'm gonna grab a shower."

Malcolm, her dad's high school buddy, was a sergeant with the White Falls Police Department. Though he wasn't the "come on over for a barbecue" type of friend, her dad always chatted with him when they bumped into each other around town. Overnight, the routines and rhythms of Jaden's world had altered; she was now the type of person who met with police.

Jaden stole a glance out the front window, where a trickster sun lured people into the cold; shards of light danced off a crystalline white stage. A siren's call to adventure, beneath which lay a killing cold that could freeze exposed skin and dull your senses. Two boys dragging plastic sleds struggled down the unplowed street, leaving perfect little postholes in their wake.

Jaden knew where they were going. They would turn left at the end of the street, then cut through a small playground to Dumpster Hill. Not the true name, of course. She didn't know its real name. No one did. The moniker for the mound at the edge of the park was handed down like an heirloom from siblings or neighborhood kids, all of whom had rolled down it in summer grass or scaled it with a toboggan come winter. She'd spent too many snow days to count hiking up and tearing down the hill, until her legs ached and her ears tingled with cold.

A flash memory hit her. It must have been one of Jaden's last true snow days, before getting older meant abandoning snow play for teen hangouts and binge-watching *RuPaul's Drag Race*. She'd walked through the door after a morning of tobogganing, nose running and toes pained with cold, to find freshly baked sugar cookies and a pot of hot chocolate still warm on the stove. The doughy smell was like stepping into a heated blanket. Jaden had spent the rest of the afternoon happily doing a puzzle with her mom and sipping at a bottomless mug.

She'd been close with her mom then; "two peas in a pod" was the cliché frequently used by others. Then puberty hit in earnest, and her mom went from being her best friend to an irritant. At the time, Jaden was at a loss to explain why her mom's attention felt like a clamp. Their silences grew longer. Jaden elected to spend time in her room listening to music, chatting with friends, or scrolling on her phone, until snow days were just like any other day.

Since she'd left for university, the distance hadn't widened but hadn't closed either. Her mom's garden-variety anxiety translated into bottomless nagging, especially with Jaden living in central Toronto, a city her mom seemed to consider to be one of the circles of hell, with transit. The barrage of warnings and paranoid texts dragged at Jaden like a yoke on her freedom.

Some part of Jaden understood that her mom felt the distance between them. Her first summer home from school, she'd overheard her mom chatting across the lawn with a new neighbor. The woman had a toddler affixed to her hip like a squirmy appendage, and her mom gushed over the little creature.

"I miss the days when you could just pick 'em up like that," her mom had said, a deep smile in her voice.

"Well, my arm certainly gets a workout," the neighbor said.

"Enjoy it. It's true what they say. One of these days, it'll be the last time you pick up your kid. And you won't see it coming or know it's happened until it's long passed."

At the time, Jaden had thought it was a silly comment. Who cared about the last time you picked up your kid? Those words came back to her now like an arrow that had finally found its mark. When was the last time she'd come home, cold or anxious or just hungry, and sunk into her mom's attention?

Right now, Jaden would give anything to hear her mother's irrational warnings and hand-wringing mutters.

After pushing herself up from the couch, Jaden headed to the kitchen for a glass of water. She could hear the shower upstairs, knew she'd have to wait for her turn. She settled onto a stool at the island, letting her mind travel avenues she would have preferred to ignore. Lack of sleep and anxiety, she told herself, almost chuckling as she followed the same worry path her mom walked daily.

On the corner of the island, her mom's laptop lay open, though the screen was black. They'd been searching through it the night before, looking through her emails for any hint at her whereabouts. Like everything else they'd tried, it had proved useless.

Frustration burbled in Jaden's chest, a noxious bubble looking for escape. She tapped hard on the keys, bringing the machine to life, and toggled to the browser. Though she couldn't imagine it would be of help, Jaden looked at her mom's search history. The usual suspects popped up—a chicken pot pie recipe, the Weather Network (why her mom didn't just download a weather app on her phone was beyond Jaden), various news sites. Jaden pulled up the history page and scanned sites she'd visited over the last week. Only one seemed out of the ordinary. She clicked.

A *Toronto Star* article popped up. A dated photo of a woman, maybe around Jaden's age, with poker-straight honey hair and thick black eyeliner, sat beneath a bold headline that read: Activist Convicted of Murder Released. She scrolled down and read.

> September 21, 2023—A Toronto woman, convicted of planning a bombing that killed a fellow animal rights activist in 1999, has been granted release. Clara Morel,

> now 43, has spent more than twenty years in prison for the bombing. Her original twelve-year sentence was extended due to violations while incarcerated. Expected to be released at the beginning of 2024—

Jaden stopped reading. She wasn't surprised by the article. It was the type of story her mother collected as fodder in her ongoing argument against the city. The *Toronto Star*, though, with its clickbait tone and sensationalized headlines, wasn't her mom's usual go-to source. Clearly, she'd been willing to forgo her prejudices to take one more pass at warning Jaden off her adopted city.

She must have been getting desperate for material, Jaden thought.

She didn't bother to finish reading the article. It would be more of the same. Toronto is the land of terrible tragedy, destroying lives. Jaden already had a collection of them on her phone, courtesy of mom texts. Hunting for hidden patterns in random clicks would not help her find her mom.

"Shower's free," her dad called from the upstairs hallway.

Clearly a crappy night's sleep and worry were messing with Jaden's mind. She shook her head free of misguided hope and closed the laptop.

"Coming," she called up, letting the article and Clara Morel drift to the further reaches of her mind.

Chapter 7

Jaden

Sergeant Malcolm O'Shea was clearly not a happy man.

From her bedroom window, Jaden watched the police officer get out of his cruiser, rising awkwardly into the cold like steam from a mug. His lanky frame and overdeveloped mustache made her think of a character in a comedy movie. He stood at the end of the driveway looking up at the house and shaking his head before lumbering forward. She didn't want to hear what he'd come to say.

The Meadowses' house sat like the dot on an *i* in a compact subdivision dripping with two-car garages and cul-de-sacs. This morning, fresh snow coated every little imperfection and pothole, making the neighborhood glitter under a trolling sunshine. Though trouble could find any postal code, it didn't often find itself on these streets.

Other than mounting an occasional search and rescue for a lost wannabe woodsman, the police always seemed to have routine work in White Falls. Not to say bad things didn't happen here—the town grapevine was alive with tales of domestic calls or drug arrests over the years—but this was not the sort of place that invited true crime curiosity. Small towns had a way of spilling secrets. Even Jaden knew, it was unusual for a local resident to just up and disappear entirely.

Her mom had been missing for more than twelve hours and still not a whisper.

Since their call to the police the night before, no one had reported seeing her mom, and no hits had come through from the BOLO on her car. An older-model Subaru, the car was also impossible to track via onboard GPS. It was as if the world had swallowed Emma Meadows whole.

As she stood on the second floor landing, out of sight of the door, a weirdly familiar feeling ran through Jaden's blood. A first-year geology class had taught her that the ground was never truly solid beneath our feet; rock shelves and tectonic plates were in constant motion, like a slow-moving sea. Our belief that the earth was constant and unmoving was an illusion, and Jaden had felt an unsettling betrayal in the knowledge. O'Shea's presence raised a similar disquiet.

She stayed on the landing.

"Hey, Malcolm. Come on in. Thanks for coming," her dad said as he led the officer through the house. "Coffee?"

Jaden moved quietly down the stairs, then perched on the bottom step like she had as a child so she could hear kitchen conversations without being seen.

"This can't be happening, Malcolm. It's either a nightmare or a ridiculous misunderstanding," her dad said. Jaden heard an exhaustion-laced wretchedness in the thin strain of his voice.

"How about I be the judge of that?" said O'Shea. "Let's go over yesterday again."

Her dad didn't react to the condescension in O'Shea's tone, but Jaden felt her head tilt and her eyes narrow. Why was she on edge like this? She closed her eyes, took a breath, tried to right the world under her feet.

Her dad launched into the story again. Jaden leaned forward.

The details remained consistent, despite O'Shea's prodding questions. Her mom had left in her car to get groceries and had simply not come home. They'd found her cell phone in a kitchen drawer, and neither family nor friends had heard from her since yesterday afternoon.

"It has to be the storm, right?" her dad said. The hopefulness in his voice gutted Jaden. "I mean, where else could she be?"

O'Shea had a thought or two, he said, but wanted to get more information before he made any suggestions.

"Jaden home?" O'Shea said.

"Ya, she'll be down in a minute. She's just having a shower. It was a long night."

There was a brief silence in the kitchen, as if both men were considering what to do next.

"Look, before Jaden comes down, I have a few indelicate questions," O'Shea finally said. "They're standard, so don't jump to any conclusions. I won't either. OK?"

Her dad didn't respond, but Jaden could imagine him nodding grimly.

"Is everything OK between you and Emma?" O'Shea said. "Any marital issues? It'll stay between us."

Jaden was offended. The officer's tone was pragmatic, as if he expected there would be trouble in every corner.

"It's fine," her dad finally said, a tint of a blush in his thin voice. "I mean, you know how it is. After twenty years together, there are ups and downs. These days, maybe a few more downs, I guess, but nothing serious."

"Anything in particular causing these downs?"

Winnie passed Jaden, glancing at her disapprovingly, before ambling into the kitchen. The dog's presence in the kitchen momentarily interrupted the flow of conversation. Instead, the lapping sound of water echoed in the silence.

"Nothing worth talking about," her dad said finally.

O'Shea said nothing, until even Jaden squirmed in the quiet.

"She's been struggling lately, I guess." Jaden could hear her dad pacing slowly, a hand absentmindedly tapping his leg the way it always did when he was thinking hard. "Don't get me wrong, it's not like she's depressed or anything. She's just been . . . I don't know, moody, withdrawn. Em had a really tough time when Jaden left for school, sort of closed in on herself a little. I thought she'd moved past that, but the last couple weeks or so she's been a little more on edge."

O'Shea cleared his throat gently.

"It's so hard to tell with her sometimes," her dad said.

"Any other changes recently? Even small things. Was she upset about something? Did she mention a problem at work? Or even an odd encounter?"

"Not really. I mean, she has her moods, you know? It can take her some time to recalibrate."

"Anything set off one of these 'moods' lately?" O'Shea pressed. His voice was soft, but Jaden heard the gentle challenge.

She stood. She'd had enough of this man and his underlying accusations about her family.

"Well, maybe Jaden?" her dad said.

Jaden felt the ground shiver beneath her feet. She froze.

"Emma is convinced that Jaden's been getting involved with the wrong sort of people in Toronto. You know how she is. She worries, all the time, about everything. And especially about Jaden. If Emma had her way, Jaden would go to online school from her bedroom." He gave an empty-hearted laugh. "A couple of weeks ago, Jaden called to say she'd be shortening her time home over the holidays. She said she needed to study, but Emma believed it was something else."

Jaden strode to the kitchen. Both O'Shea and her dad sat at the island, backs turned toward her.

"Emma and I fought about it recently. She wanted to pull Jaden out of the university. I tried to convince her that Jaden was twenty-one and we had no say in the matter anymore. But we worked that out, long before Emma—"

Her dad, sensing Jaden's presence, turned toward her. An apology and a shrug lived in his eyes.

"I'm sorry about what you and your dad are going through, Jaden. I know this must be hard," O'Shea said as Jaden poured herself a cup of coffee. "Do you mind if I ask you a few questions?"

Jaden glanced at him and offered a perfunctory *sure*.

"I want you both to know," O'Shea continued, "we're doing everything we can to find Emma. The BOLO has gone out to all on-duty officers, as well as the Ontario Provincial Police. We're all watching for her car or any sign of her. I know you called the White Falls hospital last night, but we have a line into the Sault Ste. Marie hospital as well. We have eyes everywhere."

"And yet, you can't find her," Jaden said, not bothering to hide her frustration.

Her dad set a gentle hand on her arm.

Jaden wondered if anyone ever found O'Shea's spiels to be of comfort. She suspected he said the words to lay a foundation rather than provide reassurance. What could you really say when the world had swallowed a loved one? He looked directly at Jaden.

"I need to ask you a few questions that might help us narrow down your mom's recent movements and behaviors. I know it's hard, especially right now, but it'll really help if you can share anything you can think of, no matter how trivial it may seem."

Jaden held her breath, as if she were expecting to plunge beneath water. She nodded.

"I understand your mom was a little concerned about some of the friends you'd made in Toronto."

"My mom is paranoid. She sees boogeymen behind every corner. She's never even met any of my friends there. She just hates Toronto. She always has," Jaden said. "My mom flips out if I take the subway by myself in the middle of the day. It's not rational."

"Jaden," her dad said. "That's not fair."

"Why not?" Jaden said, though there was no sarcasm in her tone. "It's true, Dad. You know it is."

Mark's reluctant nod confirmed the family dynamic.

"Has anything happened recently that made her particularly"—O'Shea paused, no doubt choosing his words judiciously—"concerned?"

Why was this man asking these stupid questions instead of being out there, looking for her mom? Shouldn't he be conducting a search?

"Nothing. There's been nothing different than from the first day I set foot on campus. She thinks that I'll face some sort of ruination the longer I spend in Toronto. It's all in her head."

The curious look that crossed O'Shea's face made Jaden regret her words.

"Do you have any idea where your mom might have been going when she left here? Did she say anything to you, either yesterday or earlier? Did you notice a change in her behavior?" O'Shea said.

"If I knew, don't you think I'd have told you already?" Jaden said.

She felt ashamed of her petulance. At the same time, the unbothered, staid look on O'Shea's face invited snark.

Her dad frowned and raised an eyebrow at her. O'Shea kept silent.

"Have you told him about the music box?" Jaden said to her dad.

His face crinkled in confusion. "The what?"

"The gift Mom opened the night before last. The strange package. She got all weird after she opened it and went up to bed right after. She said she had a headache. Remember? Mom never gets headaches."

Her dad was clearly caught off guard. He held sympathy in his eyes, but his puzzlement was genuine.

A few minutes later, a glass music box sat on the Meadowses' kitchen island. Her dad and O'Shea watched as if it were some feral creature that might scurry off the table.

"And you have no idea who gave it to her?" O'Shea asked. "There wasn't a card with it or a note?"

"Nothing," Mark said. "But that's not unusual. Emma's been at the food bank for a couple of decades now. Anonymous gifts aren't out of the ordinary. Some clients want to thank her but don't want anyone to know they'd visited."

"Any that would know her home address?" O'Shea said.

“Plenty. This is a small town. Everyone knows where everyone else lives. And if you don’t, it doesn’t take much to find it out,” Mark said.

O’Shea lifted the box to his face. It easily fit in one hand; he raised and lowered the knickknack, testing the weight of the thick glass. He ran a finger over the brass, peered at the flower etching, examined beneath, and tested the mechanism. “Pretty fancy gift for a thank-you. This looks expensive.”

“Is that important?” Jaden said, hope settling in her like a breath.

“Not necessarily,” O’Shea said. “You’d be surprised what you can find at the Salvation Army Store. Do you still have the paper it was wrapped in?”

Her dad retrieved some ripped up kraft paper from the recycle bin, the kind normally used to wrap a Canada Post delivery. Several pieces fell from his hand onto the counter. A short message was on one side of the paper, but only Emma’s name. No address or postage stamp. O’Shea looked carefully at each piece, but there were no other markings that he could find. The gift must have been dropped off at the house with a brief note scribbled on the wrapping: *For Emma, with grace.*

O’Shea lifted the lid of the music box. A pleasant tune filled the quiet room, the tinny notes like those from a kid’s jewelry box with a twirling ballerina.

Two thoughts kept going through Jaden’s mind: Who was this from, and if it was as important as Jaden believed, why hadn’t her mom taken it with her?

Chapter 8

Jaden

After O'Shea left, the melancholy tune from the music box scratched and scrabbled at Jaden's mind, digging for a memory so flimsy she couldn't decide whether it was a recollection or wishful thinking. She didn't tell her dad or O'Shea. They were already skeptical of the connection Jaden saw between her mom's absence and the music box.

Besides, the sergeant had already taken a photo of the box, written down a note in his little book, and then shrugged it away. What more could Jaden offer?

She returned to the living room, where the box sat ringed in silence. She lifted the lid and again heard the warbled tune. Something about the song jarred a sluggish memory from Jaden's mind, like smoke traveling through cold air. She'd been in middle school, maybe twelve or thirteen, and had promised to bring six dozen frosted cupcakes to a bake sale. Jaden could almost hear the drawn-out groan of her name when her mom found out that the bake sale was the next day and that Jaden had known about it for three weeks.

"Right," her mom said into what had been a lazy Sunday afternoon. "You're coming to the store with me, and we're baking this afternoon."

"What? I can't. I'm hanging out with Zelda," Jaden said. She'd punctuated her words with a whine before launching a desperate, if exaggerated, protest. "We're working on our science project."

"Cancel. I know for a fact that the science project isn't due until next month." The threat in her mom's tight lips was more incentive than the actual words.

Back in the kitchen and resigned to her fate, Jaden hooked her phone up to a Bluetooth speaker while her mom pulled out ingredients and muffin tins. If she was going to be forced to work all afternoon, she reasoned, there needed to be a wall of sound between her and her mom. Jaden chose a playlist, daring her mom to challenge it, but nothing happened. Her mom dumped flour into a mixing bowl.

Twenty minutes later, both Jaden and her mom had developed a rhythm, spooning batter into waiting muffin cups while moving their hips around the kitchen to a One Direction song. Jaden found herself laughing, despite her earlier intentions to be miserable, when a dollop of batter landed on the back of her mom's hand. It was like that in those days—a crumbly wall of Jaden's fury could be swept away by a bellyful of laughter. Hormones, she guessed now. Then, she'd been convinced she was far too complicated for simple explanations.

Jaden was in midstream explaining the differences between K-pop and J-pop, when her mom stopped stirring and stared blankly at the wall.

"Mom? Hello? Did you forget something?"

Her mom didn't respond. Jaden touched her shoulder, tentatively. Confusion stilling her with a spoon still dripping in batter.

"Mom?"

Her mom turned, looked at Jaden's face, but her eyes were far away. An Ed Sheeran song streamed through the Bluetooth speaker.

"Sorry, Shmoo," her mom finally said. Even then, Jaden could tell her mom was struggling to ground herself in the here and now. "This song. I haven't heard it in a long time."

A ghost track—unlisted on the album but snuck in at the end of another song—had popped up in the playlist. The song, "The Parting

Glass," was sung a cappella, melancholic and simple, with an undertone of loss. Jaden had only heard it a couple of times herself. In a flash, annoyance returned. There was no way her mom had heard this song before.

"What's wrong with it?" Jaden said, the snap jetting out of her mouth. Puberty had been like that, one minute laughing, the next irritation or despair taking over her thoughts.

"It reminds me of someone."

"Who?" Jaden returned to spooning batter, the eye roll evident in the shake of her head and drop in one shoulder.

"Someone I knew. A long time ago. He died," her mom said, just above a whisper.

"Whatever," Jaden said and stopped the music. "Are we done yet?"

Looking back with the benefit of maturity, Jaden could say that her reaction had been most likely rooted in her own uncertainty and teenage self-doubt. At the time, though, her reaction had smothered the moment as easily as a snuffer over a candle's flame. The rest of the afternoon passed in an edgy silence.

Jaden later learned that her mom had been right. Ed Sheeran had recorded the old Irish ballad, sung often at the close of the pub or as a final goodbye at a funeral. To this day, she'd never admitted it to her mom.

Memory was such an unreliable and unpredictable little thing, as colored by the present moment as by the past. Now that the door had been opened, Jaden traveled down long-forgotten corridors. What she saw in her mind's eye couldn't be called memory; it was as flimsy as a spider's web. Still, she smoothed it and polished it, until she convinced herself that it had meaning.

It wasn't a coincidence. That song. That music box. Something about the gift had spooked her mom. Jaden had seen her turn pale and fidgety before setting the box down carefully on the coffee table, as if any sudden movements would cause it to explode. That box was important. Important enough for her mom to leave the house on Boxing Day and head out into a burgeoning snowstorm.

And Jaden was determined to find out what it was.

Chapter 9

JADEN

The inside of the White Falls police station did not match Jaden's imagination. Instead of *Brooklyn Nine-Nine*, with an open office and bandied hilarity, there was a reception desk and an almost-empty waiting area. The room smelled of toner, while office Muzak dripped from a crackly speaker in the ceiling. Three doors, each painted with a different primary color, led into the deeper recesses of the building, giving off a creepy carnival feel.

The rubber soles of Jaden's boots squelched as she walked across the pale linoleum. With each step, she felt herself shrink inside her bulky coat. It had been forty-two hours since her mom had left the house, and they were here to formally file a missing persons report. She resisted the urge to grab her dad's hand.

A young-looking officer sat behind the reception desk talking into a headset while he tapped at a keyboard. His voice squeezed through a half circle cut out of a Plexiglas partition. Bulgy eyes and a half-opened mouth made Jaden think of a lizard in a terrarium. He acknowledged their presence with a curt nod and transitory smile, though his attention remained on a caller.

"Mmm-mmm," he said. "I see. No, I'm sorry, ma'am. We can't dispatch officers for pet rescue. Have you tried using a can of tuna?"

He listened.

"No, not for you. For . . . Fuzzy, is it?"

He glanced up, met Jaden's eye, and held up his index finger with an apologetic nod.

"That's right," he said into the phone. "With the snowstorm, he may have just found himself a little nook to wait it out. He'll probably come out when he's ready, so a can of tuna might entice him."

When he hung up the phone, Jaden could just make out the words under his sigh. "Here's hoping a coyote doesn't get it first."

Despite the overheated room, Jaden felt a rush of cold through her body.

Ten minutes later, Jaden and her dad were wedged onto a small couch deep in the bowels of the building. Shaded daylight, along with a trickle of cold air, seeped in from a small window just above eyeline. Across from them, Malcolm O'Shea sat on a blue plastic chair that squealed every time he moved. He offered them tepid water from a plastic jug, leaving behind a darkened ring on the faux-wood coffee table. As he poured, Jaden's mind flashed to the Mad Hatter's demented tea party.

O'Shea spoke as her dad reviewed a printed copy of the missing persons report, most of which had been provided to the police the previous day.

"I'm afraid still nothing from the issued BOLO. We've gotten a couple of mistaken leads but still nothing concrete. It's . . . unusual."

O'Shea sat back; the chair squeaked. Jaden felt the sound at the back of her ear like a pinprick.

"So, what does that mean?" her dad said. He looked up from the papers on his lap.

"It means we have to start thinking about other angles," O'Shea said. "Malfeasance or voluntary removal."

Squeak. Jaden kept her eyes trained on a square of reflected sunlight, about the size of a paperback book, hovering against the wall behind O'Shea. The window was too high for her to see the source. The light jittered like a small bird on a wire.

"So far, there's nothing to suggest that Emma came across bad actors," O'Shea said. "We'll keep looking, but based on what we've gathered so far, the more likely scenario is that she left of her own accord."

The words were like mismatched puzzle pieces. Jaden understood their individual meanings, but the whole didn't fit together.

"I'm not sure what you're implying here, Malcolm." Her dad's voice was a knife.

O'Shea leaned forward. *Squeak.* Jaden's insides coiled.

"Don't you think it's a little strange," O'Shea said, "she walked away without her phone?"

The tone was gentle, but Jaden could sense her dad's body language change, as if a thread pulled him straighter. The air in the room thickened. Jaden drew in a deep breath and dove in.

"No," she said. "She leaves her phone at home all the time. She only agreed to an iPhone so she could text me. I don't think she even knows how to use it properly. She hates technology. Says it makes everything more complicated than it needs to be." The childish rush of her words embarrassed her.

O'Shea nodded thoughtfully, but something about the rapid blink of his eyes and bite of his lip bothered Jaden. He didn't believe her.

Her dad was not a man prone to anger. Jaden could count on one hand the number of times she'd heard him raise his voice. He moved through conflict like an otter through the current, slick and willowy, and with a hint of playfulness. So, nothing prepared her for the menacing growl that emanated from his lips.

"Say it, Malcolm."

O'Shea shot a glance toward Jaden before meeting her dad's glare head-on.

"I thought it was something we could discuss privat—"

"Just say it. I won't hide things from my daughter." Her dad's voice was a hiss between clenched teeth as he struggled to regain himself.

"Emma's done it before, hasn't she, Mark?" O'Shea said, though it clearly gave him no satisfaction.

This wasn't the police gotcha moment that Jaden had seen on police dramas. O'Shea's body was relaxed. Empathy, cool and soft, slipped through his demeanor. Her dad was having none of it.

The stench of anger and disinfectant suddenly became overpowering. Jaden felt the juice she'd sipped that morning roil in her stomach. She turned to her dad.

"What does he mean, she's done it before?" Jaden said.

Their silence told her nothing and everything.

O'Shea held his tongue, but she could feel him watching, as if she and her father were some sort of hypothesis he was testing.

"There's a lot you don't know, honey, nor should you. You're a kid. You shouldn't be worrying about your mom or me."

"Dad, tell me." Jaden couldn't keep the pleading out of her voice. She would scold herself for it, but later, when the balance of her family was no longer teetering.

"It was a long time ago, honey. Before you were even born."

"Dad? I'm not a kid anymore, especially after this." Even as she said them, Jaden knew her words would wound, that they were a cruel manipulation. She didn't care. She needed to know.

The sigh that followed shattered an irretrievable innocence.

"Your mom and I were so young when we met," he said, the tinge of memory mellowing his anger. "She was kind and beautiful and wickedly funny. It was an intoxicating mix, and I fell hard. Harder than her. I knew she had baggage. It was obvious, the way she'd withdraw into herself, avoid even simple questions about her past. But I couldn't fault her for living a life before me."

For a breath, Jaden didn't recognize her dad in the man sitting beside her. The slow smile and distant expression belonged to a sadder person.

"She never shared the details, and I never asked for specifics. I knew she had a past she wanted to forget. For a long time, she struggled with feeling safe. She'd leave when it got to be too much for her, just vanish for a few days. I think she needed an escape hatch from her life, so she never told me where she went. In the end, I respected that. She always came home."

Jaden trained her eyes on the reflected square of light, fighting tears of exhaustion and, increasingly, betrayal. Intoxicating, vibrant, secretive? Who was this woman her dad was talking about? Certainly not her quiet, contained, parent-council-bake-sale of a mom. The image of the woman her father was describing was unreconcilable with Emma Meadows.

"The first time she disappeared, I panicked. We'd been dating for a few months by then, and I thought things were going well. We'd made plans to have a picnic, but she didn't answer the door when I went to pick her up. I let myself into her apartment. All her stuff was still there, but she was gone. After a few hours, I called the police. At the time, they didn't take a missing persons report. They said skipping out on a date wasn't technically missing."

Her dad glanced an accusation at O'Shea, who nodded.

Jaden didn't know what to make of the story. Questions, as always, vaulted through her mind. She sensed now wasn't the time to ask, but her mouth moved faster than her good sense.

"How did he know?" she said, jerking her head toward O'Shea. "If you didn't report anything, how do the police know?"

"They didn't do a serious search for her back then, but I guess her name went into the system somehow."

Her dad hung his head as he spoke, and Jaden was shocked by the weariness in the gesture, as if his body were collapsing in on itself from the weight of memory.

"It wasn't in the system, Mark," O'Shea said, not unkindly. "One of the old-timers around here remembered her name. He asked me if Emma Hobbes had done a runner again."

"So, how come I've never heard of this?" Jaden said.

"She came back," her dad said. "Six days after she vanished, I got a call from Bev at the food bank. Emma had walked into work that morning as if it were any other day. Not a word on where she'd been or why she disappeared. Bev told me she'd smoothed it over with management there and all was well. It happened again a couple of times after that. After a while, I learned to trust Emma. I knew she had some demons, and if she needed time away to wrestle them, so be it. She would always come home."

Her dad took in a long, slow breath as if the effort of telling had emptied his lungs.

"But, Malcolm, it hasn't happened since Jaden was born. Once she came into the world, Emma was rooted. The last time this happened was twenty-two years ago. How could that possibly matter now? It doesn't make any sense that she'd suddenly walk away now."

Jaden's mind lurched from one question to the next, never landing long enough for her voice to catch up. She was appalled and awed by her dad's kindness and patience. At the same time, she felt a load settle on her shoulders—twin birds of duty and guilt—and the inadvertent onus his words placed on her. If she was the one who kept her mom rooted, had Jaden's actions somehow sent her away? She looked out the window to barren trees against a bitter blue sky.

"For the sake of argument, Mark," O'Shea said, breaking a spell. "Let's say the old pattern has resurfaced. What do you think might have triggered her recently?"

Nature abhors a vacuum, Jaden thought. If nothing had happened to trigger her mom's sudden disappearances, then all that remained was Jaden.

Squeak. O'Shea shifted. Jaden flinched.

"Honestly, nothing," her dad said, defeat thick as oil in his voice.

"The music box." Jaden overlapped her dad's words. A lifeline for her in turbulent waters.

"The one you showed me yesterday?" O'Shea said.

The pity in both her dad's and O'Shea's eyes was like swallowing a stone.

"Jaden, I know that it seems like it, but that trinket has nothing to do with this," her dad said.

"It has to," she said, searching her dad's eyes, willing her belief to find purchase in him. "You didn't see her when she opened it, it was like she'd seen a—"

"Enough, Jaden."

He refused to look at her, instead offering a listless slash of his hand.

She turned her eyes away, searching for the reflected square of light to hide behind, but it had vanished.

Squeak. The sound from O'Shea's chair ran along Jaden's spine like a whip. She hurdled to her feet. Both men looked up at her. She couldn't read their expressions; she could hardly see them through the veil of her frustration.

"Do I have to stay here? Can I go?" she said, looking at O'Shea and refusing to meet her dad's concerned gaze.

He nodded. "This isn't an inquisition, Jaden. You're free to go anytime."

Though not overt, the shift in his appraising gaze was unmistakable. There was an invitation and a warning in the subtle tilt of his head.

There are moments when wishful thinking is the only course of action. We strike an unreciprocated bargain with the universe: If I don't open my eyes, my lover won't leave; if I take a different route home, my son will survive. Without cause or reason, Jaden leaned into the idea that walking out of this room would make the trouble go away and deciphering the music box would bring her mom home.

She strode out of the room, not bothering to look back. She didn't need to turn to know that her dad was standing in the hall behind her, hands at his side and a mix of dismay and incredulity warring on his face.

Chapter 10

Jaden

Cold—bitter and scarring—reached hold of Jaden's lungs as soon as she stepped outside the police station. The type of cold that made a mockery of the sun.

The mercury had been in a slow descent since Christmas Day, bottoming out the previous night at minus thirty-two degrees Celsius. Exhaust hung listlessly behind cars. The air, normally infused with the metallic tang of the lake, held no scent. The smattering of people who braved the outside darted between vehicles and buildings, heads down and hands shoved deep into pockets so that the figures looked like bent-over crones in their dark coats and hoods.

Snow squeaked under Jaden's feet as she started walking. A steady northwest wind, fed by arctic air and lake ice, leached through every layer of her clothing, whipping at residual tendrils of body heat. She didn't notice. With every step, her thoughts descended into an endless loop, replaying the conversation with O'Shea, his suggestion about her mother, and her father's disclosure. She ignored the demands of her cooling body and her buzzing phone. She didn't know—nor did she care—who was calling. All that mattered was placing one foot in front of the other and dragging herself out of the morass.

Improbably, Jaden felt her mom's absence like a fresh wound, oozing and gaping, until it reshaped the very structure of her body.

You'll catch your death walking aimless like this. She heard the echo of her mom's voice.

"You're catastrophizing," Jaden said. The street was empty, but her mind's eye saw her mom, wool hat held out, head shaking and a sigh poised on her lips.

It's not catastrophizing when the catastrophe's here. Her mom's voice swirled, wind and winter and cold taking over Jaden's mind. *Look for the easiest thread and start pulling. It's all there.*

The body will go to great lengths to protect itself when its core temperature drops; energy and blood flow shift to vital organs at the expense of the extremities, muscles tighten, and the heartbeat slows, dragging the capacity for reason with it. Jaden watched her booted feet. She no longer heard the squeak of snow underfoot or sensed the numbness in her fingers and toes. She couldn't have seen the nickel-size white spots developing on the buds of her cheeks or known that her body temperature had dropped by a full degree in the last block. She walked through a white-filled world until thought, opinion, and speculation merged into a slow-moving mass in her mind.

O'Shea was wrong. The thought burbled and groaned, grabbing for Jaden's attention. Her mom would never have walked out on the family, not without a reason. The Emma her dad first met—that lost woman looking to exorcise demons—had disappeared long ago. Emma Meadows, the woman who folded underwear and printed online coupons, would never have left Jaden to make her own way in the world. If her dad or O'Shea weren't going to believe it, then Jaden needed to prove it.

When she finally looked up—numb and long past shivering—Jaden was standing on the steps of the White Falls Food Bank.

The tidy clapboard building—once an Anglican church—had been converted years ago, when declining attendance and financial constraints had forced the diocese to deconsecrate and sell. They'd scurried off with the stained glass and other valuable tidbits, but the sweeping timber beams remained, as did the goodwill and charity. A drop-in center in the basement offered hot meals, showers, and kind words for anyone in need.

Jaden stepped inside.

The sudden warmth woke up dormant synapses, reminding Jaden of the demands of her body. Her fingers itched and tingled. A sudden flush of heat spread through her face as if a tap had been turned on beneath her skin.

Jaden leaned on the banister as she made her way to the basement, her will frozen beneath a layer of cold trapped against her skin. Her boots clunked against the wooden stairs, announcing her arrival like a crusading army. When she finally reached the bottom, Jaden landed headlong into the curious gaze of Bev Clancy.

Pushing on the door of seventy, Ms. Clancy was on the food bank's board of directors and volunteered for serving shifts when her arthritic hip allowed. She loved this place and was on top of everything that happened in the building. Jaden's mom always said, *If a can of peas goes missing, Bev knows about it.*

"Jaden!" Ms. Clancy said, tottering toward her with outstretched arms. "What a lovely surprise."

"Hi, Ms. Clancy," Jaden said, her still-frozen lips struggling to make the shape of words.

Though she hadn't been around much over the last few years, Jaden had spent countless days in this building as a kid, exploring hidden nooks, helping set up for bingo nights, and pilfering fresh-baked cookies. The familiar smells of oiled wood and yeast wrapped around her as she leaned into Ms. Clancy's hug.

"Oh my goodness. You're a Popsicle. Let's get this coat off and warm you up," Ms. Clancy said, running her hands up and down Jaden's arms. Jaden felt a welcome burn at the woman's touch.

Dinner prep was well underway. The smell of frying meat and onions drifted from the kitchen at the far end of the room. The food bank was part cafeteria, part community center, with a shelf full of kids' games and books in the corner and a bottomless supply of coffee and kind words. Under the rattle of cutlery and gentle laughter, Jaden's stomach rumbled. She melted gratefully into the care and comfort to be found here.

Ms. Clancy ushered Jaden to one of four rows of long tables nearby and fetched a red cafeteria tray piled with two cups of hot cocoa from the kitchen, each with an overflowing dollop of whipped cream, and toasted bagels. She slid a bagel with cream cheese in front of Jaden as they both settled on hard plastic chairs under the peeping eyes of the staff.

"Eat," Ms. Clancy commanded kindly. She gave a satisfied smile when Jaden nibbled at the edges of the bagel. "Now, what brings you by?"

"I—" The words withered and died in Jaden's throat.

Ms. Clancy took Jaden's cold hands in her own paper-crinkled ones. An entire treatise on compassion passed to Jaden with that touch. She felt as if she'd been careening down a hill and landed with a thump in a soft, forgiving pile of snow.

"Just start at the beginning, love. I find that's usually the best place."

Jaden recounted the last two days and all that she'd learned, including O'Shea's suspicion that Emma had disappeared willingly. The wound of possibility slashed at Jaden's voice as she stammered over parts, but she forced herself forward, all the while staring at the thin blue lines running along the back of Ms. Clancy's hand.

"I think they're wrong," Jaden said when there was nothing more to tell. "They don't know Mom. Something's not right. My dad told O'Shea that she'd been struggling, but whatever is bothering her couldn't have been that bad. I would have noticed. And even if she was upset about something, she wouldn't have just walked out on us."

The hot chocolates lay untouched on the table, a thin layer of melted cream clinging to the surface. The sweet smell turned Jaden's stomach, and she pushed hers down the table.

"You don't think she'd walk away like that, do you?" Jaden said.

Jaden leaned her head on her hands so that Ms. Clancy's crackled yellow face was framed by her fingers. Her mom had worked with this woman for over twenty years; if anyone could be called a friend, it was her.

Hope and desperation poured out of Jaden, begging Ms. Clancy to carry them forward. She wiped a sleeve across her eyes, righteous stubbornness driving back tears, and waited for words she longed to hear. It wasn't to be.

"Oh, honey. I am so sorry this is happening to you," Ms. Clancy said. She patted Jaden's hand and sat back in her chair with a sigh. "I wish I had answers for you. I really do. But the only thing I know for sure is that under the right conditions, people are capable of anything. We all do the best we can to get through the day, but we're all just fragile and fallible creatures in the end, aren't we? I've heard enough stories under this roof to know that it's impossible to know what's going on under someone's skin or to understand their choices. Could Emma have buggered off? Maybe. Did she? Well, that's the rub, isn't it?"

Jaden felt a simultaneous betrayal and affirmation, like being hot and cold at the same time.

"God's honest truth, Jaden, I don't know. What I can tell you is that Emma requested a leave of absence just before Christmas."

"What? Why?" Jaden said, her head snapping back as if she'd just been stung.

A rumble of laughter followed one of the volunteers out of the kitchen. With darting glances at the two seated women, he started wiping down the tables for dinner service. They would open the doors soon, and Ms. Clancy would be needed. She looked Jaden in the eye, and Jaden saw a battle wage. *Fragile and fallible,* Ms. Clancy had said, and the words bounced through Jaden's mind like a marble in a maze.

Ms. Clancy let out a short breath. The older woman had made a choice, and for the rest of her life, Jaden would wonder if it was the right one.

"All I can tell you, honey, is what I told the police yesterday. The last couple of weeks, Emma has been missing shifts. She just didn't show up. Which is very unlike her. I covered for her, but when I asked her if she was OK, she brushed me off, said she'd just been busy with Christmas prep."

A sound, like angry bees, filled Jaden's ears. The harder she tried to listen, the louder the buzzing, blocking out her ability to take in Ms. Clancy's words. She mustn't have heard right. Her mom never missed work. Over the years, she'd powered through viruses, snowstorms, even a tornado, to be in this basement. And, if Ms. Clancy had told the police, why had O'Shea not mentioned it?

"I believed her, at first," Ms. Clancy continued, though Jaden wasn't sure she wanted her to. "I knew your parents were hosting the big family do this year, and that can be a lot. But something else was off with Emma. She seemed jittery. Like she wasn't sitting right in her skin. And she asked me more than once whether we'd had any sketchy clients lately or if anyone had asked about her. I pressed her, but she wouldn't say why she wanted to know."

With more volunteers spilling out of the kitchen and the first few clients arriving for dinner, the room started to fill with chatter. Jaden stood to leave. Two little girls skipped past her, hand in hand, giggling as they made their way toward the kitchen, their mom trailing behind. Forgetting why the family would have come to the food bank in the first place, Jaden felt envy, hot and cloying, surge through her veins. It crept up her throat. She wanted to rip those hands apart, rub the smiles off the girls' faces, and scream at them for—

For giggling.

"Jaden, are you OK? You look a little flushed." Ms. Clancy's voice was a distant, but insistent, bell.

"Thanks, Ms. Clancy," Jaden said. She turned her back on the elderly woman and walked out the door without another word.

Chapter 11

Jaden

The house was quiet when Jaden opened the front door. She stood on the threshold, wind pushing loose snow across the entry. Only the jingle of Winnie's collar greeted her. The dog ambled toward the door, eager and confused.

Jaden knelt while Winnie happily sniffed at her coat. She buried her face into the golden, soft fur and allowed herself a sob. Her muscles gave way, her heart emptied, and all semblance of strength vanished. The dog, perhaps sensing her need, stood still, absorbing Jaden's tears. When she finally came up for air, Jaden was sitting cross-legged on the floor in a puddle of snowmelt.

A note sat waiting on the island top. For a heartbeat, Jaden thought the world had righted and her mom had left a note that they'd all overlooked.

> At Aunty Sheila's making calls. Come if you feel up to it. I've already walked and fed Winnie. Love Dad.

Disappointment slid over her like a careless wave. In its place, a sharp sliver of a thought lodged itself in Jaden's mind. What if O'Shea was right? What if this was a deliberate plan on her mom's part? Her mind railed against the idea; still it slipped back in through cracks in her resolve. What if Jaden had been the reason her mom had left? What if life in White Falls, their family, Jaden herself, hadn't been enough for Emma Meadows?

A twist of anger, raw and wriggling, sputtered in Jaden's core like a defective firecracker long after the wick had burned away. This couldn't be on Jaden. How dare her mom go away without saying anything. Without taking her phone. How stupid could she be?

Jaden yanked off her boots and marched up the stairs to her parents' room.

Standing in the doorway, she took in the room's contours and shapes. Nothing had really changed in years. A thick white duvet still lay across the bed, and a Persian-style rug in shades of sand softened the harder sounds of the wood floors. On the far wall, the framed Alex Colville print of a woman lit up a side of the room with an expanse of pale-blue summer sky over ocean. A small stack of books, a half glass of water, and a tube of hand cream lay abandoned on the nightstand on her mom's side. Though not a mess, the room had the lived-in look of a space given over to comfort rather than company. Jaden remembered lying on the thick carpet as a kid, a book in front of her, while a rainstorm raged out the window. There had been a sense of home in this room. Now it felt as unapproachable as a crime scene.

Jaden strode to her mom's dresser and yanked the top drawer. Her breath moved heavily in her chest, and sweat rose beneath her coat. She riffled through the contents of the drawers without hope of relief. Still, her hands crawled through every corner, fabric sliding through her fingers like water. She moved on to the next drawer and the next, futilely mining for answers, until a dripping trail of underwear, T-shirts, and broken promises lay in her wake.

When her legs gave up holding her, Jaden dropped to the floor. Another discarded item added to the mess.

She lay on her back in the middle of the room, staring at the white ceiling, sweat pooling in the small of her back. As her heartbeat slowed, other senses battered at her: the vanilla-and-citrus scent that followed her mom like a shadow, the plush carpet absorbing the shape of her, the ticking sound of the heating. She closed her eyes, filling her lungs, her heart, her blood. She wiped the familiarity across her body like a salve.

A memory percolated, pinpricks merging into a coherent picture.

She had been nearing the end of elementary school, staring down the barrel of puberty with her first few pimples and patches of insecurity. The utility of boys and makeup was still a mystery, but she was peering in the window of a world she would soon inhabit.

There had been three of them in the school bathroom: Jaden and two friends who had outpaced her in development. Jaden stared at her hands under a stream of water at the sink while her friends compared bra-strap colors and spoke a tantalizing language of fabrics and seams. Jaden was awed to see the blush-pink and baby blue lines snaking under the collars of their mirrored reflections.

"Um, Jaden, I think you need one too," one of the girls had said.

She pointed to Jaden's T-shirt, where the once-smooth field of her chest had given ground to inevitable mounds. Jaden was mortified.

She ran home that afternoon. Too impatient to wait until her mom came home from work, not yet understanding the intricacies of shape and size, Jaden tore up the stairs determined to find a bra in her mom's drawers. She burst into the bedroom.

Her mom sat on the bed in the unlit room, a shoebox open and a flurry of papers spread in front of her like oversize confetti.

The shock of her mom being home in the middle of the afternoon stayed her mind briefly. The urgency, though, would not be silent for long.

"I need a bra," Jaden blurted out, breathless. "Everyone has one."

She bounced slightly on her toes as she approached the bed, body poised to dive onto the mattress, limbs quivering like Jell-O at the thought of owning her own blush-pink bra. Her eleven-year-old mind, laser focused on immediate desires, hadn't been subtle enough to catch the details in the moment. Remembering now, the questions seemed obvious and needful. Why had the bedroom door been closed? Why was her mom home from work in the middle of the day? Why was the room so dark?

As happens with age and understanding, the scene now stood out differently in her mind. Her mom's strange reaction at the time took on another layer with the benefit of age and hindsight.

"Jesus, Jaden. What the hell are you doing? For fuck sakes." The last words were muttered under a breath, but Jaden heard them.

Jaden froze, knees bent before a jump, caught in the beam of a mother's punishing glare. Her mom never swore. *Lazy language,* she called it, even chastising her dad on occasion.

"How many times have I told you to knock before barging into a room? You're old enough to know better," her mom continued, hastily gathering the pages off the bed.

Tears formed along Jaden's eyelids as her moment of covetous zeal was slapped aside.

Unsure what to do, Jaden waited, poised in the moment before a leap, while her mom stuffed pages into an old shoebox. Instinct told her to shrink her voice and her expectations. She slowly dropped her heels and lowered herself to the floor, head bowed to hide her tears.

After what seemed a lifetime to an eleven-year-old, her mom finally spoke again, voice softened and papers shoved carelessly aside.

"A bra? Wow. We're there already, are we?" her mom said.

From beneath her bangs, Jaden snuck a peek at the pale smile appearing on her mom's lips. Deep worry lines between her eyes sent a more tentative message, but hope remained for attaining her heart's desire.

Jaden nodded, keeping the rest of her body still.

"OK, Walmart, here we come," her mom said. "Why don't we swing by Bulk Barn, too, and we can pick up those juice-berry candies you like."

Jaden felt confusion ebb, leaving room for a flood of anticipation.

Before they left the bedroom, her mom ducked into the closet with the shoebox. She reemerged without it, having shucked off the sad, angry woman Jaden had seen on the bed.

Jaden rolled to sitting. Sunset was approaching, leaving the room in flat shadows. Winnie watched her from the doorway, her tail wagging every time Jaden glanced over.

"All right, then. What was so important, Mom?" Jaden said, her voice fulfilling a need to break the silence.

On her knees, she moved toward the closet and opened the door. Though not her first time rummaging in her parents' closet, a sense of the forbidden still tickled at her conscience. She inched forward into the smell of stale clothing and a more pungent version of her mom's particular scent. Clothes hung neatly from a chrome rod with a shoe cubby lining one wall; on the other wall, a low shelving unit housed wicker baskets neatly filled with a mishmash of accessories. Jaden closed her eyes and breathed in her childhood.

She let memories flutter like moths through her mind until the shoebox centered behind her lids: battered orange and brown, with the Nike swoosh across the lid.

Jaden hesitated. A primordial fear of creatures that go bump in the dark stayed her hand. She couldn't see the shoebox, but she knew it was there, tucked somewhere out of sight. Finally, shuttling aside childish qualms, she moved deeper into the closet and groped into the corners for answers.

Her fingers found cardboard.

She sat cross-legged on the closet floor, examining the paltry collection of items in the shoebox. Though seemingly random, Jaden felt in her bones that a pattern lived under the surface. The box held Jaden's birth certificate, a small velvet box with baby teeth, a collection of newspaper articles from the 1990s, a few romantic cards from her father, and a student transcript from the University of Toronto in the name of Grace Elaine Hobbes.

A watermark of the school's crest—a coat of arms with a beaver and books beneath a tree—was embedded in the paper, along with the Latin words *Velut. Arbor. Aevo*, "as a tree, over time." This Grace woman, whoever she was, had been studying history. She was a good student, landing on the dean's honor list for two years, the third year only thwarted by a glaring C in a biology class.

"Hobbes," Jaden said the name out loud several times, testing its edges for familiarity, like a climber reaching for unknown holds.

Her mom's maiden name had been Hobbes, but Jaden had never heard of a Grace Elaine. Questions nattered at her. Was Grace a sister or a cousin? If so, why had Jaden never heard of her? Was she dead? Or was this a registration screwup with her mom's name? Could this connection to the school have been the reason her mom had been so dead set against Jaden attending the university?

The newspaper clippings, mostly from student-run or local newspapers, provided no answers. Dated between 1996 and 1999, they were mostly articles about student organizations, theater performances, and quirky eateries in and around the Toronto area. More than one of the articles reported on the activities of an animal rights student group with a silly name.

The transcript, however, held Jaden's attention.

She glanced at her phone. Four o'clock. There was still a chance that the records office would be open with a skeleton staff over the holidays. Jaden googled the number and hit connect.

"Registrar's office," a bored, nasal voice answered.

Jaden sat up straighter. She cleared her throat and reached for a haughty tone.

"Yes, hello, my name is Rachel Plint. I'm with Faskins and Row. I'm calling about a Grace Hobbes," Jaden said, disguising the uncertainty in her tone with a shuffle of papers that she hoped traveled through the phone.

Faskins and Row was a consulting firm in the Toronto area that often recruited on campus. Jaden had no clue what they did, but it had name recognition, and that might just be enough.

"How can I help you?"

A little surprised she was getting away with it, Jaden pushed forward.

"Ms. Hobbes has applied for a position with us and stated her qualifications and degree from the University of Toronto. A degree from a recognized university is a requirement for the position. We'd like to confirm her attendance and matriculation from your institution."

"Of course," said the woman. The click of fingers dancing across a keyboard accompanied her words. "What year are you looking for?"

Jaden wasn't sure. She hesitated.

"Let me look." There was no indication on the transcript that Grace Hobbes had in fact graduated, only the years she had taken classes.

"It says on her application that her degree was conferred in 1999," Jaden said, taking a stab at a date after a quick calculation in her head.

Click, clack. Click, clack.

"Hmm, I'm not seeing anything in our graduates list from that time. It's been a while, though. Could she have changed her name?"

"I wouldn't know," Jaden said, her natural voice slipping out. She felt deflated, as if a prize were being held just out of reach.

If the woman noticed, she said nothing.

"I'm not supposed to do this, but let me just take a quick peek at our registration records. I'll see if anything pops up."

Dead air lay heavy on the phone, interrupted only by the incessant electronic clicking.

"Here she is," the woman said, with an inappropriate amount of enthusiasm. "Grace Hobbes. Attended 1996 to 1999. Hmm."

Jaden couldn't tell if the woman's tone was curious or defensive.

"I think you're being hoodwinked, Ms. Plint. Grace Hobbes dropped out in her third year. She left midsemester, not even a record of withdrawal. Looks like she just stopped coming and got incompletes in her second-semester courses. She certainly doesn't have a degree from the University of Toronto." The woman let out a nervous chuckle. "Looks like she vanished."

Jaden hit end on the phone.

The nasal voice echoed in Jaden's mind, reverberating the way a howling wind whispered long after its passing. In dimming afternoon light, the papers lay in front of her, spokes on a broken wheel. She ran a hand over the random collection of papers. The edges of the newspaper articles, dry and brittle, disintegrated under her fingers. The words stared back at her, disjointed puzzle pieces in the absence of a reference photo for guidance.

Chapter 12

Grace

1996

The Philosopher's Walk was not what Grace Hobbes had expected. Given the name, she had anticipated *Leaves of Grass* and a barbaric yawp over the roofs of the world from the University of Toronto walkway; instead, there were preformed metal benches and interlocking brick. It was yet another way the city and university had defied her expectations. Grace hadn't yet decided if she was disappointed or enchanted.

Under dappled sunlight and with the scent of fresh-cut grass in her nose, she followed the walkway until it dumped her into the middle of campus. Eighteen and a freshman at one of the largest universities in the country, she was still getting her bearings in this new life.

Grace had almost been sent to her knees with grief when she'd first arrived in Toronto two weeks ago. Six months had passed since her parents were killed, the victims of an overeager pickup truck that had jumped the light, and the loss could run through her like lava. Her parents hadn't been there when the letter of admission to the University of Toronto had arrived, hadn't seen her graduate from high school, hadn't helped her settle into her dorm room. She had had to survive each of those moments by herself, each milestone a jagged reminder her parents were gone and never coming back.

She found it strange to refer to herself as an orphan, and yet it told an entire story in a breath, one that had instantly cut her off from the life she had known in her hometown of Winnipeg. There, among her friends and the people who knew her, she felt her existence had been reduced to a single moment of incalculable loss. Here, in a new city of over four million people, she was unknown and unknowable. If all went well, she would leave loss behind and become part of the graduating class of 2000. She could find a new life, and the remnants of the orphaned prairie girl could be stamped out.

A slow trickle of sweat ran beneath Grace's T-shirt. She looked up at the looming brick structure of the student commons building and debated turning around. She could still head back to her dorm, curl up with a Margaret Atwood book and a bowl of popcorn. It would be infinitely easier than entering a room full of strangers and pretending to belong.

"You have to try something," Jess, her best friend since kindergarten, had said that morning on the phone. "If you hate it, you don't go back. Easy. You just need to find a few friends. It's the only way to survive university."

"I have friends," Grace had said, standing in the middle of her postage-stamp-size dorm room, twirling the phone cord around her finger.

She hadn't wanted a roommate, another person with whom to share her tragic tale. Her inheritance had been more than enough to cover a single room and living expenses for her undergraduate years. Now the stark white walls stared back at her, mocking her decision.

"The custodian and the weird girl next door who tried to smuggle a lizard into the dorm don't count as friends," Jess said flatly.

"Well, not if you're being picky, they don't."

Grace resented Jess for being right. She hoped the roll of her eyes was imbued in the tone of her voice. If her friend heard the sarcasm, she chose to ignore it. She hated to admit that a congenial loneliness had started to descend, one she knew would ruin her if given the chance.

"Who knows? It could be fun. And animal rights were something you felt pretty strongly about before—"

Jess had never been able to bring herself to say the words, as if uttering them was a curse. Grace didn't blame her. Dead parents were a kind of curse. It was another reason the gulf between them was widening. Jess was in Winnipeg, meeting new people at her own university, having new experiences, and Grace was two thousand kilometers away, body and soul.

"Just try it. For me," Jess had said before they uttered their goodbyes.

Jess's words echoed in her head as Grace forced herself up the concrete steps and into the cool interior of the building. She was greeted by gray linoleum flooring and walls coated in student posters advertising everything from math clubs to fundraising events. Though quieter than during the week, the hallways still had a faint bustle with students coming in and out like bees in a hive.

Maybe two dozen people—some standing in small groups, others keeping to themselves—were milling about when Grace poked her head through the meeting-room door. The small lecture theater wasn't bursting, but neither was it echoey the way Grace had feared. The smell of sweat and nerves danced on a sigh of air-conditioning; soft laughter peppered watchful conversations. At the front of the room, a good-looking guy with wavy chin-length hair and a mischievous grin had just written his name and email address on the whiteboard.

Grace surveyed the exits. Slipping away would be easy if need be. She took a seat near the door.

"Hi, I'm Ben," said a guy two seats down from her. He extended his hand, the expression on his face a mix of hope and trepidation.

Grace looked at him for a moment, her mind slotting through the behaviors expected of her: ignore, smile, or move away. Though she assumed he was university aged, his cheeks still had lingering pillows of middle school fat. She looked down at his extended hand, not the typical greeting among her peers. Grace found it amusing.

"Grace," she said, accepting his damp palm.

A relieved smile passed over his face. He pumped her arm like he was drilling for water.

"Are you a first year?" he said.

"I am."

"Knew it. We all have the same lost-puppy look. Of course, I couldn't hide mine if I tried. Not with this face." He pinched his cheeks as he spoke, causing the last few words to drop into a sloppy slur.

Grace laughed.

Encounters with strangers could feel like waiting for a bus. One came along and you considered getting on, curious about the destination. Other times, every instinct told you to wave them on past. With Ben, there was never a question. Grace knew from her first conversation that they were headed in the same direction.

There, Jess, she said in her head as the room started to settle. *I've made a friend.*

A loud clap and bellowed *welcome* from the front of the room hushed any final mutters. Beside the lectern on a small dais, the good-looking guy was rubbing his hands together and casting curious eyes over the people gathered. A charmed smile rested too easily on his lips, as if he were born to the expression. He had the ease and confidence of all good-looking men who knew they could command a room with a wink.

His name was Konrad Sharma, he said.

Though he didn't give himself a title, it was clear he led the student club that was hosting the meeting. They called themselves Militant Animals.

"Our mission," said Sharma, "is to raise awareness through determined outreach and active frivolity."

A nervous chuckle went around the room. Sharma grinned.

"Look, I get it. You're all used to the Greenpeace model. Chain yourselves to harpoon guns, lie down with baby seals. But that's not what we're about. We focus our actions on the achievable and the less dramatic. Right now, our targets are cosmetics companies that still test on animals. I mean, do we really need, in this day and age, to torture Snoopy for a shade of lipstick?

"Militant Animals also feels that people pay more attention to a protest if it makes them laugh. Last year, for example, for one of our demonstrations, a group of us 'shopped' for makeup at a local department store wearing rabbit costumes. It hit the local press, and the store decided against renewing contracts with companies that use animal testing."

A polite spontaneous applause deepened a proud grin on Konrad's face.

"We build community and have fun for a cause." He let that sink in to their imaginations like sugar dissolving into tea, before continuing. "How many of you are first years?"

Most hands flew up; the few that didn't were attached to irritatingly knowing smiles.

Konrad affably scrutinized the new faces in the seated crowd, nodding as he made eye contact with a few of the newbies. Grace refused to be sucked in that easily. She kept her eyes turned away even when she felt his gaze linger on her.

Ben leaned toward her. "I think he just winked at you," he said in a whisper.

"Wasn't looking," she said. Though, she couldn't stop a smile from flitting through her eyes.

Other members of the Militant Animals executive team were introduced, each sharing the same confidence and glee that Konrad had brought to his opening remarks. Giddiness spread like an infection through the audience, until most were smiling and laughing with the same looseness as the presenters. Jaden kept her face closed and her thoughts to herself.

"All right," Konrad said, taking over the meeting again. His expression shifted, the grin settling behind harder eyes. He took in a breath and glanced at the ceiling before speaking. The room leaned in to listen.

"Now to some serious stuff. Yes, we care about animals. Yes, we believe that change starts with activism. Yes, we are interested in getting attention for our message."

A few heads nodded. A couple of whoops went up.

"Make no mistake, though, if you are here to incite violence, you are not welcome. If you are here to cause harm, you are not welcome." His voice dropped, and he shot a tight-lipped glare before resuming. "We do not tolerate violence of any kind, for any reason. Militant Animals is about respect and dignity, for those who agree with us and for those who don't."

Grace had to hand it to him, he knew how to use a strategic pause.

"If you can abide by that," he continued, "you are most welcome. If not, no harm, no foul. There's the door."

Konrad held his arm up and his silence. The room fidgeted. Jaden looked across the room to see more than one girl, and even a couple of the boys, with smitten looks in their eyes. No one left the room.

"And, yes," Konrad said finally, the smile creeping back onto his lips. "It is still possible to maintain your dignity while wearing an adult-size rabbit costume."

And with that, any tension shattered.

The room ignited into excited murmurs as the meeting closed. Grace heard snippets of conversation—*so cool . . . awesome . . . real deal*—and, not for the first time, found herself feeling like the adult in the room. Tragedy could do that, age you beyond your years, so that joy no longer came easily.

Over the clatter, one of the organizers invited the crowd for drinks at a nearby bar. As she shuffled toward the door, she saw Konrad shouldering a politician's toadying charm offensive while he bumped fists and slapped backs.

"Are you going to go for a drink?" Ben said, bouncing a little on his toes. "This seems like it could be a lot of fun."

He walked beside her, a messenger bag slung over his shoulder and his hips dancing to step around traffic so he could keep up with her. Ben wore his loneliness like an emblem, offering pieces of himself as a lure, poorly braced for disappointment. They didn't know each other, but Grace felt a soft spot for him. Watching Ben dodge and weave between bodies, she couldn't help wondering whether lonely people had secret means of finding each other, like moths calling silently to each other in the dark.

"I'm not sure it's my scene, I—" she said.

"Hey there, you guys! Coming out for a drink?"

The voice that cut Grace off was less startling than the firm hand on her shoulder. She felt her face bloom as she resisted the impulse to flinch.

Konrad Sharma had come up behind them, gently steering her and Ben forward. Heat from his hand seeped through Grace's T-shirt. She wouldn't have said there was an attraction, not then, but an energy buzzed at the point of contact, like a dull zap from fresh laundry.

Ben looked at Grace, offered her the faintest questioning head tilt. His expression was restrained hopefulness, though she could see the effort it was costing him in his reddening ears and tight smile.

An urge trickled through Grace, one she hadn't felt in months. Not since the day a police officer had walked into her basketball practice and shattered the world. The sensation was like a splash of cold water on sunbaked skin. The feeling was distantly familiar, a faint song, but there. Grace wanted to be around people. She wanted to be around these people.

"Sure. Why not?" she said as she followed Konrad Sharma out the door.

Chapter 13

Jaden

After hanging up the phone on the University of Toronto registrar's office, Jaden found herself unable to move. She sat in the middle of her parents' room, the phone on the floor in front of her. Images from the last couple of days slid through her head like a deranged PowerPoint presentation: her mom's face on Christmas Day, the square of light on the wall of the police station while her dad's words filled the room, the transcript from the University of Toronto in a wrongly familiar name. None of it fit together into a coherent story. And yet, here it was.

As a kid, Jaden had been curious about the imbalance in her family: the Meadowses, loud and large and ever present, and the Hobbeses, virtually nonexistent. There were no pictures, or even stories, about her mom's side of the family. She'd asked, from time to time, begging at bedtime, coming away with only crumbs.

A final bedtime conversation had eventually put an end to Jaden's curiosity.

"Where do guppies go after they turn into frogs?" Jaden had asked while she pulled a pajama top over her head. Her mom was picking up a day's worth of abandoned activities off the floor. Jaden was old enough to understand that questions could be a marvelous stalling technique at bedtime.

"I think you mean tadpoles," her mom had answered. "Tadpoles actually change into frogs. They grow legs and arms, until they're no longer tadpoles. They're frogs."

Jaden thought about the answer, considered whether it made sense, and decided it wasn't worth wondering further.

"How come bubble gum loses its flavor when you chew it?" The question popped into her head as her mom tossed clothes in the corner laundry hamper.

"That is a good question. I'm actually not sure."

Jaden could sense her window was coming to an end. Her mom huffed out a sigh on the last answer.

"What was my grandma's name?" Jaden said, crawling into bed, still tasting the grape-flavored toothpaste on her lips.

"Lilian," her mom said, stifling a yawn.

Hearing her grandmother's name had felt like unearthing a treasurer. "Lilian," Jaden said, trying the shape of it on her own lips. She liked the sound, pictured a delicate petal of a woman with white hair and a long green dress.

"Was she nice?" Jaden said.

"She was."

Jaden pulled the blanket up to her chin while her mom stuffed the edges underneath her body so she was wrapped like a burrito.

"What did she like?"

"It's bedtime, Jaden."

Her mom left the room briefly for the obligatory glass of water and placed it on Jaden's bedside table.

"What about Grandpa? What was he like?"

"Come on, honey, enough questions out of you tonight," her mom said, rubbing the back of her neck as she sat on the edge of the bed.

"What was his name? Daddy said he was a doctor. Did he fix you when you got sick?"

"Jaden, that's enough. Time for bed." Her mom turned on the night-light that projected stars onto the ceiling. Jaden couldn't sleep back then without the universe over her head.

"Do you miss them?"

Jaden saw the tear then, as it slipped from the corner of her mom's eyes. A shame she didn't understand radiated from her core, gushing to her face. It wasn't as brutal as shock, more like a sudden knowing. A knowing that left her feeling uneasy and deceived: Parents, too, it seemed, could be sad. Jaden buried her face behind the stuffed bear that lived on her pillow.

The mattress leaned as her mom's body lay beside her. Jaden peeked out from behind the bear. Her mom lay on her back watching the stars make their slow journey across the ceiling.

"Your grandparents died when I was young," her mom said quietly. "Even though it was a long time ago, it still hurts. It's kinda like having a tummy ache that never really goes away. When I talk about them, the tummy ache gets worse."

Even at nine, Jaden understood the gentle squeeze of her mom's hand on her leg. She nodded. She said nothing, but an understanding settled itself into her bones that night: Her mom was alone, vulnerable and without protection in the world. She needed Jaden to protect her.

Jaden rolled onto her side, facing her mom, and felt the rough plush of the stuffed bear under her chin. She reached a hand to her mom's stomach, felt the slow rise and fall, saw the smile that wasn't a smile on her lips, and understood enough. It was the last time she'd asked about her grandparents.

The university transcript in the name of Grace Hobbes now burned questions into Jaden's mind about the unexamined parts of her mom's past. Sitting on her parents' bedroom floor, papers spread out in front of her, Jaden understood that her mother was her own flawed story, one that Jaden had never bothered to read.

The first chapter had to be whatever had been left unspoken for all these years. And the music box was the key to unlocking it.

Jaden lurched on numb legs toward her room, where her laptop lay on the bed. She tapped the keys, and the screen jumped to life. Settling cross-legged, she navigated to the browser. She was still hunched over the computer hunting for information a couple of hours later when her dad poked his head in her room.

"Hey, you hungry?" he said, standing in the doorframe. "Sheila sent me home with casseroles, and we still have a ton of leftovers."

Jaden looked up, letting her brain readjust. She hadn't even heard him come home. Every neuron had been tuned to finding a digital thread to the music box. She had no idea what she was looking for, but she trusted that the algorithms and search engines would lead her somewhere relevant.

Stiff and still cross-legged, she took in her dad's exhausted frame with her unfocused eyes. Her own body felt bone weary, but her head buzzed from the hunt.

"I'm not sure I could eat," Jaden said.

"No, me neither. I think I might try to rest my eyes for a little bit, though. You doing OK?"

Though Jaden couldn't have said how she knew—perhaps it was the shallowness of his voice or the deep breath he took before speaking—it was clear to her that her dad needed her to be OK in this moment. He couldn't know that she was chasing down the thinnest, most careless idea of a lead and clinging to the hope in it.

"Ya, I'm OK," she said.

He nodded ruefully.

When she heard the faint click of his bedroom door, she turned her attention back to the screen.

She keyed *gold jewelry box* into a Pinterest search bar. She normally shunned the craft-and-project site as a waste of time, but desperation had a way of realigning assumptions. She waited for the hits to pop up. Her eyes burned, and an ache budded across her forehead.

A kaleidoscope of options appeared on the screen. Jaden sighed. She scrolled down, expecting nothing.

Her eyes strayed from the screen to the duvet on her bed; she felt its pull like a siren's call. Maybe resting her eyes for just a few minutes couldn't hurt?

This is stupid, she thought, giving voice to the pathetic need in her search and in herself. Hope had a way of driving you past the point of reason to a place where doing nothing gnawed at the back of your brain and going forward ate the heart out of you.

Vintage box, perfect for jewelry organization flashed past on the screen.

Jaden almost kept scrolling. Fatigue delayed her mind's ability to translate text into meaning.

She scrolled back and clicked on the embedded link. On the screen was a brass-and-glass box with an etching of flowers across the lid. Not the same as the one still sitting on the living-room coffee table but similar style and motif in the etching. The box, larger and more grandiose, was pictured open, revealing a maze of compartments. A small music mechanism nestled in the corner. The ad read:

> Clear Glass Jewelry Box—
>
> Vintage jewelry case with lid. Swiss made. Vanity metal and brass. Perfect for jewelry display.
>
> Dust-proof organizer for earrings, rings, necklaces.
>
> Originally purchased at Music Box Stop, in Toronto, near Kensington Market.

Jaden stood up from the bed and let out a strained squeal. Her stiff knees groaned with the effort, while her neck protested the sudden movement with a sharp crick. She kept her eyes on the screen, paranoid that she had misread it or that the image on the screen would disappear.

"What the hell was that?" An unexpected but familiar voice whirled Jaden around toward the door.

Standing on the threshold, arms crossed, and one delicate eyebrow raised, was Zelda Fitzgerald. Her best friend's mop of shoulder-length curls was a painfully welcome sight.

"I've been trying to reach you all day. Pick up your damn phone once in a while," Zelda said, though there was no anger in her dark-honey features.

Zelda lived up to her literary namesake. A biracial kid raised by a single mom in a small Canadian town, she had a thick skin and a razor-sharp wit. She also had an exceptional talent for seeing the world as it was and calling it out. They'd known each other so long, Jaden couldn't remember a time when they hadn't been friends. Both were now roommates in Toronto and had come home for the holidays.

"I heard," Zelda said, not needing to explain more. "Thought you could use a friend right now."

A barrage of emotions careened through Jaden—anger, despair, relief. She couldn't seem to settle into just one. In her mind, she saw a thread, bright red and thin as a whisper. She looked up at Zelda, her concerned smile on her lips.

"Any interest in a road trip?" Jaden said, reaching for her first filament of hope in two days.

Chapter 14

Grace

1996

"You've never been? How is that even possible. It's the best!" Ben said, his words melding with the chatter in the university cafeteria.

He stuffed another ketchup-laden chicken finger in his mouth while stabbing the student paper laid open on the table. Across the centerfold, a pair of highly glossed lips floated above the title of a movie.

"*The Rocky Horror Picture Show* is only the best two hours you will ever spend in your life," he continued. "We're going. Tonight. We need rice. And water guns. And a deck of cards."

Grace laughed. Not even her wildest imaginings fit those three items together, and he was still going with a list.

"OK, OK. Let's go," she said, leaning into his enthusiasm. "My Business Principles paper be damned."

"Awesome. Do you have a French maid's outfit, by any chance?"

Grace started to wonder what the hell she'd just gotten herself into.

"Never mind," Ben said. "I'll bring everything. You can be Janet. Wear something super boring and heels if you have them."

"The clothes I can manage. The shoes? The best I can do is Mary Janes."

"Perfect," Ben said with a big grin. He stood and swung his backpack over his shoulder. "I've got some errands to run now. I'll meet you in front of the library at seven. We can grab something to eat and still get there with plenty of time to get a seat at the back. We'll want that for obvious reasons."

Grace didn't have the heart to tell him they were not obvious to her.

"See you then," she said and watched him hustle between the tables toward the door.

She looked at her watch. It was a little after two. If she really concentrated, she could probably get a good chunk of her business paper outlined before she had to meet Ben. She also had time to pop into the Second Cup across College Street; the walk would do her good, and the caffeine boost from their double espresso always gave her an extra little study kick.

Outside, a rare mild autumn sun lured open jackets and daydreams of the forgotten summer. Grace scurried across the square, head down and the Violent Femmes in her headphones. She had almost reached the end of the square when she heard her name above the music.

She turned to the sound. Konrad Sharma waved at her before detaching himself from a small group, all of whom glanced at her with annoyance. She pushed away the flitter in her stomach when she recognized him.

She'd seen Konrad a number of times since their first encounter at the Militant Animals intro session. He was a constant presence at meetings and a well-known face on campus. A relaxed charm and easy laughter made him a magnetic presence in any crowd; more than once, Grace had found herself caught in the vortex and craving his attention. She kicked herself every time, her inside voice berating her mercilessly.

Don't make an ass out of yourself, she thought as he sauntered across the quad toward her.

"Hey there. Where you off to?" Konrad said as he drew near.

She debated not answering. Or lying. But what was the point? Her heart wanted Konrad to know where she was going, even if her head resented her for it.

"Coffee," she said. "Then the library to work on a term paper."

"Excellent," he said. "My plan exactly. Well, not the term paper. Coffee, then studying for the LSAT. Can I tag along?"

"Free country," Grace said, her insides squirming with excitement and a dismay in her lack of self-control. "I'm heading all the way to Second Cup on College, though. I like their coffee."

"Sounds great," Konrad said, rubbing his hands together. "Let's go!"

Four hours later, they were on their third cup of coffee and deep in a discussion about the social commentary and brilliance of *The Simpsons* when Konrad suggested they continue the discussion over dinner.

"Dinner? What time is it?"

She glanced at an oversize clock behind the cash register and was shocked to see it was nearly six thirty. The coffee shop was empty, and two lone staff had started hoisting seat-side chairs down onto the tables.

"Shit!" she said, standing up abruptly. "Shit, shit, shit."

"Whoa, I didn't think dinner was such a radical suggestion," Konrad said with a laugh.

"No, it's not that, it's—"

She stopped herself. Under the half quirk of a laugh still on his lips and the soft golden brown of his eyes, Grace was embarrassed to concede that she really wanted to go to dinner with this man, and more.

"It's just, I kinda have plans already," she said, pushing aside the petulant regret she felt. "Rain check?"

"Absolutely. Just tell me where and when."

Grace melted into the broad smile on Konrad's face before she flew out the door. Each step away from the coffee shop brought a tinge of annoying wistfulness. With effort, she pushed down the childish longing and forced her feet forward.

The temperature had dropped in the absence of the sun. Cold snuck under her now-useless sweater. As her mind cleared, her term paper deadline filled the void. She'd done nothing on it. Why had she agreed to see some silly movie with Ben? Maybe it wasn't too late? Surely Ben would understand if she canceled.

All thoughts of canceling evaporated when she saw him standing at the foot of the library stairs, backlit by a streetlight. He'd ditched his standard-issue T-shirt and jeans in favor of ankle-length black pants and a too-small suit jacket over a white T-shirt. His face was coated in white makeup with dark rings outlining his eyes. The effect had a Halloween-zombie feel with a dash of goth.

"What the—" Grace said.

"I told you, we wear costumes," he said, his smile taking over the entirety of his strange-looking face. "You didn't change."

He handed her a plastic shopping bag and started riffling through another one in his hand. "It's OK, not everyone dresses up."

"Ben, I'm—"

"I got the rice, toilet paper, playing cards. I couldn't find water pistols, but these spray bottles should work and—"

"Ben, I can't go."

He looked up at her, his face angled slightly away as if he'd just been slapped. In the dim light, Grace couldn't make out his expression behind the makeup.

"What?"

Ben didn't move. His head froze in a confused tilt, and he held a smile until time and the makeup made it slip into creepiness.

"For long, I mean," Grace said, knowing she couldn't disappoint him and recovering. "I can't go for long."

"But you said you had no plans tonight," Ben said, the smile finally dropping.

"I know. It's just, I bumped into someone at the coffee shop and fell behind a little. I still have a lot to do on my paper."

"Who?"

The challenge in the one-word question bristled.

"No one you know," Grace lied. She wasn't sure why. Something about being scrutinized by Ben in a demented-looking butler costume set her on edge.

"I'll go for a bit but probably won't stay until the end. What's the big deal? It's just a movie, right?"

If a person could be flattened and remain standing, that was Ben. Grace hadn't meant for her words to sound so snarky. They just came out. And now that they were there, standing like barbs in the space between them, she had no idea how to pull them back or undo the hurt she'd just caused. It was too late.

"Look, I'm sorry," she said, though it sounded dismissive even to her. "I promise I'll make it up to you."

"Ya, sure. It's OK," Ben said, his expression anything but mollified.

Grace gave a half-hearted smile and started walking. Her gaze stayed stolidly ahead as she considered possible restaurants for her delayed dinner with Konrad. In her wake, a sneer traveled Ben's face, morphing into a cold hurt in his eyes.

Chapter 15

Jaden

The break of the weather-sealing strip made a tiny *whoosh* as Zelda pulled open the heavy wood door of the Music Box Stop. The narrow brick building—painted in shades of canary yellow and sky blue—squeezed itself onto a block lined with Victorian town houses. The main floors of each had been converted into a ragtag line of shops and restaurants. Primary colors popped against the drab tones and gray sky of a Toronto winter.

Without glancing back, Zelda stepped through. Jaden followed.

"What the he—" Zelda said in stunned awe as she stopped dead just inside the door.

Jaden stepped around her friend and into a warped dream. Floor-to-ceiling music boxes and cuckoo clocks lined the walls. The entire room was drowned in candy-color ceramics, shiny black lacquer, glass inlays, and a hundred more materials Jaden couldn't identify. Shelves started at baseboard height and ran up to the ceiling, each briming with colors and shapes, creating a kaleidoscope of time. The girls stood motionless, mouths open and eyes wide, still unable to take it all in.

As Jaden's eyes adjusted, cues from her other senses came into focus: the sound of ill-timed cuckoo clocks, the patter of traffic outside, the feel of what turned out to be an orange tabby rubbing against her leg.

Jaden looked over at Zelda and saw a mirror of her own feelings in her friend's puzzled expression.

They hadn't noticed the door set in the corner to their left or the small counter and cash register in front of it. A sudden burst of notes from a wooden clock above the counter announced 1:00 p.m., a ring of wooden children on a wheel dancing to the mechanical tune. Something prickly and woodsy permeated the air. It took Jaden's brain a few seconds to catch up before she identified it. Tiger Balm. She remembered the camphor-and-eucalyptus combination that her grandmother rubbed onto her arthritic hands.

"He looks petrified," Zelda whispered, drawing Jaden's attention to an old man asleep behind the counter. His eyes were closed, and his head tipped back. His mouth was open a crack, as if he had been in the middle of a conversation when he fell asleep.

"I heard that, young lady." The mouth moved but the head did not.

Zelda jumped and let out a yelp. "Jeez. You scared the hell outta me, gramps."

"As well I should with that mouth," the gentleman said in a rolling French accent. He slowly opened his eyes and fixed the girls in a firm and curious gaze.

He creaked to standing and reached for eyeglasses that dangled on a string around his neck. His shoulders were square and back straight, giving the impression of a heavy life well carried. He stared at them without smiling.

"Sorry to bother you, sir," Jaden said, thinking that a little sweetness might smooth the situation.

"Well, come in, come in now. I will not bite," he said, waving them forward.

"Yes, sir," the girls said in unison and shuffled toward the counter. Something about his manner commanded etiquette.

He lifted a mug off the counter and took a small sip. Jaden could see a line of moisture along his dry lips. "Now," he said, putting his hands behind his back. "How can I help you ladies?"

Jaden reached into her backpack and pulled out the towel-wrapped music box. She laid the bundle on the counter and furtively unfolded the edges as if the box might suddenly take flight and nest itself among its companions on the shelves.

"Let's see what we have," said the man.

"We're trying to find out some information about this," Jaden said. She slid it across to him.

The shopkeeper pulled the music box toward himself and reached for a magnifying glass behind the counter. "Ah, yes, very nice. Swiss made. Finicky but beautiful."

His voice was tinged with a hint of longing that rankled Jaden. She pushed down an impulse to snatch back the box with a polite smile.

"It's a gift for her mother," Zelda said. "Is it possible to trace where it comes from? And what it's worth?" Jaden felt Zelda's faint tap against her hip and knew to stay quiet about the lie.

With shaky hands, the man lifted the box to eye level, smoothly examining the edges and contours. He held it up to the light so he could inspect it from all sides. He lifted the lid. Slowly, he turned the metal key at the bottom, letting notes percolate from the mechanism. He smiled. Jaden stiffened.

"I know this box," he said formally. "Tragedy follows it."

Jaden felt a hush descending. *Not another storyteller,* she thought, casting a glance at Zelda. Still, she tuned her ears to the man's voice in anticipation.

"A young man brought this in. Years ago, now. I remember because he was very young. Not my usual clientele. He said his father collected music boxes when he was small and that he grew up learning to care for them. He knew the art of cleaning and oiling, and how to . . . er, ajuster, the timing. He said his parents were new Canadiens. This, I understand. Moi, I am French, and this country, well, it can be difficult when you are new. I liked the boy."

The man lightly ran his fingers over the box, removing unseen dust. He reached under the table and pulled out a soft cloth, then gently rubbed at the glass as he continued.

"The music mechanism was broken. He asked if I could provide a new one. I think he had une amoureuse he wanted to impress. I was happy to oblige. We French, we appreciate romance. He knew exactly the song he wanted. Very precise, though it cost him much more for a special order."

The shopkeeper gently pushed the music box toward Jaden. His eyes lingered in admiration.

"Do you remember who he was?" Zelda said.

The man looked at her, a slight furrow of his brow gauging the question. Zelda held his eyes. The man nodded once.

"It is easy to remember this man because only a week after he collected the box, he was dead. I saw in the paper. He was killed."

"How?" Two voices in unison. Jaden felt a dryness in her mouth that made the word hard.

"Je m'excuse," said the shopkeeper. "I do not remember all. Only the young man and that it should not have happened. Not so young."

The man paused, as if memory and the specter of death had pulled at his energy. When he spoke again, his voice seemed hoarse and his blinks came more slowly.

"Konrad Sharma," he said. "That was his name. I remember because it was so unusual. A German first name and Hindu last name. I asked him about it. He told me his parents had met here, in Canada. Just like me and my Gertrude. Different worlds become a family."

Sounds beyond the lilt of the man's voice crept back into Jaden's ears, rustling up questions. She was aware of Zelda beside her and the constant soft hum of everyday life around them.

"How do you know it's the same music box?" Jaden said. "I didn't find a serial number on it."

"You're right," the man said with a mischievous smile, offering a glimpse of the charm and swagger he must have exuded in his youth.

"The song was not common, but that does not mean it is the same one I sold all those years ago. But I remember something else."

He opened the lid of the box and pointed a shaky finger to the inside hinges. Both girls leaned in. Jaden noticed she'd been holding in air like a child. She forced herself to breathe.

"Not easy to see, but if you know what you're looking for," he said, "it is there. Just under the hinges."

Jaden took the magnifying glass the shopkeeper held out to her. Like a trompe l'oeil that is impossible to unsee once it's been pointed out, the letters were obvious: *KS* under the left hinge and *GH* under the right in delicate cursive script.

"This is my work. I'd know it anywhere," he said.

Grace Hobbes, thought Jaden.

"Did he tell you the girl's name? Presumably, the woman he was ordering it for," Zelda said.

The shopkeeper looked thoughtful for a moment, his eyes unfocused as he searched his memories for a thread.

"Non," he said finally. "I never learned that. Or if I did, it has escaped." He tapped the side of his head with his fingertips.

Jaden tried to tuck away her disappointment, but Zelda didn't have that gift. "Well, can you at least remember the year?" she said with an impatient little sigh.

The shopkeeper gave her a placating smile. "The young, always so quick to judge," he said. Zelda's cheeks pinkened with the gentle rebuke.

"I do, in fact, young lady, have a recollection of the year. Though I can't be exact, I believe it was around the year 2000. My Gertrude got sick that year, and she died in 2003."

"I'm sorry," Zelda said, her face going from pink to red.

They thanked the shopkeeper for his time and headed for the door. Just before Jaden pushed out into the world, she heard him clear his throat.

"You know, I may know a buyer interested in your box," he said. The words were thrown out casually, but a glance from Zelda told

Jaden there was something more. "It is worth some money to those who collect. I could ask."

"No," Jaden said, inexplicably insulted by the suggestion. She caught herself. "I mean, no thank you. I'm not interested in selling."

Zelda jabbed her in the rib with an elbow, stopping Jaden's progress to the door.

"Sure, why not. Do you have a card?" Zelda reeled around and flashed the smile she reserved for cops and parents.

The shopkeeper handed over his card and then asked for contact details from Jaden. Confused but taking a leap of faith in Zelda, Jaden reeled off her name and cell number.

Stepping outside, Jaden was surprised to be greeted by the same midafternoon light they'd left outside, as if the world hadn't shifted with the story they'd just heard.

Chapter 16

Grace

1996

A spurt of schoolgirl laughter caught Grace's attention. She scowled at three women in artistically ripped jeans and butterfly hair clips standing beside Konrad on the far side of the room. She didn't know their actual names, but she referred to them as "the Ems." Every other female student in this place seemed to be either named Emma or Emily, so it was a safe bet. The Ems wore butterfly clips in their hair and expensive sweatshirts. Every time they spoke, Grace felt an urge to spit the sound of them out of her head.

"You didn't," one of the Ems screeched, placing a nail-painted hand on Konrad's arm.

Konrad's full-toothed grin and faux sheepishness told Grace everything. He was enjoying it. It was hard to tell the difference between raptors and prey in their flirtatious parry. Whatever the outcome, Konrad was prized quarry, and the Ems had their talons turned on him.

She didn't blame the girls, at least not entirely. Konrad was charming and intelligent and oozed so much confidence he had to wipe it up behind him when he left a room. It was impossible not to like the guy. And Grace had tried. Despite her eagerness after their coffee meet a few weeks ago, she hadn't followed up with a dinner invitation. She knew she shared the same adolescent crush as those fluttering eyelashes in front of him now but was determined to deny him the satisfaction of knowing.

The converted basement classroom that served as the Militant Animals office smelled like body odor and old grease, thanks to a vent shared with the cafeteria two floors above. High windows might have let in some extra light, but a November drizzle blotted out the sun. Grace didn't mind. The gray lighting and water-stained ceiling matched the rest of the city, even if it was wrapped in a pretty stone-and-ivy package. Despite the dreary surroundings, Emma enjoyed spending her time here. Being among these people—some she would even call friends—helped to fill the cavernous void she'd felt herself crawling into since she lost her parents.

Grace was still in mid-scowl when Konrad met her eye. She didn't need a mirror to know that the red blotches gracing her neck and face were likely flaming. He gave her a sideways smirk before turning his attention back to the Ems.

Grace looked down at her beat-up black-and-white Converse sneakers and oversize jeans. **God is dead—Nietzsche** was scrawled in blue pen across the toe box of her left shoe; the right retorted with **Nietzsche is dead—God**. She knew her look didn't exactly fit in with the Toronto-money preppy kids that dominated the school, but she didn't have the interest, or the energy, to bother fitting in. She shuffled her feet under the desk and went back to folding papers into neat little pamphlets.

"Do you think they're here for the animals or for him?" Ben said in a quiet voice.

Grace shrugged and threw an appreciative smirk his way.

Ben was the reason Grace was even here. Over the last couple of months, he'd slipped into the role of her best friend; given he seemed to be around all the time, she assumed the same was true for him. Thanks to his relentless coaxing, she had agreed to join Militant Animals. He stood across from her now, on the other side of a desk, stapling sheets of paper into pamphlets for a protest at the Metro Toronto Convention Centre tomorrow. A beauty show was planned for the next day, and Militant Animals was staging a beauty booth on the opposing sidewalk, offering cruelty-free makeovers and prizes for those who could prove they'd bought cruelty-free products while inside the show.

"Pretty obvious, don't you think?" Grace said. "They're practically salivating."

Ben chuckled, and Grace felt his eyes linger on her. If she looked up, she knew she'd see a puppy dog expression with a hint of worship. She didn't look up. She liked Ben, just not in the way he wanted. They'd fallen into the pattern of being each other's company. Grace hoped that time would dull the edges of his infatuation into a solid friendship.

She knew she was being a little cruel and that her need for companionship was stronger than her empathy. Toronto and her classmates were proving to be colder and less approachable than she'd hoped. Wherever she went, vapid buildings and hollow people left her in shade and shadow. Ben was a pleasant island in the concrete wasteland. She missed Winnipeg's intersecting rivers and the drawn-out prairie sun on her face; she missed friends and familiarity and a place to call home.

"You up for dinner after this?" Ben said.

She could sense the eagerness in his question and knew she was handing him an already broken promise. Guilt skulked through her. Then again, she'd learned that life could be nasty, cruel, and short, and if Ben was grazed in a cross fire, he'd survive. There were worse things that could happen to a person than an unrequited crush.

"Ya, sure," Grace said. She glanced up at him, consciously making her response dismissive. "But something quick. I've got a midterm in a couple of days and am way behind in my review."

The last paper folded, Grace looked around for something else to do, but everything seemed to be done. The room was emptying out, with the stragglers packing up materials and slipping on coats.

Grace rolled her shoulders and head. "Ready?" she said to Ben.

"You betcha," he said. "I just gotta make a pit stop in the little boys' room first. Meet you by the front doors."

Grace dropped the last of the pamphlets into a waiting cardboard box and grabbed her coat. As she slipped an arm in, there was a shuffle of movement in the corner of her eye. Her hand slammed into something hard. She whirled around—dropping her jacket—to come face-to-face with Konrad.

"Sorry," he said with a rueful grin. "Didn't mean to get in your way."

Grace was silent and no doubt blotchy. She hadn't exchanged words with Konrad since their quasi coffee date and now couldn't think of a single thing to say to him.

"Guess I better watch that right hook of yours," he said with a wink.

The wink woke her up. Condescending charm rang in her ear like nails on a blackboard.

"Or spend a little more time watching where you're going instead of chatting up bimbos," she said, matching his wink.

To Grace's surprise, instead of defensive dancing or feigned indignation, a warm, deep belly laugh escaped Konrad's lips and rolled through the room like fading thunder after a storm.

"Point taken," Konrad said. He picked up her coat and held it for her. "So, I haven't had a chance to touch base with you and your boyfriend yet. I like to check in with our frosh members around this time, see how their U of T experience has been so far."

Grace held his eyes, challenging him with a stare her mother used to tell her could freeze the river in July. All she read in response was genuine kindness and curiosity.

"Ben's not my boyfriend. We're just friends. We happened to join up at the same time. He's a great guy, though."

Grace caught the sliver of an eyebrow raise on Konrad's dark features.

"We're only friends," she said.

"In that case, Ms. Hobbes, any chance you'd be interested in joining me for a dinner?"

In the years to come, Grace would have cause to revisit her answer in this moment. She'd replay the encounter on a loop in her mind, reimagining a different choice, a different path. One that led her away from Konrad Sharma and all that was to come. In that moment, though, all she saw was a glint of vulnerability in the tilt of Konrad's head and a rare shy smile on his lips. She forgot about her annoyance and his arrogant charm and allowed the attraction she'd been stifling for weeks to ooze forward like spring mud under her toes.

Worst of all, she forgot about Ben, waiting for her by the front doors in a cold rain, as she slipped out a side door with Konrad and into her future.

Chapter 17

Ben

Ben Chalmers had the life he never expected.

Many, he knew, would have called his existence dull. His twelve-year-old stepdaughter referred to everything about him as "basic," though he didn't see it as the insult she'd intended. His current life was the one he'd dreamed about as a geeky, oversensitive university kid.

He'd left school at twenty-one with a master's degree in computer science, a seeded loneliness, and a dreary path leading straight to a dead-end career in the bowels of a high-tech firm. Somehow, he now found himself married to a woman he loved, with two reasonably happy stepkids and a solid career in the Canada Security Intelligence Service as a research analyst. He wasn't a spy, though he would wink and tell the neighbors that he was spy adjacent.

All of which made him wonder about the series of off-kilter choices that had led him to this moment: sitting in his car beneath the shuddering halo of a parking lot streetlamp chasing a ghost who had the potential to blow up his happy life.

He'd been headed home when the call came in, changing the trajectory of his evening. As he listened, he caught himself, yet again, rubbing absent-mindedly at the burn in his chest. He reached into his pocket for the roll of antacids that had a permanent home on his person.

"Are you sure?" Ben said over the phone to Henri, an antique dealer in Kensington Market who had a particular affinity for music boxes. "It's the same one?"

"Sans aucun doute. Without a doubt, mon ami. It is the same box. Ask the universe, and you shall receive. Two girls walked into my shop with it just today." Henri's voice was a little echoey through the speaker, but the twinkle in his voice was unmistakable.

Ben glanced down at the phone, which he'd set on the passenger seat. A screen saver photo of his wife and kids in mid-laugh grinned back at him.

He'd met Mary online over ten years ago. They'd had a short, though intense, courtship. Ben had been gobsmacked that someone actually liked him, so he didn't waste time before putting a ring on the relationship. And she'd accepted. They had a small summer wedding in the backyard of their Mississauga split-level. The kids, four and six at the time, had been young enough to accept this new man in their lives and had taken to calling him B-Dad. And just like that, Ben had a loving family. One he would go to the ends of the earth to safeguard.

The morning after he'd proposed, Ben had walked into the bathroom of his tiny apartment and didn't recognize the man staring back at him in the mirror. In the half-light of early morning, all he could see was the scared nineteen-year-old kid he'd been when his life had been blown up. The hallucination, if that's what it was, had been so vivid, Ben had run out of the bathroom and into the befuddled gaze of his fiancée.

Ben wasn't a believer in mysticism or signs from the universe—he considered himself a man guided by science and reason—so he hadn't needed a shaman or doctor to figure out the tricks his brain had been playing on him. The human psyche could be oddly predictable when it came to grappling with suppressed trauma. His unresolved past had hurtled back on the threshold of his new future.

And at the heart of it was Grace Hobbes.

Ben's memories had propelled him into a quirky little Kensington Market shop chasing the sliverest of threads. When Grace had disappeared from his life more than twenty years before, she'd taken a secret and a very particular music box with her. Ben hadn't really expected the music box to turn up at the time, but you did what you could to control your life, even if the heart of your actions was illogical. The owner was an affable man who knew Ben was searching for something lost but had the grace to hold his questions. Ben would check in with Henri, his trips to the store becoming more sporadic with time and a settled life.

To show his appreciation and honor a sort of friendship, Ben had bought a handful of music boxes from the shop, all varying designs, and listened to Henri wax about the properties of each. He'd found them pretty enough, but his interest was a charade. He couldn't have explained why he felt the need to be cagey, why he never asked outright about the specific music box, and he didn't bother unpacking the layers of meaning in the deception. All he really needed was a sense of agency, however fruitless.

That was until two weeks ago, when an anonymous text dinged through on his phone. The words were simple but carried menace.

With grace, it had read. *I know what you did.* The second text was a video of the very music box that Ben had been hunting.

Ben had called Henri immediately. Feeding a description and a partial truth about it having once belonged to a dear friend, he had asked Henri to look out for the box. The text and video had been haunting Ben, so he was only partially shocked when Henri called this evening with the news. The music box had turned up in the shop today.

What's more, Henri said he'd seen the box years before and treated Ben to a lecture on the Fates. Maybe Ben had to start rethinking his ideas about the universe.

"What can you tell me about the seller?" Ben said on the phone, forcing his voice to be casual.

"A young lady and her friend. Very sweet. Quiet. She said she wanted to learn more about the provenance of the antique, that it was a gift for her maman. But I do not think that was the case. There was something important about that box. The girl, she looked at it, like it was a . . . comment dit-on . . . a lifeline in a difficult sea," Henri said.

"Was it an estate sale?"

The thorned vine of a thought wrapped around Ben's heart.

"Non, je ne pense pas. At least, they did not say that was the case. Perhaps money issues? They were students, I believe. One wore a University of Toronto shirt. Very large. The styles today. Bwah! No care. You know?"

"Did you buy it?"

"Non. She did not want to sell. Soon, I think. The way she looked at the box, there was a difficult relationship there. That young girl, she didn't want to part with it, but she did not like it either."

Ben had one more question. The question he had been waiting ten years to ask. The reason he had nurtured this pseudofriendship with Henri. He sought an answer that would have been withheld, had they been strangers. Again, he forced a casual tone in his voice.

"Did you get the seller's name by any chance?"

"Oui, mon ami," Henri said in a soft chuckle. "I thought you might ask. It is Meadows. Jaden Meadows. I will contact her if you wish."

"Thanks, Henri. Why don't we hold off for now. I better check in with the wife. After last month's vacation, not sure she'd go for the extra expense right now."

"Bien sûr." Again, another chuckle. "That I understand well."

Ben hung up the phone but stayed in his car. An all-day sleet had finally stopped, and a smattering of parked cars were visible through the defrosting windshield. His gut kicked at him. He reached again for the roll of antacids. Forty-four years old and already his stomach was a wasteland of acid scars and tension.

He opened Chrome on his phone and googled the name Jaden Meadows and University of Toronto. It didn't take long. The girl's Instagram page popped up. Scanning the images, he found what he was looking for almost immediately: Jaden, standing in front of a stone wall dripping with ivy and between a middle-aged couple, all smiling awkwardly out of the photo. The post, tagged *#moveinday*, was from a few years ago. He expanded the image until the face of a woman with chin-length brown hair and an awkward smile filled the screen.

"Found you," Ben said, his voice tinged with awe.

The struggling streetlight above the car gave a final flicker, before the world outside went darker.

Chapter 18

Ben

1999

Ben stood by the door in the too-warm room, waiting. Members of Militant Animals filtered past him into the hallway, some glancing his way with curiosity. Konrad had asked Ben to stay behind after the meeting. That made Ben worth noting. He saw envy and admiration in the glances; he didn't want either.

This was his third year with Militant Animals, and though he'd been a regular, he worked hard not to stand out. All he wanted was to blend in with the other university kids and avoid smart-ass comments like *Where's your babysitter?* or *Who brought the kid?* Three years of learning and maturing, and still his face looked like he was a model for GapKids.

He felt pools of sweat under his shirt but refused to take off his jacket. After his conversation with Grace yesterday, there was a good chance Ben would need a quick exit. This conversation was bound to be about her. There was no chance Ben walked away from this without some damage, whether it would be physical or emotional remained to be seen.

Konrad was taking his time chatting with a first-year student with long curly hair and those clunky black shoes that all the girls seemed to be wearing. Ben leaned on the doorjamb and tried to look nonchalant, a task he was clearly failing. Konrad looked over at him with an apologetic nod and held up a finger, indicating he wouldn't be long. Watching the woman speak without taking a breath, Ben wasn't sure Konrad could deliver on that promise.

Too young to be a university student and too smart not to be, Ben had felt like a house cat dropped into a panther den his first few weeks at school. Everything and everyone seemed either strange or frightening, until he stumbled upon the notice for a goofy student animal rights group. The poster was a cartoony but edgy illustration of a corporate boardroom in chaos, with chickens and piglets roaming freely—one wearing a tiny necktie. **Join the pranksters saving animals with wit, guts, and glitter bombs!** it read.

He had met a few others like him in the group, young and eager for something to happen that pointed the way to their future. Grace Hobbes, though, had been his kindred spirit. She was a sweet girl trying too hard to be tough. Though the line between friendship and love had blurred momentarily for Ben in the beginning, Grace had always been clear about her feelings, and a close friendship had proved enough for him.

The attraction between Grace and Konrad was obvious early on: They laughed too hard at each other's jokes, locked eyes longer than was needed, and shared private smiles even in a crowd. They hadn't become an official couple until well after Easter break her first year. Grace hadn't trusted Konrad's true intentions. There was an inevitability, though, to their relationship. Eventually, Konrad's charisma and Grace's energy made up the guts of Militant Animals; they were blinding lights, washing everyone else out in their orbit.

When Ben had walked in on them late one night—Grace sitting on the copy machine in the group's classroom-style office, Konrad grinding between her legs as they kissed—it wasn't a surprise.

"Well, here's a cliché," Ben had said.

Konrad looked embarrassed. Grace just laughed.

With her laughter still ringing in his ears, Ben had closed the door on any lingering infatuation. He loved Grace; she didn't love him back. It hurt, but by then, Ben was used to life hurting.

The girl was wrapping up her monologue to Konrad, slinging her backpack over her shoulder and slowly walking toward the door. Konrad edged her forward with a sweep of his hand toward the exit and promises to chat next time. Ben felt sweat under his lip and across his forehead. He wondered if he might be starting to feel faint. He really wasn't ready for this.

When Grace had told Ben that her relationship with Konrad was floundering, he'd lent an ear and battled old feelings. They sat on a park bench on a warm early-April evening. Excited squeals from a nearby playground added a lightness to the fresh spring air. Grace fed bits of a stale sandwich to a group of pigeons who'd seen her as an easy mark.

"I just don't know if I'm all in, you know?" Grace had said, brushing a stray lock of hair behind her ear. She was leaning forward but turned to look back at Ben with wide, dark eyes.

Ben nodded. He seemed to be incapable of finding words. One pitiful glance from Grace and his body betrayed him. Feelings he'd fastidiously tried to bury burbled under the surface of his thoughts.

Even if he could speak, he had no idea what he could say based on his anemic experience with relationships. He had a girlfriend, but they'd only been seeing each other for a couple of weeks. What did he know about love advice. It struck him that Grace would have more luck talking with his girlfriend, Clara, who seemed to know a lot about everything. Ben tossed a bit of his cookie onto the ground and watched two pigeons fight over it.

"I mean, it was intense at first," Grace said into Ben's silence. "Really intense. We spent more time together naked than clothed." Grace smiled at the recollection.

Ben struggled to get the image of a naked Grace out of his mind. He felt his mouth go dry and his body respond in a distinctly embarrassing way. *Shit, not now,* he thought as he leaned forward and readjusted his legs. *Puppies and the alphabet, puppies and the alphabet,* he recited in his head.

"But lately? I don't know. Maybe law school is changing him? He keeps prattling on about the future and his career. He's even thinking of working on Bay Street. Can you believe that? Those bankers will have strokes when they find out they have a nonprofit organizer working for them."

Grace leaned back against the bench and closed her eyes. Her face remained focused and strained in concentration as she held it up to a final sliver of sunlight. The sad slip of a smile on her lips gave off a vulnerability Ben didn't often see.

He opened his mouth to say something, but again nothing came out. What could he possibly say? People changed. He had no control over that, nor did he have a right to judge.

Grace opened her eyes and looked directly into Ben's. He saw sadness and disappointment and longing. A breeze had picked up, leaving a tickle of gooseflesh on Grace's exposed arm.

"It's literally the biggest thing we fight about now," Grace said, her voice faltering for the first time. "He told me I needed to grow up if I wanted to be in the real world. I'm not sure either of us knows what the real world is anymore. Maybe we just don't want the same things. Maybe we never did."

Not knowing what else to do, Ben placed a tentative hand on her arm. He stayed like that for a minute, unmoving, as if time held itself in a loop of his own devising. His mind jumbled over words of comfort or advice, but he was distracted by the orange-vanilla scent Grace always wore, picked up by the breeze and enveloping his thoughts.

Before he knew what he was doing, Ben leaned his face toward her, his body giving in to a dormant longing that overpowered even the iron grip of his rational mind. He tipped his lips toward hers, closed his eyes in anticipation.

Grace stood, letting her sandwich cascade onto the ground to a flurry of excited wingbeats.

"What the hell, Ben?" she said and left without a goodbye, carrying a heavier burden.

Ben hadn't seen Grace since the park. He'd had no chance to explain or apologize. And now, Konrad had asked Ben if he had a minute to talk. While Ben considered Konrad a friend through Grace, they'd never actually had a one-on-one conversation in all the time they'd known each other. It was humiliating that this would be their first.

Finally, the office was empty, the only sound a faint whirring from the ventilation. The room was sticky with the lingering scents of too many bodies.

"This is a bit awkward," Konrad said, closing the door behind the girl. "I wanted to talk to you about Grace."

Here it comes, thought Ben. *This is where he warns me to stay away from her.* He braced himself for the onslaught.

Instead, Konrad stuttered.

His eyes darted up to Ben and away. He took a seat, looking like a little kid forced to sit at the grown-up table.

"I know you two are good friends," Konrad said. "She talks about you all the time. Ben this, and Ben that." He laughed uncertainly.

Ben couldn't imagine where this was going. There wasn't a hint of malice or aggression in Konrad's voice, certainly not the jealous boyfriend Ben had been expecting. Konrad seemed almost shy and nervous.

"I don't know if she told you," Konrad continued, "but our anniversary is coming up. I've been racking my brain for what to get her and keep coming up empty. We've hit a bit of a rough patch lately, and I'm really awful at these sorts of things. I wanted to get her something special, you know, let her know how much she means to me. I was hoping you might have some ideas."

Ben was dumbfounded. Was Konrad Sharma asking him for help with his love life?

"Look, sorry, this was dumb. I shouldn't be asking you this. It's not fair," Konrad said, standing abruptly and throwing out an apologetic half smile.

"No, no, it's fine. I don't mind," Ben said. "It's just—"

"Just?"

"It's not what I was expecting. I figured this was related to—" Unable to land on a viable excuse, Ben waved his arm toward the room. "I'm a little thrown, that's all." He recovered with the lie and consciously wiped the shock off his face in favor of a friendly smile. "Let me think about it."

"Great," Konrad said with visible relief. "Thanks, Ben. Appreciate it, man."

A memory came to Ben. A story Konrad had shared in a drunken gathering when he'd just started dating Grace.

"There is one thing," Ben said, though he was far from convinced it was right.

Konrad's life was the proverbial immigrant story. His dad had come to Canada as a young man, having left India with very little, except for a collection of family-heirloom music boxes. Ben remembered Konrad sharing the story late one evening, a few friends around the living room, sipping beer and sharing dreams. He talked about how the boxes had had pride of place in their family living room, until one by one, they'd had to be sold as the family aimed to put first their daughter, then their son, through university.

Most of all, Ben remembered Grace's tears as Konrad shared the story and the look of admiration and love in her eyes. At the time, Ben had longed for that look to be turned on him.

He told Konrad his idea.

"That's perfect," Konrad said, a broad, familiar grin returning to his face as he slapped Ben on the back.

They left together, and for the first time, Ben felt his shoulders straighten and his steps align with the great Konrad Sharma.

Chapter 19

Jaden

After leaving the Music Box Stop, Jaden and Zelda headed straight for their Toronto apartment, a tiny two-bedroom above a corner grocery store in Toronto's Little Italy. Low clouds that had hovered for most of the day had moved on, leaving a final gasp of sunshine on the horizon. The drive should have taken ten minutes, but construction and a blinding sunset snarled traffic on College Street. Each minute broiled under Jaden's skin.

There was too much that she didn't understand, and it ran through her blood with each torturous block. She cracked a window for fresh air, only to gulp back a mouthful of exhaust. Every streetcar and pedestrian on the road was an obstacle that Jaden had an urge to crash through.

Questions ping-ponged through her mind: How did an antique belonging to a dead U of T student find its way to her mom's doorstep? What had her mom kept hidden about her past? And a new question—one that felt like a betrayal and an accusation—what did her mom know about Sharma's death?

Finally, with daylight nearly gone, the girls breathed in the familiar notes of burnt coffee that lingered in their apartment like a stain, thanks to the makeshift roastery in the downstairs deli. Beggars couldn't be choosers in the Toronto market, so affordability and proximity to campus had won out over design and aroma. Jaden dropped her bag on the living-room floor and opened every window to clear the place out. A stream of cold air left its imprint on her skin. She welcomed the chill.

"So, what are you going to do?" Zelda said, plopping cross-legged onto the bright-red IKEA couch the girls had bought off Facebook Marketplace.

The entire apartment was a collection of secondhand and thrift finds, from the beat-up coffee table to the marigold dishes in the cupboard. They'd lived here for a year and a half, and still Jaden felt transitory in this space. Toronto never seemed to fit her properly; like a pair of jeans with the wrong cut, it pinched and prodded at her when she felt stressed or tired. And tonight, she was both.

"Right now, I need to call my dad," Jaden said. She'd texted him on the road to let him know they were making good time, but she really should check in. He would have already called if there had been any news about her mom, but still, she felt a knot of anticipation between her shoulder blades as the phone warbled in her hand. She shut her eyes, imagined him picking up, excitement and relief echoing down the phone line as he told her all was well, Mom was safe.

"Hey J-bear," her dad said, in a voice that obliterated her childish daydreaming. "You all right?"

Jaden and her dad shared a number of little routines—rooted in childhood and a little girl's adulation. He always asked the same question when she called; her role was to answer with *Right as rain, baby Jane.* This time, the words stuck in her throat.

Instead, her questions bubbled and broiled like trouble, souring the saliva in her mouth. She felt like she might throw up.

"Did Mom go to the University of Toronto?" she said. The question, an arrow launched into a void.

"Jaden, what is this ab—"

"Tell me."

"She did, for a couple of years," her dad said. No challenge or anger in his voice, only sadness.

Jaden had to push down a nausea creeping its way along her esophagus. She tasted bile and broken trust.

"Why didn't anyone tell me? This is my third year at that school. In all that time, no one thought to mention, hey, your mom went there? What the hell, Dad?"

A stewed silence dribbled so long from the end of the line, Jaden started to wonder if her dad had hung up. She was just about to try redialing when she heard a faint voice, as if he no longer held the phone near his mouth.

"She didn't want you to know," he said. "She said she wanted you to make your own decisions and not let her past influence you. Between you and me, I think she believed you'd run across the country if you knew your mom had gone to school in Ontario." A pale facsimile of a chuckle eked through the phone.

Jaden dropped onto the couch. Any other questions she'd had were washed away by the wave of implications in what her dad had just told her. Only one question floated to the surface. It was one she'd never dare ask her dad. His revelation struck her with the notion that hers was not the only love that needed protecting. Her dad was also struggling, in his way, to understand what had happened to someone he loved. Still, the question rose, its implications reaching out across the surface of everything Jaden held dear: Who the hell was her mother?

"Dude," Zelda said after Jaden had summarized the brief conversation with her dad. "That is low-key wild but pretty obvious if you think about it."

Jaden didn't disagree, but it amounted to nothing more than another maddening piece in a puzzle she couldn't see.

"What are you going to do?" Zelda said.

"I don't know. Bugger off to my grandmother's cabin and forget any of this happened," Jaden said, a sarcastic smile lifting the corner of her mouth.

The cabin wasn't exactly remote, but it wasn't easy to get to. About a three-hour drive from White Falls, it was tucked in beside a crystal-calm lake and had been Jaden's happy place for most of her life. Her dad had told her that Malcolm had local police check out the property and confirmed her mom wasn't there. Jaden hadn't been there since her grandfather's death two years prior, and it was tempting to just head there now. Disappear. Like her mother.

Zelda just quirked an eyebrow in response. Always Jaden's conscience, her friend didn't need words to share what she was thinking.

"Fine. No cabin," Jaden said. "But I do need a shower." She left Zelda to her thoughts and headed to the bathroom.

Jaden ran the water hot. The air thickened with steam and unanswered questions. Reaching to pull off her pants, she smacked her hand on the sink in the tiny space.

"Shit," she screamed.

The last dregs of energy Jaden needed to hold herself upright vanished. She slid to the floor, one pant leg still dangling uselessly beside her. What did she think she was doing? Desperation and guilt had her chasing ghosts. No, not desperation. Her mother. Her mom had her on this wild-goose chase.

"Jaden? You OK in there?" Zelda said, gently knocking on the door.

The anger that she'd been trying to tamp down all day rushed into her empty spaces. Jaden took a long, slow sip of air, giving oxygen to her fury, and pulled herself to standing. A resolution, firm and unyielding, came to her. Whatever this was, whatever her mother had done, Jaden was going to put an end to it.

"I'm fine," Jaden said through gritted teeth.

A take-out pizza from the deli downstairs and warm beer sat on the coffee table when Jaden emerged from the bathroom, hair still dripping. Without a word, Zelda cracked open two bottles. She took a gulp and offered the faintest of gestures with her head to the empty seat on the couch beside her.

Jaden could only nod. Improbably, the smell of grease and melted cheese drew a growl from her stomach, and her mouth started to water.

"I think we need to find him. Or, I mean, find whatever trail he left behind," Zelda said through a mouth full of cheese and dough.

"Find who?"

"This Sharma guy. Who else?"

Jaden agreed, but the prospect of going further meant finding out things she may not want to know about her mom. She felt like a child, reaching for a hand she no longer trusted.

With a swig of beer, Jaden grabbed her laptop out of her backpack.

"Let's do it," she said.

"Hell hath no fury like a couple of Gen Zs with laptops," Zelda said with a smirk.

If the antique seller's memory was accurate—and they couldn't be sure of anything—Konrad Sharma had died around 2000. Predictably, there were no traces of him on social media and no hits on a Google search. Like Jaden's mom, he was an online ghost, unseen and unknowable.

The music box sat on the beat-up pine coffee table. The scratched finish of the table and poor lighting dulled the glass, tainting its luster with reality.

"So, we agree that this Grace Hobbes person on the university transcript and whose initials are etched into this thing is most likely your mom?" Zelda said. She was leaning over the music box, a massive slice of pizza dangling from one hand. "I mean, it's gotta be, right? Why else would this thing just show up on your doorstep?"

Though the thought had been on Jaden's mind as well, she wasn't prepared to go there. Not yet.

"What if it's one of those tragic love stories? You know, *Romeo and Juliet* but only Romeo died," Zelda said. "Do you think your mom might have changed her name?"

Zelda's questions drilled into Jaden's head, like a jackhammer busting up solid concrete. She closed her eyes and ran heavy fingers over her forehead.

"If that's the case," Zelda continued, oblivious to Jaden's discomfort, "then it's no wonder we can't find anything online. I mean, when did the internet even start? It might not have even been around when Sharma was alive, and not all old records are digiti—"

Zelda's mid-sentence silence reverberated louder than her questions. Jaden looked up. Her roommate had turned back to her laptop and started typing excitedly. Her eyes blazed with the hunt, and a piece of crust dangled from her mouth.

"Voilà," Zelda said a couple of minutes later, turning her screen toward Jaden in a flourish. The image of a graying newspaper with The Varsity splashed across the top in bold blue letters filled the screen. Headlines and ads littering the pages hinted at the time frame: Quebec vote: students split over language and issues, Happy Gilmore—Opens Friday, The Fugees Settle the Score With New Album.

"It's the student newspaper," Zelda said, a grin on her face. "Every issue between 1881 and 2010 is digitized. If a student died in some tragedy, it's likely it was mentioned in here."

Jaden clicked the forward button, and the pages turned as if the print version had been laid on the table in front of them. Ads for flip phones shared space with articles on a women's rugby tournament. Jaden was equally overwhelmed and impressed. She looked up at Zelda, her eyes asking the question her mind was incapable of articulating.

"It's digitized only. Means it's just photos of the originals, so it's not searchable. But these types of sources are bread and butter for historians. At least until Elon Musk and his lackeys scrape it all off the internet along with the rest of history. It'll be tedious to go through, but we can flip through the pages and look for some answers."

Jaden couldn't tell if she wanted to cry or laugh. For the first time, she let herself believe that she truly wouldn't be alone in her crazy search.

"Let's do it," she said.

Wrapped in a blanket on the couch, Jaden spent the next hour flipping through the pages on screen. Because they couldn't be sure of the shopkeeper's dates, they'd started with the September 1995 issue and methodically worked their way forward. At first, every little thing caught her attention. It surprised her that the themes—tuition hikes, controversial speakers, administrative juggernauts—were identical to today's editions of *The Varsity*, as if time stood still on university campuses. *Maybe the world is like that,* she thought as she scanned an interview from 1998 with an environmental scientist who warned about the effects of global warming.

Jaden felt her eyes closing and her head dipping even as she continued to tap the forward key. Lack of sleep and days of screaming cortisol were taking their toll. She tried to force her eyes open. The rhythmic tick of the key beneath her finger was oddly lulling, and she felt her eyelids close. She was just thinking of taking a short nap when her head snapped back in response to a headline reaching her tired brain.

"Student killed in unexplained explosion," she read out loud.

She and Zelda bent over the computer.

> Tragedy struck the U of T community this week when a third-year law student was killed in an explosion. Konrad Sharma, 24, died on Tuesday when his car exploded in front of the VitaCore Laboratories in Mississauga.
>
> The explosion occurred Tuesday evening, shaking the quiet streets in the industrial park where the lab is located and cracking some windows in nearby buildings. Emergency services were quick to respond to the scene. There were no other casualties reported.
>
> Sharma was a member of Militant Animals, a national student-led animal rights organization with a chapter

at the University of Toronto. Their comical protest stunts had gained community and media attention in recent years, including in the pages of this publication.

William Pound, a third-year Law student and friend of Sharma's, said they were all in shock. "Konrad was a friend and one of those all-around good guys, you know? He was always smiling and happy to see you. Everyone liked him."

The Law School Dean, Frederic Daniels, issued a statement through his office. "The suddenness and nature of the death has shocked and saddened the entire Law Faculty. Our thoughts and prayers go out to Mr. Sharma's family in this difficult time."

The cause of the explosion is under investigation. Unconfirmed reports suggest the incident may be linked to a Militant Animals protest.

The Metro Toronto Police have issued a statement assuring the public that a thorough investigation is underway.

Detective Angela Bradford, leading the investigation, stated, "We are exploring all angles. It's too early to make any definitive statements about the nature of the incident, but there is nothing to suggest there is an ongoing threat to the public."

A spokesperson for Militant Animals could not be reached for comment.

"That's it!" Zelda said, strained eagerness in her voice.

Jaden bristled.

The story was accompanied by a black-and-white photo of a good-looking guy with a dark, well-kept beard and chin-length wavy hair. Sharma grinned mischievously at the camera with a nondescript streetscape behind him. Jaden stared into the pixilated eyes and saw nothing. No revelation or recognition. Konrad Sharma was foreign to her. She chastised herself for expecting more.

They followed the thread of Militant Animals through *The Varsity* and into the local Toronto papers with online archives. The animal rights group had been a hit on campus, its members gaining popularity and notoriety for their attention-catching stunts. A handful of articles described members dressed in rabbit costumes window-shopping at department store makeup counters or walking through the university commons wearing bathing suits in February to encourage students to wear cruelty-free products.

"Man, they walked the line, didn't they?" Zelda said with obvious admiration.

"What do you mean?" Jaden said.

"They were never too disruptive, never crossed any lines, nothing that would get them arrested or charged, but the stunts got attention. Clever, actually. They knew exactly where the line was and how not to go over it."

As if out of a dream, Jaden heard an echo of her mom's voice from years ago when Jaden was testing boundaries. *You need to know where the line is, Jaden, before you can decide to go over it. And you don't understand enough to know where it is yet.*

Jaden brushed aside the echo and delved back into the pages.

A final, short article, buried at the bottom of page eight of the *Toronto Star*, provided an update on the investigation into the explosion. According to police, Sharma was the only person on the scene, but authorities had arrested another member of the group, Clara Morel, who they believed was an accomplice.

The name Clara Morel rattled inside Jaden's head, a loose piece that wouldn't settle. She'd heard that name before, but nothing seemed to fit together. She continued reading. The woman had been arrested and convicted, though none of the details of her trial had made the papers.

In addition to Sharma and Morel, two other organizers were identified as part of the groups: Nero Estevez and Grace Hobbes.

"Damn," said Zelda when Grace's name popped up. "Your mom had some rizz back in the day." Jaden felt her hand twitch in response. The coincidence seemed unlikely, yet still her mind pushed against the obvious that Grace Hobbes and Emma Meadows were the same person.

Nero Estevez, it turned out, was a living, breathing man with an online profile and a Facebook page. A teacher in the bedroom community of Barrie, he'd filled his page with the typical shots of a middle-aged father living a suburban life—kids, husband, and grinning vacation photos. Whoever this man might have been in his youth, his social media life made no mention of activism or Militant Animals.

Jaden clicked the blue Messenger icon on Estevez's profile page and typed out a message:

> Sorry to bother you. This may sound weird, but my name is Jaden Meadows. I'm a student at U of T doing research on protest groups in the 1990s. I came across some information and a possible family link that I'd like to discuss with you. I think you may have known my mom. Would you have time tomorrow for a chat?

Just after setting her phone down, an arpeggio of notes vibrated against the coffee table, announcing an incoming call. Without thinking, Jaden snatched it and hit accept.

"Jaden? Jaden Meadows?"

"Yes," she said, suspicion prickling at the base of her spine.

"What do you think you're playing at, kid? Stop the shit, or a missing mom will be the least of your worries."

The phone went dead.

The police had warned them this might happen. Cranks and kooks, seeing her mom's name in the paper, might seek them out. She'd mention it to O'Shea when she was back in White Falls. For now, she had another priority.

The laptop dinged with a reply message from Estevez. He'd be available to meet them tomorrow morning.

"What was that about?" Zelda said, a crinkle of concern around her eyes.

Jaden looked toward the window. Anemic streetlight washed out the darkness, obliterating the stars. She thought about the night sky over Lake Superior and the never-ending points of light along its horizon. Longing coursed through her. She looked at Zelda and, in that instant, made a decision that would change everything.

"We have a stop to make on the way home tomorrow," Jaden said.

Chapter 20

Grace

1999

Grace was hit by the smell of sweat and stale beer when she sauntered into the Red Lion. The pub, located a few blocks from campus, was an effigy to the city's sports teams. Memorabilia and athlete photos—including a signed Blue Jays bat and framed ticket stubs to big games—crammed the spaces between a half dozen big-screen TVs. The appeal of the place was proximity to campus, along with cheap beer and nachos.

She'd walked the few blocks from campus under a warming April sky. The whiff of wet earth promised a hard winter's end, and it was a treat to smell something other than exhaust and concrete. A few stubborn pockets of snow lingered, but hints of green grass and spring blossoms were on the horizon. In comparison, the overstuffed bar was fetid and oppressive, with Maple Leafs fans jostling for screen sight lines to watch the playoff game on TV.

Grace weaved through a sea of bodies, dodging a couple of wandering hands, before she finally spotted Konrad. As usual, he was holding court with a rapt audience, mostly nubile first years sucking on his words like candy. He stood with his back to the wall, the gaggle of faces seated around him in a misshapen circle.

With a wry grin, he handed Grace a full pint glass when she approached.

"I ordered one for you," he said.

"Thanks," she said, not lingering in his gaze, though he tried to catch her eye. She wasn't in the mood for his charm.

"You're off to a fast start," Ben said. Grace shrugged. *What is it with men watching me?* she thought.

The warm beer sank to the bottom of Grace's empty stomach. She could almost hear it slosh around as she reached for a handful of cold nachos to soak up the beer.

Though Grace couldn't make out the details, Konrad was in an intense discussion with a blond woman wearing dreadlocks and a nose ring. Grace didn't know her name.

"What's he on about now?" Grace said, leaning toward Ben.

"Oh, you know. The usual," Ben said, sitting back in his chair with a sigh. "Companies are listening, our tactics are working, no need to escalate."

Grace raised a skeptical eyebrow.

Two weeks ago, Militant Animals had been the laughingstock of campus and Toronto. Some of the newer members had tried to organize a protest outside a local Kentucky Fried Chicken to draw attention to inhumane farming practices. The idea had been to have a small group in chicken costumes talk to the customers before they went in the restaurant to order.

In the end, only two protestors had shown, one of whom had mistakenly rented a bargain-basement duck costume. The two got into an argument over the mistake, and—in a turn of unbelievable bad luck—a local news crew just happened to be stopping by for lunch. They got video of a chicken and duck arguing on the front lawn of a fried-chicken restaurant, with the manager standing between them holding up coupons for a "duck-free" value meal. Any of the intended messaging was lost under laughter.

"They're giving him ten for effort," Ben said and took a sip of Grace's beer. "But I don't think they're really into the argument. Especially that one." He pointed with a subtle nod of his head to a brooding figure with greasy dirty-blond hair and a ripped camel-wool coat.

"You mean Heathcliff?" Grace said.

"I don't think that's his name," Ben said.

"It's not. But I can't be bothered to learn all the newbies' names. There's too many of them. Nicknames are easier to remember." Grace shot a wry smile at Ben, who was obviously pleased to be in on the joke.

Grace and Ben were now veteran members of Militant Animals, and it was easy to see change was coming. The group had ballooned. Cute little stunts—like putting on rabbit costumes and crashing the lobby of the Eli Lilly building—had been their bread and butter, but attention was waning and some of the newer members were pushing for more traditional protest. Words like *childish* and *useless* were being bandied about, still in low whispers. Konrad was leading the charge against it. He'd been putting up a good fight, using charm and flirtation to bring members to his side. Grace wasn't sure which way it would go.

"One botched protest doesn't demand a complete redo of our mandate and vision. Besides, there's no such thing as bad publicity, right?" Konrad had said at the last meeting.

He'd faced down a room of stoic glares, his normally effortless charm stale and pallid in the aftermath.

"This isn't about publicity," someone had shot back. "It's about change."

A number of heads nodded with low concurring murmurs. Out of the corner of her eye, Grace caught the tilt in Ben's head. She turned to look at him, surprised to see even a hint of disagreement with anything Konrad had said. Ben just raised an innocent eyebrow and shrugged.

"Come on," Konrad said, drawing Grace's attention back to the group. "You can't be serious here. Militant Animals was built on fun for a good cause. Chaining ourselves to butchery process lines and throwing paint in fur stores is not going to get us where we want to be."

"Says who?"

A cascade of overlapping voices had followed, some agreeing, some arguing. None of it heading to a good place. Grace watched Konrad.

For the first time, she understood the meaning of the term *crestfallen*. Maybe it had been a trick of the light, but Grace could have sworn the glow that trailed Konrad like a shadow had sputtered in that moment.

Grace had been dating Konrad for almost two years, and even she was losing faith in his leadership. She wouldn't have said that their relationship was tumultuous, but neither was it storybook. Konrad was passionate and sweet and all in about everything he did. Grace was tentative, suspicious, and more comfortable with one foot out the door.

Konrad was nearing the end of law school, and it was hard to ignore the distance percolating between them. Every little issue festered in the void. A relationship that had once been breathless and needful had become pale and sickly, though neither had the will to euthanize it.

The Militant Animals rift had recently wormed its way into their relationship. The issue had been lurking for weeks, like a predator waiting for its moment. Both had been aware of the strain, but neither had yet given it voice.

That had all changed two nights ago at Konrad's place, when a quiet night with friends turned into something more.

Konrad's apartment was perched on the ninth floor of a boxlike high-rise building. Late as usual, Grace stepped into the sunlight-bathed living room to the smell of stale coffee and tension. Konrad stood, backlit by the windows. Grace couldn't make out his expression, but she knew that bearing. Ben stood facing him, arms stiff, like a bull waiting to charge. Clara, a newer member and Ben's girlfriend, sat in the corner of the couch, watching.

"Look, it's not that big of a deal," Ben had said, glancing at Clara.

The target of their discussion, it turned out, was Maple and Loon, a Canadian cosmetics company that had built a national reputation around their cruelty-free products. The company had recently been bought out by a large conglomerate that didn't share the same ideology. Some members of Militant Animals had been advocating to take spray paint to Maple and Loon stores across the city, making the message indelible.

"What the hell, man?" Konrad said, his voice low with restrained incredulity. "You're talking about vandalism."

Grace slid onto a chair by the door and kept silent. She had already had a similar conversation with him the night before. It had not gone well.

"Look, we're not talking about hurting anyone. It's just about ramping up the intensity of our protests. Maple and Loon has a well-established reputation, and a lot of people will keep buying their products without knowing there's been a change in policy. And cute and cuddly isn't cutting it anymore. No one is listening," Ben said.

Clara bobbed her head gently in agreement and offered an encouraging smile.

Grace was still working through how she felt about Clara. The girl-next-door looks and anime-character voice sat oddly next to her environmental and animal rights activism. If Grace were being honest, she also felt a hint of animosity toward the girl. Ben was changing to accommodate this new relationship—eschewing things he used to love, wearing preppy shirts, and listening to the most abhorrent top 40 music.

"Konrad, man, this is about shaking things up." Ben threw a sideways glance at Clara, who smiled coyly. "If we let these companies pull the wool over the public's eyes when we know better, we're complicit."

"Oh, for fuck's sake," Konrad said, his frustration bubbling to the surface. "This is insane. Grace and I won't be part of it."

Three sets of eyes bored into Grace. She'd been silent and watchful until then. Konrad's words left her cornered. An anger, familiar and satisfying, surged through her bones. Who was he to drag her into his little squabbles? Why did he believe everyone in his life had to follow his lead?

She looked into his eyes—amber brown and disturbingly intense—and saw a plea for reason. She looked away.

"I think what we've been doing isn't working," Grace had said with finality. "It's time we bring a gun to a gun fight." Though she wasn't sure she believed her own words.

A loud collective groan rumbled through the pub. The Philadelphia Flyers had just scored a third goal against the Leafs. Grace didn't much care, but she was annoyed by the spittle of beer that had landed on her jacket when the guy behind her had shot up his beer-holding hand in exasperation. He mumbled a half-hearted apology before turning back to the game. Grace decided it was time to leave.

There was no point talking to Konrad tonight. He was in full oratory mode; she could almost see the thought bubbles over his head while he pretended to listen to others. A battle for hearts and minds was underway, and Konrad was losing. Grace didn't want to be pulled into the middle again.

If she were being honest, what she wanted was her boyfriend back. Two years ago, he'd made her feel like the center of the universe, and now she was just another obligation in his overscheduled life. Grace knew she wasn't being fair. She didn't doubt that he loved her, but she did doubt his ability to hold all those priorities in his heart. Something was going to give; better she be gone before it collapsed.

"I'm outta here," she said quietly, tapping Ben on the shoulder. "Tell him I had to study." She nodded at Konrad, who was still deep in conversation with the dreadlock woman.

"I don't blame you," Ben said in a conspiratorial whisper.

Grace waited until she was on the sidewalk before slipping into her coat. A faint trace of warmth still lingered off the sun-kissed concrete. Night had fallen, though not darkness. This city never found its way to true dark. Jaden looked up to a murky gray sky despite being cloudless. More and more, she found herself craving the sight of stars.

"Grace?"

Grace turned to see Clara. "I thought that was you." Her light-blond hair glowed under the yellow streetlight. "Are you coming or going?"

"I'm just on my way out," Grace said.

"Sure, but um . . . if you have a few minutes, I'd love to go for a quick coffee."

Grace's surprise must have been evident on her face, as Clara laughed softly. "I promise, I won't bite. I just have something I wanted to run by you."

Grace hesitated. Clara hadn't suggested a drink in the pub but a one-on-one discussion away from the others. Curiosity won out.

"Sure, I have a little time now," Grace said.

Chapter 21

Jaden

Zelda had, unexpectedly, been against meeting up with Nero Estevez. They climbed into the car in Toronto, and she launched into a running rant that brought them past the city limits. Jaden couldn't be deterred. She let the sound of Zelda's voice fade into background noise.

"Zelda, I get it," Jaden finally said, interrupting Zelda's tirade of statistics on internet stalkers. "I get it. But I'm still going."

They'd left early enough to avoid the real guts of Toronto rush hour, but still a steady stream of cars had bobbed and weaved through six lanes of traffic like leaf-cutter ants coming out of a nest. Zelda's tirade softened into accusatory silence as the sky lightened and the highway squirmed beneath them. Jaden marked time by the silly names of passing communities—King City, Strange, Snowball—that flew past. She let her curiosity recede in the rearview mirror.

The road was clear and dry, most snow and ice unable to withstand the plows, thaws, and sun-warmed asphalt. It took over an hour before concrete and steel finally gave way to a semblance of trees and farmers' fields. Even then, every few kilometers, urban sprawl popped up again: an outlet mall, an exit sign plastered with restaurant and gas station logos, the scars of a quarry pit. The city had tentacles, stretching into surrounding lowlands like the roots of a tree. Pockets of green space were a form of resistance. It remained to be seen who would win.

When they exited the highway toward the city of Barrie, Zelda took another pass at dissuading Jaden.

"You know this is a bad idea, right? I mean, a colossally bad idea?" Zelda said.

They followed a commercial strip of road lined with gas stations, chain restaurants, and box stores. A handful of small businesses still clung to the edges, but with the likes of Home Depot and Starbucks as the anchors, this road could have been transplanted into any other city in the country.

This isn't exactly the type of place where shady or untoward deeds happen, thought Jaden. It was suburbia at its most dull.

"So you've said," Jaden replied.

"You have no idea who this guy is. He could be a freak or a stalker. Who knows if his Facebook page is even legit? Don't you think it was a little weird how quickly he agreed to meet a stranger?"

"Hmm-mmm." Jaden double-checked their direction against the map on her phone.

"Are you even listening?"

In truth, Jaden hadn't been. She was watching for a distinctive red, white, and yellow sign while trying to breathe away the stabbing irritation building in her chest. Answers lay ahead; she could practically taste them. She wouldn't let Zelda's fears, no matter how reasoned, derail that.

"Come on, Z. It's not like I'm meeting the guy in a dark alley or a sleazy basement. It's Tim Hortons. Nothing bad ever happens at a Timmies."

Jaden's attempt at humor did not land well with Zelda.

"Whatever. If you don't think psychos are happy to hang out at a Tim Hortons with everyone else, you're delusional." Zelda punctuated herself with crossed arms and an explosion of air.

"Look, if you're so worried about it, just come in with me," Jaden said, working hard to keep her voice level. "I promise, if you get a bad vibe off this guy, we leave. No questions asked."

Jaden flashed a questioning smirk to emphasize the point as she eased the little Mazda into a parking spot between a black pickup truck and a cherry red Tesla. Zelda's sideways glance and dropped shoulders were all the answer Jaden needed. She leaned across the seat, tapping shoulders with her best friend.

"We've got this," Jaden said.

Zelda shook her head and responded with a begrudging grunt.

The smell of fresh-brewed coffee and fried dough hit them as soon as they stepped through the door of the coffee shop. Orders of "double-double"—two creams and two sugars—overlayed a soft chatter as customers popped in and out for their morning fix. Only a few people—mostly seniors—sat at the melamine-topped tables.

"See," Jaden said as they lined up to order. "We're in a public place, in a town we don't live in, and there are crullers. We're all set."

Zelda's sarcastic sneer would have been funny any other time.

They were settling in to a table at the back of the restaurant when Nero Estevez walked through the door. He was easily recognizable from his Facebook pictures. Zelda stopped Jaden from waving with a touch of her arm. "Give it a minute," she hissed. "Let's check him out first."

Wearing a wool navy peacoat and a red scarf, Estevez shuffled his leather boots against the walkway mat, even though the ground outside was bone dry. His nose lifted, as if an unpleasant smell had just caught him off guard. He lazily scanned the room. With dark-plastic-framed glasses, tailored jeans, and a stylishly trimmed five-o'clock shadow, he looked more like an online influencer than an aging activist.

"Fine," Zelda said in a whisper. "He looks OK."

Jaden waved him over.

"I take it you're Jaden?" he said, looming over them. He lingered on the *you*, stretching it out with an eyebrow pop and brow furrow. He cast a slanted glance at Zelda before his eyes settled back on Jaden, an expectation and a demand in his gaze.

"I am. Nice to meet you," Jaden said.

Rather than taking Jaden's outstretched hand, he slid onto the seat across from her. Zelda shuffled to the other side of the table, a restrained scowl brushing her lips. Estevez wore a rich brown-and-cream argyle sweater under his coat and a slim wedding band on his finger.

"So, you wanted to know about Militant Animals?" he said, leaning back slightly in the chair. The tips of his fingers brushed at an unseen crumb.

Jaden nodded. Suddenly, she felt young and foolish. What could this man tell her that she hadn't already learned from the newspapers? If he had indeed been a student activist, clearly that version of him was no longer part of his life.

"May I ask why?" he said. "Your message said something about a school project and a family connection."

"We think her mom is Grace Hobbes," Zelda said into Jaden's silence.

His body language was unfazed but for a flinch of an eyebrow at the name and a slight narrowing of the eyes. When he spoke, there was a small flare of the nostrils.

"Think?" he said.

"It's possible she changed her name," Jaden said.

"I haven't heard that name in a long time," he said. "Is there a reason you haven't asked your mom this question?"

Jaden shrugged. Nero sighed.

A moment passed. Straight-backed and one hand lying gently over the other on the table, he seemed disinclined to continue. His gaze, when it finally landed back on Jaden, was critical but resigned, as if acknowledging the past was a shadow he could never outrun.

"All right," he said finally, a battle wavering in his eyes. "Ask your little questions."

Jaden began.

"What can you tell me about Konrad Sharma?" she said.

"Konrad? My, my, you are full of little surprises, aren't you? Konrad was the de facto leader of Militant Animals," Nero said, sarcasm imbued in the qualifier. "And my friend."

Zelda and Jaden cast quick glances at each other.

"Do you know what really happened to him?" Zelda said, leaning in.

"You mean do I have some inside track on why he was reduced to a pulpy mess by an explosion? No, sorry."

This was not going the way Jaden had hoped. The molded-plastic seat was hard and hot against her backside. She flailed around in her head for something, anything, that would get the conversation on a stable track, only coming up with childish platitudes.

"I'm sorry," she finally said, fighting against a burn in her eyes. "I just want to know what's happened to my mom."

Almost without taking a breath, she told him about her mom's disappearance and the convoluted route that had brought them to this moment. She watched his face as he absorbed the story, noted a tiny wrinkle under his eye, like a slow-motion twitch.

"The press had it all wrong at the time. Militant Animals wasn't a typical protest group with angry demonstrations and impassioned calls to action," Nero eventually said on an exhale, his expression tittering between suspicion and empathy. "The group was just a loose collection of misfits, kids really, trying to feel important and have fun. After the"—his lips puckered and eyes hardened—"accident, rumors started, of course. There always are when these things happen. People love a scandal, don't they? And the press ate up every crumb. But Konrad wasn't some radicalized activist. He was a nice guy who made some terrible decisions."

The picture Nero painted was completely at odds with the Konrad Sharma described in the news articles at the time.

As customers flitted in and out behind him, Estevez explained that he had left Militant Animals months before the explosion happened. Like everyone affiliated with the group, he'd been questioned by police at the time, but that was the end of it for him.

"Why did you leave?" Jaden said.

"A combination of things," he said. "The group was getting too big, too many new faces, too much arguing. And, frankly, the ideas for stunts were getting stupider. But mainly, I grew up. I met Michael, my husband, and had more important things to do." He shrugged.

"So, what do you think happened the night Konrad died?"

Jaden saw the truth dangling in front of her, ripe and rich.

"I wish I knew," said Nero. "I wasn't involved. No one was. He was alone when it happened."

Disappointment echoed inside Jaden's head.

"If anyone knows, it's her," he said. A blush of red and a flash of darkness in his eyes, more than his tone, betrayed his feelings.

Jaden held her breath.

"Grace?" Zelda said, just above a whisper.

"No," said Estevez, with more ridicule than Jaden thought possible in two letters. "Clara Morel. I have no doubt she was the one responsible for the whole mess."

That name again. Disparate shapes fit into place, like a warped tangram puzzle. Jaden had first seen the name Clara Morel on her mom's computer, the article concerning the woman about to be released from prison. She hadn't thought anything of it at the time, assuming it was random. Stupidly, she hadn't made the connection when the name popped up again in the archive's pieces. Hearing it spoken jogged the connection.

"Konrad was moving away from Militant Animals before the explosion happened," Nero said. "He was in law school, leaning more into his career. And the group was changing. He started to think it was time to leave. I don't know how Clara pulled him back in, and I don't care what the reporters said about him. There's no doubt in my mind that Konrad had nothing to do with what happened. If anyone was responsible, it was her. I'm glad she's rotting in jail."

Jaden had been peeling at the cardboard sleeve on her coffee cup, ripping strips, trying to get the courage to ask the one question that felt like an anvil. Eyes locked on the small pile of cardboard she'd created on the table, she pushed the words out.

"Have you ever heard the name Emma Hobbes?"

Zelda placed a hand on Jaden's knee, stilling the jittering of her leg under the table.

"Emma? No. There was never an Emma that I knew," Nero said. "Just Grace. She was Konrad's girlfriend."

Jaden heard a distant ringing in her mind, the sound familiar but just out of each, like an earworm that wouldn't let go.

"Do you know what happened to her? To Grace?" Zelda said, relieving Jaden of the burden.

"No idea. I haven't talked to any of them since university. Not Clara, not Grace, not even Ben. They could all be in Timbuktu for all I know."

"Who's Ben?" the girls asked at the same time.

"Ben Chalmers. He and Grace were a strange package. I don't think they ever dated, but he followed her like a devoted little pup. Wherever Grace was, there went Ben. At least until he started dating Clara. After that, I don't know what happened. I was gone by then."

And just like that, another thread was dropped in front of Jaden. She scrambled to pick it up. Zelda, ever the researcher, beat her to it.

"I don't suppose you know where we can find pictures of all these people? The paper only had photos of Konrad. It'd be helpful to put faces to all these names."

Nero sighed and rolled his eyes.

"Fine," he said on an annoyed sigh, though his relaxed shoulders suggested he was softening toward them. "I think I have an old group photo somewhere. I can text it to you when I get home."

Jaden hesitated. Zelda's warnings floated in her head, like tendrils of fog. She knew further contact crossed a line. Yet hunger gnawed at her. She thumbed at her phone on the table. She could just share a picture of her mom, ask him if Grace and Emma were the same person. But she wanted more. She wanted undeniable, physical, irrefutable proof. Nothing other than the source would unravel her mother's secrets.

She nodded and mumbled a thanks.

"Do you still protest?" Zelda said.

"Oh, hell no. I teach civics. I wouldn't hear the end of it from my little buggers if I was still that stupid." The words were harsh but affectionate. For the first time, a touch of humanity reached Nero's lips. For all his uptight exterior, he clearly had a soft spot for his students. "I'm still a vegetarian, though. Can't let go of everything." He smirked.

They were partway back to White Falls when Jaden's phone chirped, begging for her attention. She glanced at the screen but couldn't see the sender. A denser forest had crept forward as the highway moved out of the lowlands and onto the Precambrian backbone of the continent. The trees, scragglier but hardy, took root over granite slabs. The snowpack drew higher, and the temperature dropped as they moved farther north. They were headed home, beyond the reach of the sprawling concrete Toronto beast to the south.

"It's from him," Zelda said, on the edge of irritation. She'd kept her opinion to herself when they left the coffee shop, but Jaden could feel her disapproval.

This stretch of highway would have been called empty in the summer; in the winter it was as barren and desolate as the backside of the moon. There were hours to go before home, and the day had already slipped into afternoon. The sun, rushing toward the horizon, left stretched shadows of evergreens over the road. Though the car heater was on high, Jaden shivered when she looked at the ice-lined forest.

When they crossed a small side road that was wide enough for them to stop, Jaden pulled over, carefully maneuvering the car so they wouldn't dip into the surrounding drainage ditch. She left the engine running. There was always a danger, no matter how infinitesimal, that a cut engine wouldn't restart, and you'd be left with nothing but snow and trees and the long wait for help.

"Open it already," Zelda said.

Jaden clicked on the message; it sprang to life, revealing miniature faces from another time. She tapped at the photo, expanding it to fit her screen.

The photo was taken after a charity race. The figures wore matching T-shirts, tired grins, and numbered bibs. One woman, smiling from center screen, wrenched Jaden's attention. She was crouched in the front row, a fist extended above her head and a look of triumph on her face. Beside her, Konrad Sharma, with an ear-to-ear smile, draped a lazy arm on her shoulder. She magnified the image further until the woman's face filled the entire screen.

"Bingo!" Zelda said.

Zelda's voice was small and far away to Jaden's ear, as if the world had dropped off into an abyss, and all that remained was the hum of the engine and the photo in front of her. Jaden couldn't pull her eyes from the screen to recalibrate.

The woman looking up at her was undeniably and unmistakably a younger version of Emma Meadows, her mom.

The tail end of daylight drifted through the living-room window when Jaden arrived home in White Falls. Deep shadows and stale air filled the house, as if neither had bothered to move in the time Jaden had been away.

The familiar smell of home, tinged with worn wood and lemon, wrapped itself around her. Winnie, as usual, ambled toward the door, her tail keeping time behind her. Over the long drive, a fantasy had rooted itself in Jaden's mind—she would step through the door to be greeted by her mom and a world of cleared-up misunderstandings.

"Hey, sweetheart," her dad said as he emerged from the kitchen.

Jaden looked into the face of a changed man. His usually boyish face was drawn, with pockets of deep gray under his eyes. Unwashed hair had tamed his persistent cowlick, and he was wearing the same clothes he'd had on when she'd last seen him two days ago.

"Hey, Dad," Jaden said.

She leaned into his bracing hug with utter relief that the size and strength of his arms had not diminished.

"Glad you're back," he said, his voice raspy. He pulled away and turned his always inquisitive eyes on her. "How's the apartment? All good?"

"Ya, it's fine, Dad. I worked it all out."

"Good, good. Mom's gonna read the riot act to that landlord when she gets back."

Jaden knelt to pet Winnie, and to hide her face. She lay her forehead against the dog's soft shoulder and breathed in the familiar dusty-sweat smell.

She had no words. How could she explode his hope? She felt tears burn her throat. In the daze of the unexplainable, Mark Meadows had decided to trust and wait. Did Jaden have a right to take that away by sharing what she'd learned about her mom's past and her growing suspicions? Would it change anything?

"Don't worry, sweetie," her dad said. He knelt beside her and placed a warm hand on her shoulder. "Mom'll be home before you know it," he said. She saw the look in his eyes; the phrase had become his mantra.

Jaden kept her eyes on the floor. She couldn't bring herself to shatter his illusion, so she held her tongue.

A high-pitched double chime crashed into the quiet.

Jaden had started to hate the sound of the doorbell. The electronic jangle raced over her nerves, settling at the base of her neck, squeezing muscles and tendons into an impenetrable knot. She'd given up expecting good news or even answers at the sound. No doubt, there was another well-meaning neighbor with a casserole dish standing at their door. Good intentions laced with unintended cruelty.

“It was a long drive,” she said. “I’m going to take Winnie for a walk.”

Without taking off her coat or boots, Jaden tromped through the house and slipped out the back door. Dusty afternoon light left a blue-gray tinge across the snow. The back walk hadn’t been shoveled since the storm. Calf-deep snow slid up her leg. She didn’t care. She made her way through the backyard toward the front street. The only car parked on the block was a dark-blue SUV a few doors down. She saw the outline of a driver behind the wheel but nothing more in the fading daylight. Jaden kept her head down. She was in no mood for pretend sympathy and faked gratitude.

Beneath her, the asphalt was painted with intricate webs of skim ice, frozen tendrils hardening now that the sun had drifted low. Winnie loped happily beside her, occasionally bounding through patches of soft snow as they rounded the cul-de-sac. It was the kind of winter weather—on the edge of melty—that tricked you into thinking winters were survivable here. Jaden knew better.

Chapter 22

Ben

1999

A breeze came in through the open window, bringing whiffs of spring rain and new growth. Outside, pale new leaves swayed comfortably. Evening light created a hint of enchantment in Grace's walk-up apartment, with dust motes riding currents of air. At another time, Ben would have sunk into this space as if he were coming home. Tonight, it felt like he'd crossed into a foreign land.

The words had arrived so organically, Ben couldn't remember when casual references to violence became part of the rhetoric around them; there hadn't been a before and after moment when they'd slithered forward. They simply arrived, nesting and reproducing, until Ben sat in a corner listening to people he loved discuss a bomb.

What had started as a lazy conversation sharpened when Clara pulled a set of plans for a homemade explosive device from her bag. Grace and Clara were now bent over sheets of dot matrix printouts laid out like a morbid map on the coffee table.

"How could we be sure no one gets hurt?" Grace said.

The conversation had started as a hypothetical. Finals were just behind them, and the long, hot days of summer lay ahead. Four of them were staying in Toronto—Clara for spring session, Ben and Konrad for summer jobs, and Grace because she had no home waiting for her elsewhere. The two girls and Ben were having a postfinals celebration and finishing off the last of the weed. Pearl Jam's deep, mournful vocals and distorted guitar seeped from a crackly speaker.

"Good question," said Clara. "I think you could adjust the amount of explosive, couldn't you? Maybe you only use a tiny bit if you want a small explosion. Enough to make a bang but nowhere near enough to cause damage. You'd also have to make sure the area was empty. If you planned it right, I bet you could make it pretty foolproof."

The question at the heart of the discussion had been like dozens of other stoned speculations between the friends: What if we backpacked through Europe next summer? What if we started a business selling bracelets? What if one of us ran for city council?

Imagination took flight aboard hypotheticals, making them feel like the world was theirs for the taking. Tonight, though, the question had a practical edge: What if we made a small bomb to rattle a cosmetics company's cage? It hadn't been anything more than fantastical speculation. Until it wasn't.

Ben couldn't stop himself from interjecting.

"How could you possibly know the right amount? You'd need an explosives expert for something like that."

Both women glanced his way, but his words didn't land.

He'd noticed a closeness developing between the two women over the last few weeks. They'd started laughing at inside jokes that didn't include him, rolling their eyes collectively at his interjections, forgetting him when plans were being made. It irked him more than he cared to admit. What was the problem, exactly, that his best friend and girlfriend were getting along? Isn't that what he should want?

Still, when he saw them through the window of a shop last Saturday afternoon, he was hurt. Clara had blown off her plans with him, saying she'd scored some extra computer-lab time. She was working on a final project for her Intro to Programming class, she'd said, and needed all the time she could get. Grace, meanwhile, had told him she had study group. The term was just about over, exams looming like an axe around the corner. Ben didn't question their stories, not for a second.

Not wanting to waste the entirety of a sunny afternoon, Ben had decided to stroll toward Chinatown. Maybe pick up an order of garlic ribs and find some of those chocolate-covered coffee beans that Clara loved to munch while studying.

He'd spotted the two of them through the front window of a little bakery along Spadina Avenue. He watched long enough to notice the half-eaten piece of cheesecake that sat between them, to see Grace throw her head back in laughter, and to feel a stab of rejection pierce through his flesh to his spine. He thought about going in, asking to join them. But then, if they'd wanted him there, they wouldn't have lied to him.

He'd walked back to his apartment, garlic ribs and coffee beans forgotten.

He was thinking about that humiliating, lonely walk back to his apartment as the third hit from a joint reached his brain. He lay back into the armchair, inhaled the skunky smell, and let Clara and Grace's conversation slip past him like a stick dropped into a river.

"That'd be the easy part," Clara said, a tinge of annoyance in her voice. She rarely appreciated reality marring her imaginings. "You know, I think we need to consider something like this for real. Imagine the splash it would make, pun completely intended."

The living room filled with the women's lazy, giddy laughter. Ben regretted that they'd finished the entirety of the joint.

Grace and Clara continued to talk about logistics and possible targets. Ben watched their conversation as if witnessing a slow-motion traffic accident. He could see where it might go, but part of him still denied the possibility of any real danger.

"Seriously, though. What if we could pull it off?" Clara's voice quavered with a contained zeal. "These plans pretty much show us how."

"Where'd you get these anyway?" Grace said, still bent over the pages, one hand tugging at her ear, the way she always did when her mind was working through a problem. It was this, more than the words, that set off uncomfortable bells in the back of Ben's brain, though he was too stoned to make sense of them.

"Computer lab," Clara said. "I swear, someone just left them sitting on the printer. I was gonna throw them out, but then I saw what they were. I was curious. No one will miss them."

Clara, an engineering student, spent most of her spare time in the computer lab. The internet was just starting to take hold, and her class project was looking at how to build better search tools. Ben loved the way Clara's mind worked and had been attracted to a beautiful girl more interested in STEM than makeup. He never imagined that she'd use her creation to locate and print designs for a lethal weapon.

He heard the next words as if through water, his mind refusing to accept the possibility.

"You know. It could be done," Clara said. "Maybe it's just what we need to reenergize our crew and get people talking?"

With the mingled smell of wet earth and marijuana still in his nose, Ben drifted on an unfamiliar sea. A threshold had been crossed, and he struggled to cling to the boundaries. These two women were closer to him than family; their words mattered. He trusted them, admired them. The idea that they might be in the wrong was too remote a concept to grasp.

"Are you being serious right now?" he said.

Both women looked up at him. Grace's brown eyes, kind and watchful, though always with a touch of anger; Clara's, green, alluring, and calculating. An unnatural quiet permeated the room; not even the sound of traffic bled through the open window, as if the world outside stood still, waiting for the answer. Ben understood enough to know he was trapped in a moment of his own creation, like an insect who willingly waded into the amber.

"Maybe," Grace said casually, though her cheeks reddened with the effort.

Clara, standing behind Grace, shot him a knowing smile and flirtatious glance. The pot he'd smoked had obliterated his ability to read the room, and he leaned into the invitation in Clara's eyes with a lascivious grin.

Years later, waking in the dark and chasing memories, Ben will recognize that a different reaction in that moment might have changed so much about what was to come. Had he pushed back, maybe the events that followed would have been altered. Instead, he shrugged and let them unfold toward tragedy.

A rattle of the apartment door disturbed the conversation. Clara and Grace craned themselves awkwardly around, but Ben had a clear view of Konrad Sharma's face as he loped into the room. A flicker of disappointment crossed his features, replaced in a breath by Konrad's usual electric grin. His face shone with a thin veneer of sweat. An elegantly wrapped box was tucked beneath one arm, while the other balanced a bottle of wine and a bakery box.

"Hey," Konrad said lightly. "What's going on? Seems intense in here."

"Nothing. Just hanging out." Clara was the first to answer. She stacked the pages on the coffee table.

"Okaaay," Konrad said. His eyes met Ben's, then shot a glance to the package under his arm.

Pieces fell into place. The wine, the bakery box, the present. Konrad had expected to find Grace alone.

"Clara, we should get going?" Ben said. He stood, though the room took a little spin until his head adjusted. He really was more stoned than he'd intended.

"What? Why?" Clara's voice sounded shrill against a sudden twitter of sparrows out the window. Outside, the evening was soft and delicate as spider silk and held a promise. Inside, a foul current stirred the air.

Konrad moved around the couch toward Grace, his smile still warm, though there was wariness in his slow, deliberate movements. "What's this?" he said, bending over the coffee table.

"'Cause, we need to go," said Ben, reaching for his backpack and holding out his other hand to Clara.

"Don't—" Grace leaned forward from the couch, trying to grab for the pages. It was too late. Konrad was looking at them. His index finger pushed them around as if they were an infection.

"What the hell?" Konrad said.

In all the time that Ben had known Konrad, he'd never seen the man truly angry. He'd seen counterprotesters try to bait him, administrators try to dismiss him, and the occasional jealous boyfriend try to fight him. Not once had Konrad's demeanor changed from a gentle chuckle and an easy slide into more comfortable terrain.

Konrad's low growled words now might as well have been a yell. A steel jaw and half-open mouth showed the ridge of his upper teeth. There was anger, yes, but something deeper and primal. A threat and an attack in conjoined syllables.

"Why the fuck is it here?" Konrad said, his eyes locked on Clara.

Clara stood. Her lips raised in a laissez-faire smile. "It's nothing. I just found it at the lab. Thought it was interesting."

"That's bullshit," Konrad said.

Konrad had moved to the front of the apartment. Backlit by evening light, his features blurred, and his edges seemed to expand, taking up the whole of the living room. Ben waited for a reaction from the girls, but their blank, guiltless expressions gave away nothing. He looked back at the snarl on Konrad's face and tried to decipher his meaning, like lines on a page that might link to a discernible pattern.

"Your girlfriend didn't tell you, did she, Ben?" Konrad said, redirecting his ire. "Guess it's hard to see the truth when you're chasing her ass all the time. She's the one who's been pushing for more confrontation, gathering followers like some deranged 'cult leader.'" The air quotes were all the sarcasm needed.

The accusation released, Konrad's shoulders sank. His anger had exhausted itself, leaving only a young body blocking the sun.

Clara gazed up at him, her face a mask of incredulity and concern. "Konrad," she said. "I don't know where you heard that, but it's simply not true. You're starting to sound paranoid."

Rumors had been spreading for a while about some members wanting to intensify efforts, be more direct. Like everyone else, Ben had had theoretical conversations with Clara. Maybe Konrad's head just wasn't in this anymore? Probably time for him to step aside for some new blood. He tried to remember who had started the discussions. Could Clara have been the driving force behind the tensions infecting the group?

Ben looked at Clara—the soft, ash-blond hair that had lain across his pillow, the rose gold lips he'd craved, the blush of anger on her cheeks—and dismissed the idea.

There was no way Clara was the cause. Sure, she'd been interested in hearing about new tactics and had a passion for animal welfare, but Konrad's accusation was ludicrous.

Clara grabbed her jacket from the back of the couch. She made her way to the door, turning her back on Konrad. Perhaps a mistake. His next words spun her around, like prey alert to the gnarling teeth of a predator.

"I think campus admin and maybe even the police might be interested in learning about what our little Clara's been up to. Creating an explosion. Isn't that what you've been suggesting to everyone? And using university property to do it too. Sure, you keep pretending it's a joke, but this isn't the first time you've brought it up, is it?" Konrad said.

His next words were softer, almost gentle, but no less intense. He turned to look directly at Clara, his eyes pinning her in place like a spider trapped under a glass. "It's not a game, Clara. This is real life, and I won't let you take people down with you. Stay away from me and stay away from them."

Four bodies stood in that room, locked in a vortex of tension and recrimination as the day's sunlight gave a final shudder.

"Get out," Grace said; her voice matched Konrad's in intensity.

Ben followed Grace's gaze and realized, to his bewilderment, that her ire was directed at Konrad.

Ben watched events play out, a spectator to a drama that had been unfolding for weeks. He really was too stoned to think clearly. Konrad looked to Ben, his eyes asking a question, and Ben felt nothing: not anger, not resentment, and surprisingly, not even admiration. Konrad was a wounded animal, a has-been, and no longer the leader they needed. He had turned a languid afternoon into something deeper, with cruelty licking at the edges of the moment. Ben thought about intervening, pulling them all back from the black hole they were heading into, but he had no control over which way it went. He never did. He watched Grace circle the room, like a feral character on a stage.

"Who do you think you are?" she said. "Coming in here like some smarter-than-thou asshole, flinging around unfounded accusations. If you can't accept that things are changing, the least you can do is be respectful and not slander anyone with a different opinion. You think that Clara's responsible for your lack of leadership? You're embarrassing yourself and me."

Grace tilted her head apologetically at Clara. When she turned back to Konrad, she slammed her small hands into his chest, shoving him onto his heels.

"Get out," she commanded.

Konrad stumbled, and the boxes in his hands fell to the floor. She shoved him again, harder. This time, he was braced for it. His body held firm. Only his eyes betrayed the depths of the wound.

Ben remained in place, incapable of rewinding what had just happened and unable to move forward through the implications. Konrad walked out the door on a muttered curse. The beautifully wrapped present and box of pastries lay abandoned in a heap on the floor.

Ben heard words spoken to him then, slow and distorted, as if he'd stepped into a *Charlie Brown* cartoon and the mangled voices of the adults were speaking. He looked at Clara, then Grace. Both stared at him expectantly. He was supposed to do something, but he didn't know what.

"I said, you should go too," Grace repeated, her tone soft but no less firm. "Clara and I still need to talk about some things, and you need to sober up. You are way too stoned for this."

Ben heard the echo of a buzz in his head, as if a bee were hammering against a window trying to get out. "But—" he said, with no thought of what else he could say.

"It's all right," Clara said. She cast a glance at Grace before she spoke again. "We got this. Go home, Ben."

Ben stood a moment longer—the sting of the dismissal settling in—before he left. As he closed the door behind him, a fleeting thought drifted through him like smoke: Neither woman had met his eyes when he'd been told to leave.

Later, when the moon was visible at the top of the sky, Ben found himself back at Grace's apartment. He'd cleared his head of the weed and the unsettled fear that crept under his skin. He'd walked four hours through congested streets and under the crisscrossing streetcar lines, as if the answers could be found in the low brick buildings and Chinese groceries in Chinatown. Though almost midnight, the streets of Toronto were still alive, feeding on the warm spring night.

The hallway was dark. Ben knocked at Grace's door. There was no answer. He tried again, holding his breath to better hear movement inside. Nothing.

He took the spare key from above the doorframe. The lock gave easily.

"Grace? You home?" he called into emptiness as he stepped forward. No answer came.

Ben had once read a novel about a man who could play with time, moving it backward and forward at will, adjusting the dial until the outcome of his life was more to his liking. In the end, the man met a gruesome fate, a cautionary tale about the abuses of power. Still, not for the first time, he yearned for the capacity to hold mastery over time, to take lessons learned far too late and replay parts of his life, as if the previous scenes were merely rehearsals.

Streetlight through the unshaded windows was enough to see around the room. The loathed pages on the coffee table were still there, along with the glass music box and crumpled gold wrapping paper. Ben lifted the lid to the box. Tinny notes reverberated in the hollow space.

The song was painfully beautiful. The first time Ben had heard it was in this very room. A cold winter night, sipping hot chocolate with Baileys. Content, though not drunk, he and Grace had fallen to swapping childhood stories. He'd told her about bullying and the plight of a small, overly smart kid in high school hallways. She'd shared details about the deaths of her parents. As the night deepened, Ben learned about the song her mother had sung to her every night when she was little—an Irish lament about love and leaving.

That very same song now filled the space around Ben. It slipped across him like a hair shirt, one he would carry for the rest of his days.

Chapter 23

Jaden

Within sight of the house, Jaden let Winnie off the leash. The dog raced ahead, treading a well-carved path born of instinct and habit. Jaden sighed with relief when she noticed the blue SUV from earlier was no longer parked on the street. Whoever had dropped by had made a quick stop, sparing Jaden their cloying sympathy.

By the time Jaden noticed the police car in the driveway, it was too late. Winnie was already scratching at the front door. She cursed the dog under her breath and rushed over to grab her collar.

The front door opened just as Jaden reached the end of the driveway. It crossed her mind to duck behind the car, but she quickly brushed the idea aside. Childishness had no place here; besides, Winnie had already announced their return.

Jaden turned back to the house to see the gargoyle-like form of Malcolm O'Shea in the doorway. His grim expression and firm stance told a story she was not interested in hearing. Dozens of thoughts careened through her mind, exploding like malevolent fireworks before blowing to ash.

"Jaden," O'Shea said. His voice, though quiet, skimmed over the snow. "Can we talk?"

There were moments when the mind was forced to choose, rational response or give in to the primordial demands of the nervous system. Living in a wilder part of the world, Jaden had learned to lean into her instincts in the face of cracking lake ice or a lurking coyote. There was no such response now. Her only answer to O'Shea's question was to freeze, as if she could blend in with the gray sky and concrete of the driveway.

"It's OK, Jaden," O'Shea said, as if luring a wounded animal. "I just want to talk. Nothing else."

With effort, Jaden placed one foot in front of the other and followed Winnie into the house.

Jaden knew something was wrong as soon as she set foot inside. Some people fill the frame of the lives around them so completely, their absence is an immediate void. Jaden's dad was one such person.

"Where's my dad?" Jaden said, turning a critical eye on O'Shea.

"An officer has taken him to the station," O'Shea answered, though there was no relief or triumph in his eyes, only sadness and concern.

"Why?"

"I think we should sit down."

"No, tell me now." Jaden hated the histrionic strain in her voice.

"We have a lot to talk about. It's best if we take a seat." O'Shea placed an irritatingly gentle hand on her elbow.

The edges of her vision blurred, narrowing to a tunnel that encompassed O'Shea and the slimmest of views of the living room, where he was directing her. She had trouble catching her breath. Her chest moved in short, sharp jabs. She was sitting but didn't remember doing so.

"I'll get you some water," O'Shea said.

The officer was a talking shadow, gliding from the room on an unseen current.

A warm, steady weight leaned against Jaden's leg. The feeling ran up from her shin and thigh. She reached without looking and felt a silky mass beneath her fingers. Spreading her palm flat, she twined her fingers into Winnie's plush undercoat. Sounds trickled back. Jaden heard a glass slide across the coffee table, smelled the dry pine of the Christmas tree.

She took a deep sip of water, looked O'Shea dead in the eye, and said, "Now, why the hell is my dad at the station?"

O'Shea didn't answer her question, but he gave her the answer she needed in that moment.

"There's been a sighting of your mother's car," he said.

Her mom's Subaru, he said, had been spotted via security camera in the parking lot of a small cottage resort between here and Lake Superior Provincial Park. The properties were mostly summer cabins, but two of them were winterized and occasionally rented to ice fishers. The resort offered self-check-in with key boxes, so the manager hadn't called in the sighting to police until a guest complained that their cabin hadn't been cleaned properly.

"It's not uncommon for drifters or local kids to break into these types of cabins over the winter. It's one of the reasons the owners installed cameras," O'Shea said.

Unfortunately, rather than video stream, the cameras were time lapsed, taking a photo every few hours, so they had a series of still images. All they knew for sure was that the Subaru had arrived late on Boxing Day and was gone by the following morning.

"Where is she then? If you found her car, you must know where she went from there," Jaden said in a bark. Anger spilled over her best efforts to contain it.

"We don't know."

O'Shea held her gaze and let Jaden's eyes bore into him without expression.

"So, what are you doing to find her then?"

To his credit, there was no pity in O'Shea's next words. Only cold facts.

"We've done a preliminary search of the cabin, and traces of blood have been found in the kitchen. We won't jump to any conclusions yet, but it's enough to not be incidental."

He let the words fall, giving Jaden time to absorb all they could mean before continuing. Winnie lay on the couch beside her, her head on Jaden's thigh. The deep tick of the radiator pulsed the passage of time.

"There wasn't a lot of blood, but it was enough that we need to look into it," O'Shea continued. "Someone had broken into the cabin through a rear window, but we have no confirmation it was your mom, only that her car had been in the parking lot. The manager said there hadn't been any bookings since the middle of November, so he hadn't been by there in a few weeks. The break-in could have easily happened weeks ago. We're looking into it."

O'Shea explained that the snow over the last few days had obliterated any tracks, human or vehicle.

"There are a couple of snowmobile and ski trails in the area, so we're starting with a search of those and will broaden out if needed. Without a definitive point of access, we won't start a full ground search," O'Shea said. "It would be like looking for a needle in a haystack."

Jaden almost laughed. The cliché pretty much summed up the last few days.

"We've called in a provincial forensics team, but they won't be out until tomorrow. Sorting through the evidence will take some time, as will the lab work. The blood traces might confirm your mom's presence, or they might not be related. Now that we have access to the photos from the security camera, we've also looked at other known persons in the vicinity."

The last was said with a slight bend of his chin and lift of the eyebrow.

Jaden reached for a blanket at the end of the couch and wrapped it around her shoulders. She didn't care if O'Shea noticed her slight rhythmic rocking as he took her through the next steps.

"We're going to focus on the forensics for now. The BOLO is still active, but our working theory is that your mom may have accessed the cabin for a few hours at most, maybe to meet someone or maybe to regroup. We can't yet determine if she was there of her own volition or with someone. The fresh snow makes it impossible to track where she may have gone after.

"There are a couple of towns along the snowmobile route. Poplar Bay is only about five klicks up trail, and it gets pretty frequent use, including by skiers and snowshoers. We're not discounting the possibility that Emma accessed another mode of transportation to leave the area, though it's much more likely she left in her own vehicle. All avenues are being explored."

O'Shea's calm, smooth voice grated against Jaden's nerves and muscles. She felt like a coiled spring waiting for its moment.

"You still haven't answered my question," Jaden said slowly, refusing to look at O'Shea. Her anger had abated but not disappeared. It ran just beneath her skin, hot and flickering.

"Jaden, were you with your dad all day on December twenty-seventh?"

The abrupt question made no sense. Dates were meaningless, empty boxes on a calendar that spoke only to the passage of time since her mom had disappeared.

"Of course. Why does that matter?" she said.

"I'm asking you if you were with your dad for every moment the day after your mom disappeared?"

Though his voice hadn't changed, there was an ominous message carried on the words.

"Yes."

"All day? You never left each other's presence for any period of time."

"Why are you asking this?"

"Did you know your parents had a life insurance policy?"

Jaden shook her head, stunned. This was starting to feel like a bad cop show.

"It seems your dad expanded their life insurance policy six months ago. Had he talked to you or your mom about that? It's a pretty substantive increase. In the event of death or declaration of death, the policy pays out five million dollars."

"No. Neither of my parents mentioned that," Jaden said, her jaw tightening.

It was like watching a car wreck in slow motion. Jaden could see the slide but couldn't find a way to turn into it and right the trajectory.

"You see, what we're trying to figure out, and I'm hoping you can help me out here, is why your dad's car would have also turned up near the very same set of cottages on December twenty-seventh."

Crash! In the back of her mind, Jaden heard the crunch of metal. She jumped up.

She stared down at the uniformed officer still seated on the chair. She wanted to slap the composed look off his face.

"I think you should leave now," she said.

She had intended for her voice to be a whip, but all she could hear was a squeak of a scared little girl clawing for reason.

Chorus

She liked the way Konrad unconsciously chewed his lower lip when he was studying. It made him look studious and thoughtful. Sitting a few tables over in the concrete-and-glass reading room of the Robarts Library, she'd been watching him out of the corner of her eye for the last ten minutes, evaluating. Every time he bit his lip, she pinched the back of her hand, counting the seconds in between like tracking the time from thunder to lightning. Every now and again, Konrad turned a page in a thick green tome laid out in front of him and scratched notes on a yellow legal pad. He had the look of someone with a future, she decided.

Shit.

Her thoughts were shattered when three others clambered onto the seats around Konrad. She recognized them, of course. They were all members of the student group that he led. Their voices echoed against the brutalist architecture, pooling into an incomprehensible hushed echo. A librarian gave the group a nasty look, and they settled behind a short, guilty giggle.

Unlike Konrad, the trio carried themselves with the self-conscious bluster of senior students who knew they belonged. They'd been around long enough to learn the campus rhythms and wanted the world to see it, so they sashayed into quiet spaces and winked at the annoyed librarian. Konrad, she'd learned, was in law school, already on his way to something better than what his student group could ever offer.

It wouldn't be long before he left the rest of them behind. He was on a path, one that she'd studied intimately. In the annoyed glances he shot their way, she could already see his equation starting to shift and rebalance.

The only problem was her. The wannabe grunge princess who was holding his hand and holding him back. The same brunette she'd seen Konrad with after the group's meeting the previous week. The roots of her bad dye job were obvious or intentional. Either way, they looked cheap and trendy, just like her worn out Converses. It was beyond her what Konrad saw in the girl, but it did seem like the relationship was entrenched.

She looked away when Konrad leaned over to kiss grunge princess. That girl couldn't possibly understand what Konrad needs for his future.

By the time she looked back to where Konrad had been, only the goth princess and her little tagalong friends remained.

Konrad had left, likely to someplace more important. She watched the remainders. They were slumped over books, sharing a bag of Sour Patch Kids on the table between them, bodies relaxed. When two of them reached in the bag at the same time, fingers grazing, they didn't even look up. There wasn't a romantic spark, more an ease and acceptance.

One of them was cute in a Leonardo DiCaprio, shaggy-haired sort of way. Round face but with an earnestness in his features. He'd been at the front of the room when Konrad spoke the other day, had spoken about his own experiences with the group and why he'd enjoyed his time among them. Not riveting but there had been an honesty in his voice. A likable face.

The variables in her equation were shifting slightly. An inevitability as she gathered data and ran simulations in her head. The key was learning enough to identify the weak points and use your strengths to compensate. It was demanding and not always as precise as she would have liked, but such was the way given the consistent frailty of people. You worked with what was in front of you and managed the risks as best you could.

That's the trouble with equations, she thought. Sometimes, they required dedication and sacrifice. And not just her own.

Chapter 24

Jaden

On the last day of the year, Jaden woke in her childhood bed. She was still wearing her clothes from the day before, along with a rank smell of body odor and sleep. Her mouth was desert dry, gluing her lips together with a sticky residue.

She had lain awake half the night waiting for her dad's footsteps in the downstairs hall. When sleep finally came, it dragged her into a welcomed, though restless, oblivion. Eyes still closed, she straddled two worlds, aware of her surroundings but incapable of escaping clinging dreams where lucidity was an afterthought. Her head spun, recent events echoing in her mind like a series of twisted GIFs: the threatening phone call, O'Shea's accusations, her mom's past. All of it spun until a single macabre image appeared behind her eyes—a kitchen dripping in blood and her dad standing over the carnage.

She sat up abruptly. The house was silent. She didn't need to look to know it was empty. Her dad had not come home.

Jaden wiped at her eyes, as if that alone could banish images from her mind. The sun was up, struggling against the will of a winter morning. A cold, flint gray light seeped through the window. She shivered. In the glare of reason, it was like she'd lost pieces of herself and had no way of retracing her steps.

Absurdly, a childhood song popped into her head. Whenever she'd misplace something—a pencil case or a purse—her mom would torment her by following her around singing the same tune.

"What was lost can still be found," Jaden sang quietly, the words absorbed by the soft surfaces around her.

Unanswered questions pricked like mites. Had her mom been at that cabin? And where had she gone? How did her past and the sudden arrival of some old music box play into all this? Jaden had no answers, and the feeling of powerlessness burned in her chest.

"What was lost can still be found," she sang louder, letting her voice fill the room.

Jaden knew only one thing with absolute certainty: She needed to find her mom. She felt like a child, scared of the dark but too stubborn to admit it. Emotions slammed against her thought, trapped in a roiling sea of anger. Her mom was gone; her dad was caught up in the blind zealousness of a police officer. She wanted—no, needed—to blame someone, but the house was empty. Her anger was a beast hunting for a target.

"What was lost can still be found," Jaden screamed until her throat hurt and all breath had left her lungs.

Her phone warbled from the nightstand, the number unknown to her. She considered not answering. Hiding behind voicemail. She accepted the call.

"How are the holidays going with the family, Jaden? That sure is a cute dog you have there," a now-familiar voice said. It was the same off-kilter growl from the call earlier in the week; only this time the words were sharper and firmer in the absence of background noise.

The warm phone battery pricked her palm.

Jaden hung up and tossed the phone on the bed. A sudden flash of the blue SUV from the day before galloped through her mind. The faceless shape in the driver's seat, unmoving as Jaden turned her back and made her way up the block with Winnie. She had no proof of the connection, but her gut was telling her there was a link. The caller wasn't some rubbernecker feeding on an unfurling drama. Randomness had no business in her life right now.

She slunk to the bedroom window and peeked through a gap in the curtains. The street was empty. Fear ran rampant through her mind, slamming into a guilt that clawed its way up her throat, threatening to consume every part of her.

Her mom hadn't caused this. Someone, a coward or a kook, was responsible for what was happening to her family.

"Fuck you," she said as she drew herself to full height and threw open the curtains. "This ends now."

Jaden stood in the lobby of the White Falls police station, facing down the reptilian-looking reception clerk. It was not going well.

The clerk's eyes flitted in a circle between her face, the lobby, and his computer screen. He scowled in response to Jaden's defiant glare. She held her ground. Behind her, a burgeoning lineup of people oozed impatience and complaints. In their black puffy coats, they reminded Jaden of crows on the side of the highway waiting for a roadkill buffet.

Jaden had stormed into the police station, dragging with her a wind of evidence. If O'Shea wasn't prepared to consider alternatives to his theory, then Jaden would make him. She had the music box, the articles from her mom's closet, and Nero Estevez's photo of the Militant Animals group; it wasn't a full story yet, but it had to be enough to help her dad.

"As I've told you already, Ms. Meadows, Sergeant O'Shea is currently unavailable," the bug-eyed clerk said, trying for stern nonchalance. The words may have been polite, but the tone dripped a monotone sarcasm.

Jaden wasn't fooled. The jitter of his pupils and deepening lines around his mouth gave away the effort it was costing him to be dismissive. A mug on the desk proclaimed **I DON'T DO MORNINGS** beside the snarky face of a cartoon cat. Jaden imagined reaching over the plexiglass and smashing the mug against the side of the clerk's head, crumbling his last act of resistance.

"Time to move it along, honey," one of the crows said from behind her.

"I'm not leaving until I see Sergeant O'Shea," Jaden said.

She ground her weight into her heels and fixed her eyes above the clerk's head. On the wall behind him, the words **PROTECT, SERVE, HONOR** glowered in blue and gold against a white wall. Jaden resisted the temptation to scoff.

Caws and sighs amplified from the lineup behind her. Jaden didn't turn around. She gripped her backpack like a talisman and swallowed the crows' grumbling along with the clerk's annoyed contempt like bitter medicine.

Finally, the clerk reached for the phone handset on the desk and hit a button. He swiveled his chair so that he faced the wall. Jaden couldn't make out his exact words, but his body language was translatable. O'Shea would see her.

A few minutes later, Sergeant O'Shea marched into the waiting area. It was only ten in the morning, but a five-o'clock shadow filled in the folds of his chin. A loose button hung limply at the stretch of his belly. She caught whiffs of musk and a winter fire as he drew closer. She wondered if he'd spent the night outside.

"Jaden, this is not helping," O'Shea said quietly. "I told you I'd call if—"

"I found this," she said as she thrust the backpack out to him. "I think it matters."

O'Shea stared at the backpack. His tight lips and hitch of an eyebrow made it clear he was still deciding what message to convey. Finally, he accepted the bag and motioned for Jaden to follow him.

The remaining lineup of crows watched her walk across the lobby and through a yellow-painted door marked **PERSONNEL ONLY**. Arm at her side, she let her middle finger drop toward the room, a passive satisfaction.

Flickers of pity and exasperation warred on O'Shea's face when he asked her to take a seat. They were inside what looked like an unused office dressed in the same institutional taupe as the rest of the station. A small modular desk with a powerless monitor faced two wobbly guest chairs. O'Shea placed the backpack, gently, on the desk as he took a seat. Jaden felt like she'd been called to the principal's office.

"I found these news articles and a transcript for Grace Hobbes in my mom's closet," she said as she thrust her hand deep into the backpack. She came up with the papers and the music box, along with printouts of the articles she and Zelda had found online.

Jaden described her internet search, her meeting with Nero, and her certainty that Grace Hobbes was her mother. She mentioned the names Clara Morel and Ben Chalmers, disappointed by the absence of reaction on O'Shea's face. Jaden's words vaulted over each other, tumbling and crashing into a semicoherent mess that explained everything and nothing. O'Shea tried to interrupt her a couple of times, but she barreled on, her voice rising when it looked like he might speak. If she stopped talking, if he refused her, then she had nothing but waiting. And that could never be enough.

"My mom never mentioned any of this before, not once," she said. "This old music box must be connected. It must be! She was perfectly fine until this thing showed up. I know it looks like she's left us, but she wouldn't do that. I think this music box might have belonged to her when she was Grace and maybe someone was trying to send her a message. And there's this Ben person. I think if you subpoena his records, or whatever it is you do, then maybe you can find him, and he can tell us more about what happened to Grace—"

"Enough, Jaden," his voice, calm but firm, silenced her.

A long, slow seep of air escaped O'Shea's mouth. Jaden smelled coffee and cooked meat on his breath. She didn't dare look him in the eye, though she could tell a battle raged between kindness and exasperation. He didn't speak until the outcome had been determined.

O'Shea pursed his lips and nodded. She was about to be placated, as if she'd spent the last ten minutes trying to convince him that the

Easter Bunny was real. She was suddenly too hot and too cold at the same time.

"You should know that we've looked into your mom's movements in the days before her disappearance," O'Shea said. "In addition to the leave of absence she'd taken from work, there are other indications that she left voluntarily."

Voluntarily?

"I'm telling you, she didn't just up and leave," Jaden said, edging dangerously close to a whine. Why was the air in this building so thick and syrupy? It was like they were intentionally making it uncomfortable to breathe.

"I know it's hard to imagine, but even good people can do unexpected things sometimes. Even the people we know and love." O'Shea's saccharine attempt at sympathy roiled Jaden's stomach. Bitter liquid filled her mouth.

Love?

Jaden landed on that word in her mind like an anchor. This wasn't love. This was insanity.

This man clearly did not know her mother. Her whole world revolved around the house and the food bank. She'd told him. Her dad had told him. Her mother had no extended family, no real friends. The woman shuddered at even the idea of going to the next town for dinner. Where would she possibly go?

"She'd never do that," Jaden said. God, she hated the whisper quiet of her voice. "If she's left, it must be for a reason. Maybe she was kidnapped or—"

"You should speak to your dad," O'Shea said, not unkindly. "I can't tell you anything more at this time, but you should speak to him."

Jaden wanted to slap the man.

Belief has a way of obliterating what the senses perceive, letting us sink into the way the world should be, rather than how it is. Most of the time, we're right—we believe in the goodness of a stranger, we have faith the storm will pass us by, we trust in the safety of the road we're on—until we are horribly, life-alteringly wrong.

A bowl of oatmeal cooled on the table in front of Jaden while she sipped at a weak cup of tea. Around her, the usual morning crowd at Nick's Diner filled up on runny eggs and gossip. The smell of bacon and burnt toast swirled through the room every time the front door opened.

She sat in a corner booth. A few locals recognized her—clearly having heard her story—and flitted knowing glances her way or chittered empty, kind words. Jaden barely noticed. Her eyes were trained on the police station across the street. They hadn't arrested her dad, not as far as she knew. She believed he'd be walking out that door any second, and she would be there, waiting for him. She scanned for his familiar shape, each second yearning to see his loping gait on the station's front steps.

"Another pot?" said a waitress with badly dyed blond hair and a kind smile.

She gestured toward Jaden's cold tea with her head while gathering dirty plates and cutlery from the surrounding tables. The diner had quieted after the morning rush, the clatter dulling and customers thinning out. A country song floated from a nearby speaker, the singer complaining about a lost love over the drawl of a steel guitar.

Jaden, struggling for words and reason, just nodded.

The waitress returned a short time later with a single-serving teapot and a scone that she slid across the table. "Fresh out of the oven. No charge, hon. Thought you could use a little comfort food."

The small act of kindness and the yeasty warm smell of the pastry lodged themselves in Jaden's throat.

"Thank you," she said, her voice thick.

Tears were coming too easily now. Jaden sniffled and poured the amber liquid into a fresh cup. The first sip of peppermint tea loosened her throat and opened the floodgates.

Not wanting to humiliate herself further by crying in the fishbowl of the diner, Jaden made her way to the bathroom. Mercifully, it was empty. She peered under the stall doors to confirm. Muted sound and forest green walls offered unexpected calm in a strange storm. Jaden found her way to the sink and took heaving breaths. She wouldn't cry, not here, not now.

She splashed cold water on her face. Felt the trickle down her neck and relief in her swollen eyes. She was leaning over the sink when she heard the bathroom door open and close.

"Jaden?" a man's voice said.

Jaden whipped around. Water splattered from her cupped palms onto the tiled floor. The faucet continued to run. She felt her heart, an alive creature.

A middle-aged man in an ill-fitting parka and brown Blundstone boots stood beside the now-closed bathroom door. He held a pair of leather gloves in one hand; his head followed the darting of his eyes like a sparrow sensing danger. He had positioned himself in front of the room's only exit. Electrified strands of thinning hair reached for the ceiling while his free hand edged into his pants pocket.

Jaden's eyes were trained on that hand. Every muscle stiffened. She braced herself, calculating whether her body force alone could knock him off balance enough.

"I just want to talk," he said, pulling a roll of antacids out of his pocket and popping one into his mouth with one hand.

His eyes, finally done flitting through the room, settled on Jaden. "It's about your mother."

Chapter 25

Ben

Standing in the women's washroom of a backwoods diner, Ben took in the same small build, deep-brown hair, and narrow cheekbones that had lived in his memory for nearly twenty-five years. The girl looked so much like Grace, Ben thought he might double over from the pain of it.

The eyes, though, were different. Instead of Grace's milk chocolate brown, the girl's eyes were a stabbing blue with flecks of gold.

She had spun around when Ben said her name, like a night creature caught out by the light. Water trickled down her neck, slipping beneath the collar of an oversize sweatshirt. Blotches of red bloomed on her cheeks.

Shame, bitter and burning, spread from Ben's gut. She was a child, lost in a story she couldn't possibly understand, and he needed something from her. An orange blaze traveled the length of his chest and into his throat. He swallowed it down.

I know what you did. The words from the text he'd received reverberated in his head.

Ben had never told his wife or his employer about his time with Militant Animals or Konrad Sharma's death. A sin of omission, he reasoned. After Clara Morel's trial, he'd walked away from the whole thing, letting it fall like mud at the bottom of a puddle. He couldn't predict the aftermath if Grace was trying to rip open old scars, but he knew nothing good would come of it. Some truths needed to stay buried.

For the first time in his marriage, Ben outright lied to his wife. He told her he'd been called to Ottawa for a few days, where the main offices were located. She raised an eyebrow at the timing but didn't question it. Last-minute trips weren't unusual in his job, and he hadn't taken holidays over the Christmas period this year. He knew it was a sacrifice—skipping out on his family to tend to his past—but there was a greater evil if all the details came to light. One he couldn't allow to be unleashed on his family.

This girl was his link to Grace, and nothing else mattered right now. Whatever Grace had meant by sending him the video of the music box, Ben needed to stop it before she went too far again.

He'd found a path to Grace Hobbes, now known as Emma Meadows. Her disappearance was all over the Facebook accounts of White Falls residents. Friends and neighbors sharing worried messages and callouts for help, good intentions that he could pick over like a carrion beetle over a carcass. He didn't believe for one second that Emma Meadows's disappearance was a coincidence. He saw a pattern.

He was self-aware enough to know there was a creepiness and a crime in what he was doing—stalking and following a young woman—but principles could be bent a little before they shattered. The girl wasn't the objective. And Grace had fired the first shot. It could only have been her who texted Ben the music box video. Konrad was dead.

I know what you did.

He didn't know what game Grace was playing, but he was determined to find out.

"It's about your mother. I need to talk to her," Ben said.

Memories clung to his mind like viscous tendrils as he watched Jaden Meadows's eyes widen, then narrow with suspicion. His voice echoed off the bathroom stalls.

"You and me both," the girl said.

She stepped back and crossed her arms. A stifling chemical-rose-cleanser stench invaded Ben's nose. Harsh light against white tiles hurt his tired eyes. He sighed to himself. He really didn't want to be here, doing this.

It hadn't been hard to track Jaden down. All he'd needed were her name and phone number, which Henri had provided. Ben's job as a research analyst made him particularly adept at online tracking. Ten thousand hours at anything made you talented; eighteen years made you cunning.

Jaden lived a typical Gen Z social media life, sharing everything from the meals she'd eaten to her class schedule. Following her account was like opening a vault. He split open her life as easily as wielding a carving knife. Posts and comments provided a taste, but the unintended morsels from the autoshared locations and overlooked background details were the meal. Ben had everything.

When her location popped up at a Tim Hortons in Barrie, an hour and a half drive north of Toronto, he knew she was going home.

Ben had gotten in the car in Toronto and followed a thick ribbon of highway north. He was a city boy, born and bred in the suburbs of Toronto. He'd never imagined the ice claws that reached over the highway in winter or how much he would cling to the road for fear of the bitter endlessness beyond.

God, he thought, driving past an abandoned gas station whose roof had caved in beneath a crushing snow, *this place sucks the life out of things without so much as a blink.*

With each kilometer north, winter grew deeper and bolder. Ben shivered every time the outside dashboard thermometer dropped by a degree. By the time he'd gotten his first peek at Lake Superior, the temperature outside was minus seventeen degrees Celsius and the snowbanks along the road would have swallowed him whole given the chance. Worse, beyond the ridges of snow on the side of the highway, all he'd seen was thick, unwelcoming forest filled with black-needled pine trees and endless expanses of nothing.

"I'm not here to cause you any trouble, Jaden," Ben said, staring at the quarry that had pulled him into this wilderness. "I just need to talk to your mother. She reached out to me."

Jaden's body language changed. Her drawn shoulders and straight back relaxed. Her head tilted, and eyebrows crinkled in confusion. Ben could see the questions on her lips, so he waited.

"You know my mom?"

"I do."

"When did she contact you? Is she OK? What did she want? Do you know where she is?" Jaden stepped forward with each question, her gaze now studying Ben as if he were a map she could read.

The bathroom was warm. Electric heat, too high for the small space, ticked along the baseboards. Ben felt sweat slide along his back and a flash of dizziness. The girl really did look like her mother. His mind slipped back in time again. He was having a difficult time controlling that in her presence. The bathroom shimmered in his mind's eye to another time, another place, the eyes in front of him morphing from probing blue to milky brown and enraged.

"What did you do?" Grace had said, a snarl overlaying sobs. "What the hell did you do to him?"

A light spring breeze rose around them. It wasn't cold, not really, but Ben had felt a chill so deep in his bones he wondered if his body had forgotten the touch of warmth. Grace sat on a small bench in a postage-stamp-size park about a block away from campus. He'd followed her here, chasing her as she ran away from news that had altered the trajectory of both their lives.

A call had come early that morning requesting his presence at the office of the dean of students that afternoon. The day, he remembered, was cool for spring, as if still hanging to the edge of winter. Pockets of dark clouds mustered within a blue sky, the weather not able to decide which way it wanted to go. He'd stepped off the streetcar, hands shoved deep in his pockets, feeling like a kid called to the principal's office.

He was ushered into a nearby meeting room, where a stocky police officer with untamed eyebrows and accusatory glances had shared the news with no preamble. Konrad Sharma was dead. Ben's first thought was that it was a prank; he sat wordlessly waiting for the punch line.

"You hear me OK, son?" the officer had said, one eyebrow reaching for his hairline. "Your friend, Konrad Sharma, was killed last night. We're still looking into the exact chain of events, but preliminary evidence suggests it wasn't an accident. He was found in a car with what we think was a homemade explosive device."

The words seeped like poison through Ben's skin. His mind and body, aware of the threat, hardened, trying to distance itself. He didn't breathe, didn't blink, waited for the shock to roll over him like a rogue wave. It was no use. Blood, lungs, heart—they were all infected. Bile vaulted to his mouth, and he vomited, painting the floor with coffee-colored sludge and chunks of undigested Eggos. The smell rose like a rebuke until the room was putrid.

After the dean called maintenance, they moved to a smaller office. Ben, the police officer, and the dean crammed themselves into a closet-size space barely large enough for their three chairs. He sipped from a glass of something cold that had been handed to him and tried to think.

"Now, Ben, you're not in any trouble here," the dean said, though Ben hadn't registered a single thing about the man, other than a voice like tepid water and a bald head. "I know this must be a terrible shock. The officer here just wants to talk to you. You don't have to say or do anything you don't want." Ben had the distinct feeling the last was addressed more to the officer.

The officer in question loomed even larger in the small space. He had a litany of questions, for which Ben had few answers.

When was the last time you saw Konrad? Do you know anyone who might have wanted to hurt him? Did Konrad tell you what he was doing last night? Were you involved in this in any way?

I can't remember, no, no, no. Ben was a skipping track of nothing.

After what seemed like hours but had only been about twenty minutes, the officer told Ben he could leave but to expect a follow-up in the next few days. He offered half-hearted condolences beneath a crumb-filled and graying mustache.

Grace was exiting the room opposite when Ben stepped back into the main office.

Head bowed and on shaky legs, she was grabbing for tissues held by a female officer at the door. The office staff held their breath, hoping no doubt that tragedy would pass them by if they didn't sip from it too deeply. The show, Ben later learned, had been going on all morning with members of Militant Animals invited individually to hear the news and be evaluated. The desk receptionist, her hands on a silent keyboard and mouth agape, stared openly as if a carnival act were being rolled out in front of her. A wave of loathing at the sight of her face threatened to upend Ben's stomach again.

"Grace," Ben said, his voice coming out like a croak.

He stumbled over the look of disgust and fury she threw at him. It was like being adrift on an endless lake, with only the night sky to guide your way.

Grace ran out the door.

Ben finally caught up with her beside a small patch of city-kept green space a block away from campus. The air held a whiff of damp soil, rotting leaves, and exhaust from the traffic crawling past. A small crowd of teenagers gawped and whispered as they eyed the two strangers in a motionless battle, before they walked by into better lives. Ben ignored them; his eyes and questions were trained on Grace. Something was irreparably wrong, and he was only starting to understand.

"You did this. You killed him," Grace said. The words came out in staccato blubbers, sobs feeding on the available air in Grace's lungs.

"I didn't," he said, his mind reeling over a reality that was vaulting forward without him.

"I would have never," Grace gasped.

"Grace, I don't know what happened. An explosive? I mean, that was never part of the—"

There are moments when pieces slam into place in the mind, rocketing images with so much force that the mind has difficulty seeing the whole until it is far too late. Realization, when it comes, is not the slow dawn of connections but a white-hot blade slicing through to your soul.

Ben knew in that moment what had happened. A car, an explosion, Konrad.

He looked at Grace. She was shivering and pale despite the warmth of the evening, as if a winter wind had come to claim only her. She had no breath for words, but her eyes—soft brown wells of loss and regret—told him everything he needed to know.

Ben staggered backward. The pieces shuddered into place like a demented game of *Tetris*, leaving behind a grisly picture.

Clara, meeting secretly with Grace, the looks that had passed between them when they thought Ben wasn't looking, the impatience with his questions. Demands within Militant Animals for more aggressive action. Ben heard a crashing in his head, like storm-engorged waves against a cliffside.

"What did we do, Grace?" Ben said, closing his eyes.

He wasn't sure he had the strength to withstand the answer.

He hadn't realized that he'd closed his eyes until he opened them again. Grace was gone. It was the last time Ben had spoken with her.

"I'll answer all your questions, but first, does your mom have a music box?" Ben finally managed to say to the girl in front of him. "Made out of glass with brass edges and corners. Maybe she's mentioned it was a gift from an old boyfriend? She's probably had it for a long time."

The air in the bathroom was thick with the heat, and he was starting to get faint whiffs of urine beneath the reek of the failed cleanser.

For the first time, the girl looked afraid.

"I don't know what you're—"

"Don't, kid. I know your mom has it. You have no earthly idea what's going on—only she does. Hell, I'm not even sure I know, but you've been asking around about the very same music box, and I want to know why." The unexpected anger came hard and fast.

Three other people in all the world knew about that music box. One was dead, one was in prison, and the third had recently disappeared shortly after he'd received the text. Clara could not have gotten access to his phone number—or a burner, for that matter—from behind prison walls. It wasn't a stretch to point the finger at Grace. He was not going to play games, even if it meant frightening a naive kid in over her head.

"I think you know where your mom is or at least have a better idea than me, and neither of us has the time or the inclination to let things lie. I want any information you have," Ben said as he flashed his government identification. He doubted she'd look closely and was relying on the very naivety he was exploiting to make her think he mattered.

Jaden stared at him, mouth half open and confusion distorting her features. They were interrupted by voices and a rattle of the door behind Ben.

"Who are you?" Jaden said.

"I'll be in touch," Ben said as he turned to leave the bathroom. "Soon."

Chapter 26

Jaden

Jaden tore out of the diner. Cold air flooded her lungs, tensing muscles and tendons as she ran across the street to the police station. Her breath jackrabbited short, shallow gasps. Thoughts dive-bombed her brain so quickly, she couldn't capture one before it scattered like confetti. More than once, she almost lost her balance as waves of dizziness crashed over her on the short sprint.

This was proof. The mantra skipped in her head.

Proof the music box mattered, that it had something to do with her mother's disappearance. She would tell O'Shea about the man in the bathroom, demand they arrest him, and finally, there would be answers. She hadn't realized she was still running until her hands slammed into the front door of the station. The echoing bang crashed into the lobby.

A half dozen people, perched on waiting-room chairs, looked up briefly before returning to the infinitely more interesting dramas of their own lives.

The bug-eyed clerk behind the reception desk recognized Jaden immediately. His slow slide of a gaze up to the ceiling told her everything she needed to know. She let her breathing slow and drew herself to full height. Battles could be waged and won but only if she believed that to be true.

Her first step across the lobby changed everything.

Just as she placed a foot down, a green door to her right opened. O'Shea stepped from the darkened hallway into the fluorescent lights of the lobby. He wasn't a big man, but his haggard bearing and grim expression filled the doorframe. He met Jaden's eyes, and she registered a flicker of surprise, before gloom poured over his whole body.

O'Shea stepped aside. Trailing behind the officer like a child on a tether was Jaden's father. His eyes were red and raw, but he held himself straight despite the handcuffs drawing his arms together in front of him.

"Dad," Jaden said, her voice part yell, part plea.

When he looked up, a crowd of emotions crossed his face, each vying for dominion. In the end—her dad being the man he was—a gentle smile settled comfortably on his lips, if not his eyes.

"It's OK, honey. Everything's going to be OK. I'm all right," he called to her.

Jaden crossed the lobby. O'Shea tried to stop her, but her glare threw him off. He nodded gravely and stepped a few paces back.

"What's going on? I don't understand?" Jaden's words vibrated with fear and confusion.

"It's nothing. A little misunderstanding, that's all. I've called a lawyer friend of mine from work, and we'll get this all cleared up in no time."

Jaden turned her anger and confusion on O'Shea.

"This is wrong. You have it all wrong. There's a man. And the music box. He knows my mom. Or said he knew her. I know he's responsible. Or involved. Or . . ."

Jaden's words made no sense, even to her. Desperation warred with uncertainty and too little sleep, jumbling thoughts with emotions until all she felt was a chasm of grief so deep she thought she might fall into it forever.

"Time to go, Mark," O'Shea said, stepping closer.

"No!" Jaden said. "What's happening? You need to tell me what's happening."

O'Shea just looked at her with a stupid hangdog expression and pulled gently at her dad's elbow.

"I'll call you as soon as I can and explain everything," her dad said over his shoulder as he was led away through another door. The hallway beyond was so dark, all Jaden could make out was a bright-red exit sign hanging from the far ceiling. The door slammed behind O'Shea, and Jaden was left with nothing but questions and pitying looks from others in the lobby.

In that moment, two thoughts rang out as clear as a summer blue sky.

The first, and hardest, was that nothing she said in this moment would make any difference. She saw the warning and conviction on O'Shea's face. Anything she said would be dismissed as the ravings of a scared little girl desperate to help her father.

The second, and the one that clawed at her chest, was that her family was in very real trouble with no one to help them.

Chapter 27

Ben

Ben had watched from his car as the girl stumbled out of the diner and bolted across the street toward the police station. She passed so close to his vehicle, had she only turned her head, she might have met his eyes. But she didn't turn.

Emma Meadows's disappearance was public now—spread over social media and the local radio—and law enforcement knew tragedy brought unwanted attention from all sorts of people. He didn't think they'd act on what had happened at the diner, not immediately anyway. But just in case, he slowly pulled out and drove casually down the street. Just another passerby in the eyes of the locals.

Clearly, Ben had rattled the girl. The satisfaction he felt was tinged with guilt for having bullied a young woman into telling him the truth, if not by her words, then her actions. Still, he needed to know more and whether she knew the whole story or not. Jaden Meadows was his link to Grace.

Needs must, he thought.

The stuffy phrase triggered a long-ago memory, the hurt in it still fresh despite the years. The week after Ben had suggested a music box as an anniversary gift for Grace, Konrad had come looking for him again.

Finals were looming, and Ben had sought out his favorite hideaway, a little-used corner of the library surrounded by stacks, tucked away from the maddening crowd. He often came here to study or just be alone.

Konrad's arrival was announced by a cheerful whistle and the jangle of change in his pocket. The noise started a full thirty seconds before his form popped out from behind the shelves. Ben tried ducking lower. It was futile.

"Ben, my man!" Konrad said to a chorus of *shh* from three girls huddled at adjoining study carrels.

Even when he wasn't making noise, Konrad's presence was like an electric pulse, interfering with the flow of light. Some perfunctory small talk did nothing to dim the wattage burbling just under the man's skin. Ben wasn't in the least surprised when Konrad pulled an old-fashioned, if pretty, brass-and-glass music box out of a leather shoulder bag.

"What do you think? Grace'll like it, right?" Konrad said.

Everything about Konrad, from his fidgety stance to his goofy grin, screamed ease and unquestioned self-confidence. Ben admired—and hated—him for it.

One look at the Victorian-inspired piece of kitsch, and Ben almost felt sorry for Konrad. Nothing about the dilapidated antique was Grace's taste. She liked solid, natural, and modern, with sleek lines and simple designs. Konrad's box was ancient, brittle, and dated, its facade etched with curlicue flowers.

Ben could have laughed, could have rolled his eyes, but something in Konrad's puppy dog look stayed his snark.

"Ya, it's pretty," Ben said with a faint nod.

"Do you mind keeping it for a bit?" Konrad said. The flash of his smile and rove of his eyes made it clear he expected agreement. "I don't want Grace stumbling across it accidently at my place."

"Uhmm, I don't know," Ben said. "I mean—" He couldn't think of a suitable excuse.

“Please, man,” Konrad said, throwing a high-wattage smile and wink his way. “I wouldn’t normally ask, but I can’t think of anywhere else where Grace won’t stumble across it. Sooo, needs must?”

“Sure,” Ben said, resigned. How could he deny the great Konrad Sharma, he thought to himself, working to keep the sarcasm out of his eyes.

“Terrific. Thanks. You’re a peach.”

Konrad sauntered off, pleased with himself and oblivious to the weakness of will in Ben’s response. His whistling could be heard through the stacks until the elevator finally swallowed him.

Ben looked at the chintzy little thing on the table and sighed. He lifted the lid and leaned in to hear the pale notes from the music mechanism. He wasn’t sure what exactly he had expected to hear, perhaps *Für Elise*, *Edelweiss*, or something equally clichéd.

What he heard ripped at his heart.

The delicate notes in that quiet space rose into a song that spoke to love and loss and an understanding of Grace’s unique history.

“How did he—” Ben couldn’t bring himself to finish the thought.

He suddenly understood what he’d been distantly aware of for some time but had stubbornly pushed away, as if denial could vanquish reality. His world tilted, resetting his path from the moment before, and after, Konrad Sharma had come around a bookshelf and winked at him. An irrefutable and life-altering fact pounded against Ben’s head, battering its way into his stubborn consciousness—Ben was not the only man who truly knew and loved Grace Hobbes.

In that moment, with the notes still nattering at his ears and a blind fury in his eyes, Ben had hated Konrad Sharma beyond all reason and wished him dead.

The little motel sat at the junction of White Falls and the highway. Time had somehow ignored the pastel pink structure, with its vintage sign announcing the name of the place: the Come for a Rest Motel. Ben liked the sound of the words.

"Come for a rest," Ben said to the slumbering forest surrounding the little motel.

In the back of his mind, a song bloomed with relentless acoustic guitars and fiddles, along with an Irish pipe.

Come for a rest, the mantra repeated in his head, edging toward memory and desire. *Come for a rest, come for a rest.* "Home for a Rest," the title of the Spirit of the West song emerged like a prayer.

No, there would be no home for him. Not tonight. Not now that he was so close to finding answers. It wasn't just his curiosity he needed to satiate. Grace held secrets that could upend his life.

He couldn't leave town. Not yet. It was clear that the girl knew more. All he had to do was follow where she led.

Chapter 28

Emma

2002

The sun was warm on Emma's neck as she spread a blanket on the beach. Rays seeped under her skin, filling her cells, while her bare toes dug into spring-kissed sand touching the cooler layer beneath the surface. The air still carried an edge of winter, so Emma wore jeans under an oversize cable-knit sweater she'd found at a thrift store.

This early in the season, the beach was empty. Not even spring shoots had arrived on the spindly branches. Emma closed her eyes, heard the caw of gulls, the whisper of a breeze over dried grasses, and the lap of water against a gentle shore.

Old Woman Bay. That's what Mark had called this little strip of sand on the edge of Lake Superior. Emma liked the name. It suited the horseshoe-shaped cove. Behind her, the lake was an unending expanse of slate blue, stretching into the horizon and infinity. It terrified her.

"Come on in," Mark called from the water.

The ice had barely melted. The water, when she'd tested it, hit with a cudgel of cold. Mark called it the coward's polar plunge, a dunk in the lake when the air was warm enough to take the chill out of your bones after.

"Forget it," Emma said over her shoulder with a cackle. "You want to shrivel your balls, you go right ahead. I'm staying right here where I can still feel my limbs."

"Suit yourself," he said before dunking beneath the surface.

Two years, and two winters, she'd lived along these shores. Though the lake was a slumbering beast now, she'd learned firsthand its mercurial nature. Those waters would turn fierce and unforgiving given the opportunity. She could respect the water, even admire its beauty, but she would never trust it.

The winters, though, had brought an unexpected solace. Locked in by the snow and ice, White Falls seemed to repel the world outside, a buffer against memories and grief. It never lasted, of course. Eventually, the snow melted, and the real world came crashing through. The reprieve had allowed her to be Emma and let Grace Hobbes float away with the spring thaw.

She turned. Only a gentle ripple could be seen in the spot where Mark had been standing. She waited. Ten seconds. Twenty. Not even a beat of legs or a flash of his moppy hair. Thirty seconds. She hadn't noticed that her feet had brought her up to the water's edge until cold stung her toes.

"Wooo!" Mark's voice echoed against wood and rock as he thrust up from the water. "That's refreshing."

"You idiot," she said to him, though not with malice or anger. She'd learned early on that Mark was a child of nature, cradled by these waters and at his most confident when he was immersed in the wilderness that surrounded White Falls.

Emma understood the appeal. After landing here like a castoff from a storm, she'd managed to carve a small place for herself. Thanks to Mark, she found a job at the food bank, a small apartment, and a semblance of a life.

Mark, and everyone else in White Falls, knew her as Emma. She'd introduced herself that way when she first met him, wrapping the identity around her like a carapace. She hadn't expected to make a life here, with a husband and a job. When it became clear that White Falls would be home, at least for a little while, she shed Grace entirely, like a spider leaving behind a copy of itself when the old body no longer fit. Grace—with all her mistakes and foolishness—was not welcome here. Grace was a person Emma no longer recognized, a woman capable of killing the man she'd loved.

Emma, though, had no baggage. She was fun and flirty and unfailingly kind. Emma was happy to spread out a blanket on an unexpectedly warm mid-spring evening and gaze into the golden orange sunset with a smile.

"Hungry?" Mark said as he stood beside the blanket, water rippling across lean muscles and darkening the sand at his feet.

Though they'd been friends for two years, this picnic was only their second date. Emma always understood that Mark wished for more. He never asked, never pressed, only waited. They might have continued that way forever if Emma had decided it was so. She'd started to feel something more recently. Despite herself, desire sputtered like the ripple of a small stone on a calm lake. Mark had a warmth and goodness that was infectious.

"Starving," Emma said. "Let's eat."

His grin ignited a small ember. She didn't know if it was love or lust or something else altogether. Her eyes traveled the length of his chest, noting the edges of muscle made firm from weekends camping, climbing, and hiking in the backwoods. His damp hair sprang to life as it dried in the sun, adding to a boyish charm that undulated under his skin. The caution that she'd carefully cradled for two years was starting to crack.

She pulled a warm crusty loaf of bread from a backpack, along with soft Brie and smoked sausage made by a butcher downtown. From a small cooler, she took out a bottle of chilled white wine and two glasses.

"Fancy," Mark said, settling in beside her.

"Well, I needed to do something a little special for a second date." She felt the blush as she spoke and at Mark's contentedly surprised glance.

"So, it's dating, is it? I'm good with that," he said with a wink.

Emma looked out at the lake. The sun had dipped to the edge of the water, exploding its color over the surface until it was impossible to tell where sky and water met. Gold, red, and orange blended together into a tableau that could steal your heart.

This part of the world could either kill you or seduce you, she thought. Tonight, Emma decided to let herself be seduced.

The beach was still empty. Only a few straggling gulls and the occasional sparrow watched as Emma moved to straddle Mark, who sat with his legs out in front of him, eyes closed against the sudden brightness. He kept them closed as Emma leaned in and kissed him lightly, tentatively, like a butterfly testing the safety of a leaf. Soon, she too closed her eyes. Mark wrapped his arms around her and pulled her down, blending their bodies and their lives into a single whole that obliterated the entirety of the world while feelings long buried exploded into the light of a dying day.

A month later, Emma knew.

Her period was never late. The telltale absence would need to be confirmed, but Emma didn't need a test to know what her body was telling her. Once again, one night had turned her life upside down and she would need to reshape the future she'd anticipated.

Chapter 29

Jaden

Jaden wandered through the empty house on New Year's Day, a cup of cold coffee in her hand. Silence scraped along her skin like a raw scab until she felt like she was standing in someone else's house. Fear and doubt dragged at her while sludgy thoughts quarreled for her attention.

An idea had come to her in the dark hours of morning, when rational thought was a rare commodity. It was still there, though, when the sun rose and remained while she packed a few essentials in an overnight bag. A loose plan was forming in her mind, born of desperation and a desire to take control of something, anything. The bag now glowered at her from the kitchen counter. It told her what she needed to do, but her mind still warred against itself.

As he'd promised, her dad had called the previous evening.

"It's honestly not a big deal," he said, a cheery strain in his voice. "Things got a little heated, that's all. They were suggesting"—her dad paused, searching for the word—"stuff that just didn't make any sense, and I sort of lost it."

"What stuff?" Jaden said.

"They're trying their best," her dad said. "They're just spinning a bit, grasping at straws. It's the easiest answer, isn't it?"

"I don't understand. What's happening? What's the easiest answer?"

The silence on the other end wrapped Jaden in a vise grip.

"The husband," her dad finally said. "When they can't find an easy answer, they suspect the husband."

Jaden choked on the insinuations.

"It's OK, honey. We'll get this sorted out. Right now, they're just holding me for obstructing a police officer. I might have gotten a little difficult with this OPP officer who came in to talk to me. Malcolm just wanted to calm me down. I'm sure it'll be OK."

The White Falls police was collaborating with the Ontario police. When an OPP officer started pushing the theory that her dad might have harmed his wife, he started yelling in the officer's face and pushed him. Malcolm arrested him. It would take a couple of days for the paperwork to be processed given the holidays, so her dad waited in a holding cell.

How could Jaden tell him about the crank phone calls or the stranger who'd approached her at the diner? What would be the point? There was nothing he could do. She'd already tried to tell O'Shea, who dismissed her as a ranting child.

"My lawyer isn't worried," he continued into Jaden's silence. "He doesn't think it will come to anything in the end. We just have to wait for the process to grind along. I probably won't be able to leave town for a few weeks while they sort this all out, but I'm sure I'll be home soon. It was really stupid of me. I should have kept it together. I didn't really give them a choice. Don't worry about me, honey. I'm OK, and Malcolm feels bad. He's even sneaking me in a milkshake from Nick's."

Your parents never prepare you for the moment when your roles will reverse, that point in life when you become your family's keeper. It comes so gradually—you help your dad with a new app, you thread a needle whose eye your mom can no longer see, you do the shopping when one of them has the flu—the change organic and natural. In the wake of her dad's shaky platitudes and tight voice, the moment hit Jaden like a comet boomeranging around the sun. He'd been lying.

And she needed to protect him from the truth.

A light icing sugar snow was falling as Jaden stepped out of the house, Winnie by her side. A chitter from above drew her attention to the puffed-up tail of a gray squirrel warily eyeing them. Jaden's foot slid on a patch of snow-covered ice. Her arms windmilled while her body twisted to avoid crashing to the ground. Righted, but standing awkwardly, she froze to let her mind catch up with her body. The squirrel's continuous natter now sounded like laughter.

"Come on," Jaden said to Winnie, who stood sure footed and patient.

Jaden opened the back door of her dad's RAV4, and the dog hopped up. The smaller wheels of her Mazda didn't have the best traction in deeper snow, and she'd need it on the back roads. She knew it wasn't the best plan, or even a good one, but her grandparents' cabin seemed like the only viable option in a sea of flawed choices. She couldn't lay her problems on her dad's shoulders, not right now, and reaching out to extended family—no matter how well intentioned—would only result in laying everything back at his feet. The cabin was far enough to get away from whoever was stalking her but close enough to get her home quickly when needed.

The inside of the RAV smelled like her dad's aftershave, cedarwood and musk, with hints of wet dog. She inhaled deeply as if she could carry the smell of home with her for the next few days into wherever this story led. She almost turned back then, still unconvinced by her plan, but in the end, she turned the key.

An hour later, Jaden found herself passing through Lake Superior Park. She hadn't intended to turn off the road, but grief and nostalgia could be toxically cajoling. The familiar bends and dips in the highway and the glimpses of the water's shore felt like coming home in a way. She sensed a pull, like the arc of a tether ball drawing her toward the lake. The car turned, almost of its own volition. She needed to let Winnie out anyway, she reasoned, as she slowed the car into a circular asphalt parking lot ringed by trees. In her core, though, where childhood visions of rainbow dragons and warrior princesses still lived, her soul hoped for the impossible.

She could just make out the lake through threadbare trees. Jaden let Winnie out of the back seat. The dog hesitated, raising a quivering nose to the air. Warm Sundays, birthdays, graduations—they'd all been celebrated here, making it a familiar place in summer. In winter, scents and scurrying creatures vanished, leaving only empty air and a breath-stealing wind. Winnie could not know this place in this iteration.

"It's OK, girl," Jaden said, more to reassure herself.

Suddenly Winnie stood stone still, nose poised toward the lake, alert. Without warning, the dog took off, legs pumping and body targeting a quarry.

There were no other cars in the lot. No one else was here. Unless.

Jaden ran after Winnie.

Dried, crackling remnants of leaves clung to a few branches. The pathway to the beach lay beneath inches of snow, but Jaden spotted the break in the trees easily enough. Tucked into clunky winter boots, her feet, heavy and clumsy, followed the path under an anemic sun.

The rational mind had a way of retreating in the face of deep longing. Jaden knew it was impossible. Still, she ran, her emotional center holding dominion, telling her there was always a chance that Winnie had caught her mom's scent.

As she ran, Jaden pictured fine sand, lapping waves, and her mom standing ankle deep watching the parting of the water from the horizon. Crashing through the trees onto the beach was a shattering disappointment.

Winter had stripped the sparkle out of the lake surface, leaving only iron gray water greedily licking the snow-covered beach. The wind moaned its complaints as it ripped through the bare trees. Snow piles, caught by shards of driftwood or rounded granite stones made smooth by the waves, dotted the beach like grave mounds.

Jaden shivered.

Winnie rolled in the snow on shore, snapping up mouthfuls with glee. Occasionally, she'd look back at Jaden, a tilt of her head, before the wind distracted her and she tore after another imaginary playmate.

A streak of memory came to Jaden. A Sunday afternoon just after high school graduation. One of those early-summer days when white clouds dotted the sky and everything seemed right with the world. Jaden had already accepted the offer to the University of Toronto and was heading into a summer filled with bush parties, last hangouts, and the anticipation for what lay ahead.

They'd come to Old Woman Bay for a family picture to celebrate Jaden's graduation. Her dad hummed as he pulled containers from a bottomless cooler, setting out potato salad, sandwiches, and cold sodas with relish on a sun-warmed blanket.

"Come on, it's tradition," her mom had said through a coaxing smile.

Jaden lay back, sunglasses and hat warding off the worst of the sun, while a fading hangover still lingered across her forehead.

"I'm eighteen, Mom. Kinda past the whole treasure hunt thing, don't you think?" Jaden said. "Dad, tell her."

"*Tradition*," her dad sang out, stealing tunelessly from *Fiddler on the Roof*.

Jaden sighed happily. "Fine," she said, pulling herself to her feet.

The Cheshire cat grins on her parents' faces were almost enough to make the whole charade worth it. They walked toward a large ancient maple at the end of the beach that had no business still being alive. Thick bark and deep roots had protected the tree from the worst of Superior's storms, but the branches were frailer with each season. A thick, low branch stretched out from the trunk, reaching for the water's edge, though it would never come close. Inside a V of the tree sat a perfect little cubby, smoothed and shaped by decades of rain, wind, and scurrying creatures. When she was little, Jaden's parents would secretly stash gifts in the tree, telling Jaden wood sprites had left them for her. The practice had slowed as Jaden moved through her teen years, the sprites falling by the wayside along with Santa Claus and the Tooth Fairy.

In her memory, Jaden could barely reach a hand up to the cubby. She would stand on her tiptoes and pat blindly for the offered trinkets—a pack of gum or a ZhuZhu Pet—quickly loved and forgotten. She was surprised that she could now look down into the cubby, where a gleam of metal caught dappled sunlight. She took off her sunglasses, convinced her hungover eyes were playing tricks. The gleam remained. She reached in and closed her hand around the unmistakable shape of keys. Car keys.

"No!" Jaden exclaimed, spinning to look at her parents. "You didn't."

Her parents stood side by side. Her dad draped a lazy arm around her mom.

"It was your mom's idea. She figured it'd be easier for you to travel back and forth to school," he said. "Happy graduation, sweetheart."

Her mom just beamed.

Jaden dove toward her parents, hangover and headache forgotten, and wrapped them both in a fierce hug. "Thank you, thank you, thank you," she'd said, until words and breath were exhausted.

Jaden looked to where the old maple still stood, its branches stripped and barren by winter but unbending. She walked along the beach, her boots sinking above her ankles in fresh snow. A flock of sparrows spied on her from the safety of a nearby bush, their beady eyes distrustful and cautious in her presence. She didn't expect to find an answer in the tree or meet one of the wood sprites, but memories and tradition could give her strength.

A few feet away from the tree, she was startled by a flash of fuzzy pink.

Logic and reason told her it was a coincidence, but her heart wanted to believe. Laughter, deep and manic, rose from her core like a geyser. It flew from her lips, unbidden and uncontainable. Jaden leaned over, hands on her thighs, trying to suck in breath between debilitating gales.

Huge, round eyes stared up at her from the crux of the tree.

Could this be a bizarre coincidence or the universe messing with her? She approached the tree, reaching cautiously forward. Her fingers grasped the pink strands of a two-inch-high Troll doll, with stubby legs and a broad-lipped grin.

"Well, I guess it's as good a sign as any," she said to the universe, though only Winnie heard.

Jaden had collected the silly figurines as a child. Unable to part with them entirely as she grew older, she'd stashed her collection in the back closet of her grandparents' cottage, her intended destination.

"Thanks, Mom," she whispered, not at all believing her mom had anything to do with it.

Jaden stood, the doll clasped in her hand, watching the endlessness of Lake Superior until her eyes watered and her cheeks stung from the wind. Though a lake in name, the breadth and voracity of the water was closer to that of a sea. Another country, she knew, lay beyond the light of seeing, and an infinity of stories lived along these shores; Jaden's was only one of many. It was time to go, but still she lingered, waiting for a miracle that wasn't coming.

By the time Jaden turned toward the car, even Winnie was shivering and whining from cold. She waited for the heater to offer a spittle of warmth before she put the car in drive and headed back to the highway.

The dark SUV sat on the side of the road about fifty meters from the Old Woman Bay parking lot entrance. Jaden recognized it immediately, even from this distance. It was the same one that had been parked in front of her house two nights ago. She pushed down on the accelerator.

The RAV responded, its winter tires gripping the road comfortably despite the powder-light snow coating. The Troll doll stood on the dash, like a mascot. Jaden looked at its amused little face and made her decision.

She pushed the speed of the car around one bend. Then the next. She heard Winnie topple slightly in the back seat, felt the pull of the steering wheel in her arms.

She was going too fast. She didn't care.

"Steer into the slide," she said, though whether to herself or the Troll she wasn't sure.

On the first straight stretch of road, she caught sight of the dark SUV in the rearview mirror. It was gaining. Fast. Jaden had already pushed the car beyond her comfort level, but she accelerated faster.

It made no difference. The larger SUV, with its more powerful engine, continued to close the gap.

She knew this highway, though. Understood where melt and runoff could make a bend treacherous. All she had to do was make it a kilometer farther.

She saw the turn ahead and felt her heart skitter. She approached faster than she thought possible, luring the SUV. She hit the edge, saw the web of black ice across the asphalt, and hit it. The wheels started to skid underneath her, and she turned the steering wheel into the slide, letting physics take over, and the trajectory bowed to accommodate her direction. The wheels gripped the road once again, and she kicked out of the bend like a slalom skier.

She stopped the car at the top of the next hill and waited. From here, she had a clear view of the SUV as it hit the curve. She watched the vehicle travel sideways, the wheels losing contact with the road. She recognized the shudder as the driver cranked the steering wheel against the slide and deepened the skid, sending the car spinning 180 degrees, off the road and into a narrow ditch, facing the opposite direction.

Jaden stayed long enough to watch the driver's door open. She pulled out her phone, aimed the camera lens. The driver crawled out slowly. She saw him look back toward where she'd stopped. *Click.* Phone poised, she snapped a series of photos of the exact same man who had approached her in the diner bathroom. She was close enough to recognize him but not so close that she could read his expression.

With miles to go, Jaden got back into the car and pulled away. For the first time in days, she felt in control.

Bridge

Her ears were still ringing as she stepped through the apartment door. The unnatural quiet hit her first. She'd never been in this place without chatter and laughter filling the empty spaces. A wave of nausea engulfed her. She doubled over and closed her eyes to keep it at bay. Air seeped through her nose, into her lungs, filling her belly—her body freely doing what her mind couldn't countenance.

The apartment lights were off, surfaces and furniture only visible under pale streetlight from an uncovered window. The heel of her steps reverberated on the warped wood floor. She stopped. Held her breath. Waited for voices that would never come.

She walked around, checking rooms, looking into corners, letting her mind settle into the slow steps. The apartment was empty. He wasn't here.

Confusion and something like despair rained down like hail. Her head throbbed against the night, the thump of it keeping time with her heartbeat.

He was supposed to be here.

A glint caught her eye. On the coffee table, the glass music box lay like a talisman or an unwanted trinket. She couldn't decide. She knew what it was. Of course she knew, and it shattered her heart.

She lifted the lid. Heard the tinkle of notes, slow and warped.

And finally understood.

He wasn't coming. He would never come. He would never choose her, despite everything she'd done for him. How far she'd led him away from the mire of his own life.

Ben wasn't here.

Loss, betrayal—they wove and welled through her mind like a pale pattern on white cloth. She pulled at the threads until a picture emerged, clear and biting. She'd been abandoned.

Sides of the equation thrown maddeningly into the air.

The effect was like a steel door slamming in her mind. The reverberations spread to her lungs, her heart, her knees. It wasn't anger or fury. It was something deeper, an incessant thrum through her body that would build into vengeance.

Without thinking, she grabbed the music box and headed to the door. She let her body do what her mind couldn't. She pulled a scarf off a hook by the front door and wrapped the box, tucking it under her arm.

Voices rose from the street below. She ignored them.

Struggling sconces in the hallway cast weak shadows as she walked out of the building and into a new future.

Chapter 30

Jaden

Striations of gray and white clouds, like waves against a shore, filled the sky as Jaden turned the car onto the little laneway. Tendons of blown snow stretched across the plowed gravel drive leading to her grandmother's cottage. Jaden drove carefully on tire-tracked grooves to avoid getting stuck in the edges.

The entire drive, she'd kept an eye on the rearview mirror. She didn't think the stranger would have been able to get his car out of the ditch on his own, but doubt and paranoia were an awkward cocktail. Her cell phone had been turned off before even leaving Lake Superior Park. She didn't need technology betraying her.

The only menace now was an approaching storm.

"You'll wanna get where you're going before the storm," a grocery clerk had said when Jaden stopped for provisions and a new SIM card. "Storm's coming in from the southwest tonight. And that means there's gonna be ice."

Not much older than Jaden, he had a gruff voice, with a hint of wisdom and suspicion. Jaden was used to that around here. This far north, even White Falls was considered southern Canada, and locals were always a little wary of "cottagers." While winter weather could be ruthless, ice storms could have a particularly destructive edge, downing trees and power lines more readily and turning harmless roads into skating rinks.

The car reached the end of the cottage laneway well before the first drops fell. The well-loved A-frame log cabin waited for Jaden like an embrace. The building showed its age, its brick red tin roof peeling in places and a few more weathered porch planks bowing with the seasons.

She may look a little old, Jaden thought, *but the bones are strong. So is the insulation.*

Her grandparents' cottage had been Jaden's home away from home every summer of her life until school and adulthood had taken her too far away. Entire days had been spent in the woods around here traipsing through thigh-high ferns, along granite sholes, and into the cooling kiss of the lake.

Jaden took in a slow, lung-expanding breath as she stepped out of the car. The smells of cold pine and memories seeped into her nose. Winnie, meanwhile, ran around sniffing at the earth, looking for the shadows of the creatures who'd left behind deeper scents. The dog raised a leg to remind them she was the keeper of this territory.

The key waited for her beneath a chunk of granite by the porch steps. She climbed on the wraparound porch and glanced back up the laneway, relieved at the nothingness behind her. The front door opened with an easy creak. Inside, Jaden caught whiffs of wood and lavender beneath the smell of dust and old ash. Two large front windows lit up an open living room and kitchen area. Beyond the reach of light, a single hallway led toward the back of the cottage, four bedrooms and a bathroom poking out of it like leaves on a branch. It was a home of sorts, and safe.

Jaden dropped her bags on the kitchen table. The cabin was cold. She moved through the rooms, cranking the floorboard radiators, and then stood back in the living room, her coat, hat, and mittens still on. It would take a while for the rooms to warm, so Jaden decided to take a short snowshoe to loosen her legs after a long drive. She pulled up the hallway hatch and climbed down a short set of stairs into the root cellar, where the snowshoes lived, along with a shelf of her grandmother's preserves. It was dark, but an outside-facing, ill-fitting door at the end of the cellar let in enough light. Jaden and her cousins used to scare each other by sneaking through the rear cellar door and knocking on the floorboards from below.

The cellar didn't scare her, but Jaden knew spiders and the occasional critter liked to winter in this space. She wasn't in the mood for a close encounter, so she grabbed the first set of snowshoes she could find and climbed back into the light.

A veneer of snow lay over the surface of the lake. Lacelike ice kissed the sandy shore and thickened into an opaque white, entombing the water beneath. It looked solid enough, but looks could be deceiving. Years ago, Jaden had watched her older cousin crash through the ice when the family was up for a February weekend. They'd been sledding the day before at the same spot, all of them tumbling and running on the ice. Jaden still remembered the look of shock on his face as he sank chest deep and scrabbled futilely to pull himself out. They'd had to use a scarf to drag him up, his shivering and muted lips trembling from the cold.

Jaden looked up to a darkening sky. Striations of rain, like the tendons of a behemoth, moved across the horizon. The storm was coming.

Pellets started hitting the tin roof and windows just as the last light of day slipped from the sky. In the cabin, bone-dry wood lit easily, and a fire nestled into the hearth. The space was cozy, with a few dim lamps keeping out the night. Jaden finally took off her hat, though she kept on two layers of socks against the cold-dappled wood floor. She made a package of instant ramen noodles and a cup of hot chocolate on the battered electric stove.

After eating, she typed out a text to her dad through WhatsApp: Don't worry. All fine. Back soon. The cell coverage was spotty, flipping in and out as if someone at the cell towers were playing tricks, but a message usually went through, eventually. He would get it when they released him tomorrow.

Jaden turned her attention to the fireplace, where a fire bobbed and weaved as it fed on oxygen and bone-dry wood. Her mind wandered untethered. Her breath came easier, longer. The fiercely delicate flame danced, lulling her until her slow blinks turned into sleep.

The old woman's face is cragged and crackled like the bark of the surrounding trees. A blood-black sky rises behind her. Tendrils of wild gray hair creep over her hood, writhing in the wind. Her pale skin glows beneath a round winter moon. Jaden stands on the cottage porch, watchful and afraid, but unable to run. A sound, like rushing water, fills the air, over which the woman cackles and screeches. Despite the winter cold, water rises, knocking over trees while the woman, cloaked and utterly calm, stands rooted. The water laps at Jaden's feet, then her knees. Her heart bashes against her chest while every muscle in her body is locked by the woman's steel gaze.

The slam of a car door shook Jaden from her half-sleep dream. Her eyelids peeled open to the burn of car headlights spilling in from the front window like an unwanted guest. Winnie's nails scrambled on the pine floors as the dog paced and jumped at the door.

Jaden cursed. She jumped up from the couch and moved toward the door, grabbing a pot off the stove top as she passed. Hidden by the section of wall between the door and the front window, she lifted the thin curtain. The glare of the headlights assaulted her eyes; beyond was only darkness.

What could she do if the stranger from the diner had tracked her here? Hit him with a soup pot and run? She felt terrified and ridiculous all at once.

Jaden crouched down and waited.

She had a view of the door, but couldn't be seen by anyone looking in. Footsteps ground against the porch. Winnie scratched harder at the door and whimpered. Jaden splayed her back against the wall. Her thighs burned from holding a crouch. The flimsy door lock toggled as if someone had inserted a key. She would have a second, maybe two, once he stepped into the room. She held her breath. She heard the door handle toggle. Raised the pot above her head.

The door creaked open slowly. Jaden tried to see his face, but the angle and glare of the car lights made it impossible. She heard steps on the old wood floor. Winnie stood on her hind paws, reaching for the stranger, tail wagging.

Stupid dog, Jaden thought. *Fat lot of good you are.*

Before she could think anything else, Jaden jumped toward the advancing shadow and screamed, the pot ready to descend, hard.

"Ahhh!" the figure yelled, lurching backward. One fist flew to their chest, while the other held an arm up in defense.

Jaden froze. Squinted against the headlights at the shadow within. Her heart still lurched in her chest. She flew through her senses: the slap of cold against her face, the hum of an engine, and a waft of vanilla and citrus.

"Mom?" Jaden said, still unsure whether she could trust her eyes.

"Jaden? What are you doing here?" her mom said, the sound of her voice like cold water over a burn.

Jaden stood on a threshold in her mind. The woman in front of her had walked out on her family six days ago, vanishing into a storm like some creature of legend. Anger, betrayal, and relief warred against each other as her body decided how to react to her mother's miraculous reappearance. In the end, it wasn't even a question. The little girl, desperate for her mom, overpowered all with her need and her despair.

The pot clattered to the floor. Jaden ran into her mom, wrapping her arms around her shoulders, testing the solidity of her, terrified that this was a mirage and if she blinked, all would be lost.

Her body collapsed, an invisible string that had been holding her upright and pulling her forward for days—to Toronto, to the police station, to this cabin—severed at last. Her mom's arms wound around her waist, crushing and warm, holding Jaden up. Fear and tension eked away like cold soapy water slushing down a drain.

Jaden stepped back, not releasing her mom's shoulders. She studied her face, taking in the cascade of emotions—wonder, confusion, relief—flitting past her eyes. Questions swirled into an incomprehensible morass in Jaden's head. Until only one rose, a toxic necessity and a demand.

"Where the hell have you been, Mom?"

Chapter 31

Emma

Emma had left White Falls to protect her family.

When she'd opened the music box on Christmas Day, old habits, born of trauma and fear and a foul history, had sprouted in her like a relentless vine, strangling reason. It had been cowardly to leave without saying a word, but she would never have left had she tried to tell Mark. One look at his kind, reassuring face, and she would have told him everything. Emma would just as soon bend the winds as show him the depths of her ugliness.

Standing on the threshold of the old cabin, in the face of her daughter's question and the anger behind her eyes, Emma couldn't fathom where or how to begin. How did you let your child know you were a coward and a killer? She'd spent Jaden's whole life protecting her from monsters, but what if the only real monster was Emma?

"I'll tell you everything, I promise," Emma said, buying time. "But let's catch our breaths first."

Jaden nodded, and in her daughter's round eyes and knit brow, Emma saw the stubborn toddler who she'd ushered back to bed in the dead of night with a glass of water and a mother's assurance that the monsters under the bed had indeed been banished. It nearly broke her.

"Let's unpack the car, and I'll make us some tea," Emma said.

Jaden didn't move. Only watched her mother, a startled deer deciding whether to bolt.

"It's OK, sweetheart," Emma said. "I'm here. I'm not going anywhere."

She looked into Jaden's eyes as she spoke, her hands firm on the girl's trembling shoulders, and watched what she hoped was acquiescence settle into her bones.

"Ok," Jaden muttered and walked past Emma into the blaring car lights.

When Jaden tromped back into the cottage, carrying shopping bags and a determined look, Emma had to stop herself from bending over in relief. Her daughter had chosen to stay. It was almost enough, for now.

Emma hadn't had a plan when she drove out of White Falls. The panic attack she'd had a few days ago in the grocery store had wiped her mind of past, present, and future, leaving only a shell of blood and bone and withering skin. When she'd turned onto the highway leading out of White Falls, she'd let the road guide her, until a hammering snow, more than reason, told her to stop. The storm was vicious and calculating, forcing her off the road into the parking lot of a small complex of cottages that she'd hoped were empty. She sat for hours, waiting for the snow to subside, running the engine sporadically to stay warm, and checking the tailpipe to keep it free of snow. In the quiet and isolation, her long-denied past came hurdling back, pummeling her until she was battered and bruised by memory.

Emma let her mind weave through the past, threads drawn on wishful thinking and bygone echoes. She had thought only two people could have known the significance of the music box—one was dead, the other lost to time—but what if she'd been wrong? What if there was a third? Someone just as involved in the incident that had torn her life apart from the inside all those years ago. Someone whose location was a matter of public record.

By the time the storm started to abate and space could be seen through the falling snow, a destination and the semblance of a plan had taken shape. No longer a decision in her mind, it was an inevitability.

Emma needed to find Clara Morel and ask for the truth about the night Konrad died.

"How did you know I was here?" Jaden said.

The cottage was tidy and warm, bathed in undulating firelight. They settled into the couch—Emma with a cup of tea and Jaden with an open tub of ice cream and a spoon. The patter of ice rain against the windows was background noise to the cocoon of the cottage. It would have been easy to forget the world outside, as if time could stand still and mother and daughter could stay in a loop of their own making for eternity.

"I called Zelda," Emma said, the white lie surprisingly smooth on her lips. "The rest was a lucky guess."

Emma had turned east on the highway pulling away from the little clump of cottages, back in the direction of White Falls. Predawn twilight—that moment before light split sky from earth—eased the darkness. She kept her eyes fixed on the horizon and pressed down on the accelerator as the car careened past the turnoff to home.

The drive hurled by in a blur. Crowded forests gave way to granite shelves veined with nickel, then veered south past thinning trees and rolling farmlands chiseled out of rock-rooted ground, until finally Emma found herself white knuckled on an eight-lane expressway sharing space with lumbering transport trucks. She had only a loose plan, didn't know enough to call ahead or consider what needed to happen to speak with an inmate at the Cedar Ridge Women's Correctional Facility. All she knew was that she had to try.

Emma found a cheap bed-and-breakfast near Kitchener, perched within sight of the busy Highway 401 corridor like a scab. The city was a combination of industrial factories and high-tech firms. Emma felt claustrophobic from the minute she exited the highway, despite the green spaces sprinkled about like confetti.

The room was an eruption of floral patterns laced with a choking chemical smell that vaguely resembled roses. The main advantage of the tiny space was that the proprietor didn't take payment until the end of the stay. Emma wasn't ready to tell Mark what she was doing, and running her credit card would alert him to her whereabouts, bringing more questions that she had no capacity to answer.

Cedar Ridge—the current home of Clara Morel—was a twenty-minute drive from the B and B.

Using a library internet terminal, a pay-as-you-go phone, and her birth name, Emma had been able to put in a request to visit Clara. The request had been denied outright by the authorities. Clara would be released in a little over two weeks, and it would take at least that long to do the requisite vetting on Emma. They had, however, said they could let Clara know Emma wished to speak with her. If Clara agreed, Emma could be put on an approved phone-call list.

"Since it's the holidays," a stern-sounding woman had said to Emma, "I'll see if I can put a rush on the request. The girls can get a little lonely this time of year, and hearing from a friend can help."

The unexpected humanity in such a dour tone confused Emma. She muttered a befuddled thank-you before hanging up.

Emma holed herself up in Kitchener, waiting. She'd driven past the facility a few times, but all she could see from the road was a functional cube of a building and glimpses of razor wire. In truth, there was no need to linger in Kitchener, but where else could she go. Home wasn't an option, not until she knew she could protect her family.

By the fourth day, her resolve started to crack. Emma paced the short space between the bed and the dresser. No call had come in. The room smelled of old grease and stupidity. A pile of discarded take-out containers lined the small dresser. She stared at the remains, examined a trail of gloppy red sauce spilling over an edge, not remembering whether she'd even eaten whatever was inside. Loneliness and regret crept up her spine, until her rational mind started to hold sway again, convincing her of the futility and pointlessness of her vigil.

That's when the phone finally rang.

"Ms. Hobbes?" an unfamiliar male voice said.

"Yes," Emma said.

"I'm calling from Cedar Ridge about your request to speak with Clara Morel."

Emma felt the muscles around her stomach clamp down, until breath was impossible.

"The inmate has indicated she is not willing to add your name to the call list at this time. In response to your request, however, she has attached a message that I am allowed to share. Would you like me to read the message?"

Emma wasn't sure if the word she'd spoken in reply was understandable, but the caller continued, his voice thick with boredom as he read.

"Not now, Grace. But I'll see you soon. Clara."

Emma hung up the phone and immediately dialed Mark's number. Heard the click. Her heart rabbited. She strained to hear his voice over the thrumming of her pulse.

An automated voice told her the person she was trying to reach was unavailable and that the mailbox was full.

Her stomach plummeted.

She tried Jaden's phone.

"The number you have reached is not in service. Please check the number and try your call again," the same automated voice said.

Every tendon, every muscle, every neuron told Emma something was wrong. Jaden was never without her phone, and she should be home, in White Falls, well within the range of any cell tower. And why would Mark's voicemail be full? Panic rose in her blood, hot and urgent like molten lava in her veins.

Emma ran out of the B and B to her car.

One thought hurdled through her head, a disharmonious looped chord: She needed to protect her family at all costs. She didn't know what Clara was planning, but her every instinct told her it would be bad. A line lay in front of her, one she swore she would never cross, but promises and convictions meant nothing in the face of danger to the people you loved. Alone, Emma wasn't enough to repel whatever was coming.

She needed a gun. And she knew one place where she could get one.

Emma tried to call Mark and Jaden again and again as she drove, nearly drifting into a passing motorcycle as she hit redial. Her ears rang with the reprise of the automated voice, announcing her family was unreachable. She thought about calling Sheila, her sister-in-law, but knew within seconds the entire Meadows clan would be flooding her with questions she couldn't, or wouldn't, answer. She couldn't face that. Not until she talked to Mark.

Scrabbling for a lifeline, she called Zelda. If anyone knew what was going on with Jaden, it would be her daughter's best friend.

"OMG, I'm literally shaking right now! Thank the universe, you're back," Zelda said. "Jaden's been going out of her mind."

The accusation was clear, but Emma couldn't be bothered with that now.

"Are you with her?" Emma said. "I need to talk to her. She's not answering her phone."

"What do you mean? Isn't she at your place?" The concern in Zelda's voice was unmistakable even with the miles of digital waves between them. "She texted me that she was heading home after the police station."

"Police station? Zelda, you need to tell me what's going on, now!"

It took a little more coaxing, but Emma could be very convincing when she needed to be. Zelda told Emma everything she knew—the police looking at Emma's disappearance, Mark being taken to the police station, and Jaden, alone with all of it.

"When was this? When did he go to the station?"

"The day before yesterday," said Zelda. "Jaden's been texting me. She went to the station yesterday, and they told her to go home, that Mr. M. would be out in the morning. I think she's still waiting to hear. Though, come to think of it, I haven't heard from her today."

"Did Jaden say anything else?"

"Not exactly."

"This is not the time to play games with me, Zelda. If you know anything more, you better fucking tell me."

Emma knew she was being curt and that cursing would shock Zelda enough to open up. This child was going to tell her everything Emma needed to know, or she would shake it out of her.

Zelda unloaded a story that had clearly been weighing on her. She told Emma about Jaden's obsession with the music box, the trip to Toronto, and the meeting with Nero Estevez. Emma had to pull over on the side of the road. With nothing but deep forest and blue sky to witness, she listened to a child recount scenes from her own past, ones she'd tried to hide for over twenty years.

She waited for that familiar feeling of drowning to overtake her, expected her body to fight against the confrontation with memories. Instead, she drew in a slow, steady breath and felt a buoyancy in her chest and limbs as if the air around her had lightened. She looked out the car window to the bare trees, swaying in a gentle wind, and caught the outline of a hawk on one of the upper branches. The bird's head slowly scanned the ground, surveying its domain or hunting for its next meal.

Emma could tell there were blanks in Zelda's story, but she suspected it wasn't because she was holding them back. The girl was scared and slipped easily into the role of a child in the face of a parent's stern demand.

"And you have no idea where she might have gone?" Emma said.

"I honestly thought she was at home. She didn't say anything el—" Zelda paused, her mind clearly reaching for something.

"What is it? Anything might be important."

"I mean, a while back, she joked about going to her grandma's cottage to hide out, but I didn't think she was serious. School's back in next week. I couldn't imagine she'd head up there alone."

Of course she would, thought Emma as she hung up on Zelda and put the car in drive.

The miles under the wheels couldn't go past fast enough. Emma pushed the accelerator. Though she knew it was impossible, the distance markers seemed to grow farther apart. What if something had happened to them? Or what if they were so angry, they were refusing to answer? The same persistent thought hammered at Emma's head: She'd broken everything.

Emma watched Jaden absorb the account of her conversation with Zelda.

The child Emma had sent off to university was still there, beneath the ill-fitting maturity, but Emma had to admit, her daughter was becoming a woman, with her own successes and mistakes. There were things from which Emma could no longer protect her.

Emma gently started asking Jaden to fill in some of the blanks of the last few days and tell her everything Zelda may have left out. In response to some of Emma's more pointed questions, Jaden squeezed her eyes together, a habit she'd had since girlhood when she was concentrating hard. Emma resisted the urge to gather her daughter in her arms for fear of interrupting. Jaden shared everything—the music box, the drive to Toronto, finding out about Konrad. And everything she'd learned about the explosion that killed Konrad. Emma's past spilled out of her daughter's mouth like a bed-time story.

"What did this guy look like?" Emma finally said when Jaden told her about the phone calls and the man at the diner.

"That's easy," Jaden said. She pulled out her phone from her back pocket. "It's not great quality, but I grabbed a few shots where his face is visible."

Jaden opened Photos and handed it over. She saw a man standing beside a car clearly having just spun off the highway. He had a shaken and befuddled look and seemed like a caricature with a useless overcoat in front of a snow-heavy forest.

Emma should have been shocked by the face she saw on the screen. The clatter of her past smashing into her present should have been a warning. Instead, Emma felt a full-bodied explosion of anger, as if a brooding storm had finally been released. She stiffened, and her grip tightened clawlike around the phone.

Emma knew the man in the picture, and she despised him.

Chapter 32

Emma

"Mom, what's going on? You know who this guy is, don't you?"

Emma looked into her daughter's beautiful blue eyes, faintly almond shaped, with thick brown lashes. She took a shaky breath to calm the raging wrath. She reached a hand to Jaden's cheek and felt the baby-soft skin, unlined by age or regret. Let it sooth her.

"I love you, J-bear. You know that, right?" Emma said, desperately needing Jaden to understand that above all else.

"I know. I know. I love you, too, Mom." Jaden's tone was impatient but sincere.

Emma felt her heart enfold itself in the layers of meaning those three simple words could hold.

"That man is Ben Chalmers. He was a friend of mine, and Konrad's, when we were at university. Or at least, he tried to be, for a time."

Once she started on the story, it was like the release of spring ice downriver. She gathered all the details she could remember and let them flow. Whether it would destroy or nourish the ground of her relationship with Jaden, she couldn't know, but she could no longer treat her bright, precocious, and inquisitive daughter like a child.

"I met Ben in first year. He was a brilliant kid who finished high school early. We were close, for a while. Maybe a little too close. He had a crush on me, and I took advantage of that when I needed company. I needed a friend. I was young and a little too careless of other people."

Outside the cabin, the ice storm had come up in earnest now, pellets hammering at the windows and the wind viciously seeking cracks. Emma pulled a blanket from the back of the couch and slipped it around Jaden's shoulders.

"Somewhere along the way, Ben changed. He started seeing this girl."

"Clara Morel?" said Jaden.

"How did you—" Emma's astonishment rendered her speechless.

Her past was clearly not as well hidden as she'd believed. Emma felt the layers of time slip away. Shame, her constant companion, doused her budding anger as memories flooded back. She imagined them all, faces unencumbered with the cares of time, brimming with confidence and arrogance.

"We thought we were so grown up and worldly, didn't we?" she said almost in a whisper. "But really, we were a bunch of dumb kids chasing ambitions."

There was something about a simmering fire that invited confession. Perhaps it was the orange glow softening hard-edged surfaces or the false feeling of anonymity when all eyes were trained on the hypnotic dance of flames. Your mind shifted from the here and now, traveled through doors normally shut tight in the cold light of day. Whether it was the fire, time, or a lifetime of guilt, Emma felt her mind loosen, carrying her voice with it. The events and people that shaped you never truly went away, only drifted into your subconscious, casually nudging your life choices like distant puppeteers, until you pulled them back into the light.

"There was a group of us," Emma said, opening the floodgates on her past. "We wanted to get more organized. The silly stunts were fine, but we got it in our heads that we weren't being taken seriously enough."

"Who's we?" Jaden said, guiding the flow, pulling details.

"Clara and I. Ben, too, though I don't think he was ever as convinced."

Emma hadn't let those names pass her lips in over twenty years, and in the last two days, she'd uttered them repeatedly.

"Ben and Clara started dating in my third year, and all of a sudden, we had this voice in our ears telling us what we wanted to hear. It nudged me toward something more. It made so much sense at the time. Clara had these great ideas and a real conviction that they would work."

The idea that Clara and Emma had nursed in a stoned haze after final exams had somehow taken on a life of its own, despite Konrad's tirade against it. A handful of people had gathered in a beaten-down apartment whose owner Emma didn't even know. Some she recognized from Militant Animals, others were new. They carried an anger in their voices that resonated with Emma at the time. She'd found a community but was still unable to douse this anger she'd felt at the world.

When Emma closed her eyes, she could still evoke that exquisite pain of being young and believing you needed to crash down the door to your future. Through her mind's eye, she watched Konrad pacing in a dingy basement apartment. The smell of mold from the walls had migrated into the furniture, and a scarf-draped lamp emitted an eerie orange glow.

Emma walked through the front door, dragging in a smoky cold with her. She saw Konrad turn and watched the breath silently leave his chest when he saw her. His face was expressionless, but she knew his bearing. He was angry.

"Look, it's not that complicated," someone was saying as Emma joined them. "We take their weapon and use it against them. Easy-peasy. No one gets hurt."

"What the hell, man?" Konrad said, his voice low with restrained incredulity. "You're talking about a fucking explosive."

Emma slid onto a chair by the door and kept silent. She knew Konrad was against the whole idea. She had already had a similar conversation with him the night before. It had not gone well.

"Get over yourself, Konrad," the speaker said. In the last few weeks, voices had become more vocal, pushing back against Konrad and the status quo. "No one is going to get hurt. It's not like that."

Emma was relieved to see Clara there, perched on a chair back, as delicate as a bird. She watched the speakers, head titled in amused curiosity.

It was only for effect, the argument continued, a little pizzazz. It was meant to put a scare into the right people. An idea just crazy enough to seem plausible.

"For fuck's sake," Konrad said, his frustration bubbling to the surface. "This is twisted. This is not what Militant Animals is about."

"Maybe we should take a little break," Clara had said in that sickly sweet voice of hers. "I would hate for anyone to say something they regret."

But it was too late.

"How would you know what Militant Animals is about?" Emma, then Grace, said, cold eyes boring into Konrad. The words were slow and bitter, intended to wound. "You're never around. All you care about anymore is your precious law career."

The slash hit its mark. Hardness fell over Konrad's face, a plague mask to inure him against the vitriol. He met Emma's eyes.

"Listen to me," Konrad said softly. "You can't be serious about this. Someone's going to get hurt."

All faces turned to Emma. She felt unexpectedly cornered. She looked into Konrad's eyes—dark-brown pools that she had lost herself in so many times—and saw a plea for reason. She looked away.

"I say we do it," Emma had said with finality.

Emma had been gratified to see Clara's eyes widen in subtle surprise.

Emma closed her eyes against the memories, bitter and scalding with age. When she opened them again, she saw Jaden's face, earnest and beseeching answers.

I was so stupid, thought Emma. She'd never intended to go through with it. She'd only wanted to wake Konrad up from his law school stupor. Maybe she'd hoped it could reignite his passion for the cause, and for her.

She tried conjuring Konrad's face again, the way she had a thousand times after his death, but nothing came. The details had smoothed away over the years, lost to time and the vagaries of memory, but his eyes, and the disappointment she saw there, were as sharp as claws.

Clara's voice, as Konrad had walked out the door, echoed down through the years, until Emma heard it in her mind like a clarion call: "Good riddance."

It was the last time Emma saw Konrad Sharma alive.

How could she admit to her daughter that she had a part in all that? Some things needed to remain locked away, the monster sealed into the deepest, darkest cave, away from knowing.

The music box sat, toxic and blameless, on the coffee table. Emma's eyes darted to where firelight warped and reflected on the beveled glass. She reached for it, opened the lid, and let the familiar tune seep into the air. She cast her mind back and plunged forward.

"It was Konrad who picked this song. It's impossible, but sometimes I think he knew what was going to happen, that he wouldn't be around long," Emma said. "Do you know the words?"

"A little. It's a traditional Irish song, isn't it?"

"It is." Emma took in a breath and quietly sang the tune. "But since it fell unto my lot / That I should rise and you should not / I'll gently rise and softly call / Good night and joy be to you all."

The hush that descended after the last note was piercing. Emma closed her eyes to hold back tears and focused on the comforting crackle of the fire. She felt Jaden's hand take hers and smiled sadly at the solace there.

"I don't know what happened that night, whether it was Clara's fault or Ben's or one of the other's. What I do know is that Konrad shouldn't have been there. Clara told me she and Ben would take care of it. I thought all we needed was a little spark. I never wanted an explosion."

As if on cue, a log fell deeper into the fire, sending glowing shards up the chimney. Emma was silent for a long time. She still hadn't decided what, if anything, to tell Jaden about running away from Toronto and finding Mark, and the safety and certainty she found in White Falls. She wouldn't have said it was love in the beginning—Konrad was still too much with her then—but she found contentment and stability and a loving home with her husband. What else could anyone hope for in life?

"After Konrad's funeral, I couldn't take being in Toronto anymore. I was scared. The police had questioned me, and there were all kinds of rumors. So, I left. Ben tried to talk to me, but I wouldn't see him. By then, I knew the type of person Clara was and how far she'd gone. I blamed her, sure, but couldn't separate her from Ben. He might have been my friend, but he shouldered some responsibility. He brought Clara into the group, into our lives, and they were still together when it all happened. I didn't know how deeply involved he was, and I couldn't trust him. I couldn't trust anyone. When Clara was arrested for manslaughter, I closed that chapter of my life entirely. Left Ben, as well as Grace Hobbes, behind and never looked back."

Emma closed the music box and stared into the blackness out the window. She drifted through memory, revisited the people and experiences that had shaped her days and her dreams about the future, remembering the woman she had been and the path she'd taken to the here and now.

"And now it seems, Ben doesn't want to leave well enough alone," Emma said, more to herself than Jaden. "I don't know where he's been all these years or what he hopes to achieve now. Targeting you was a mistake, though. It needs to end. All of it."

The young woman Emma had once been, with her anger and devotion, was still a part of her, with one notable exception: The youthful Emma—or Grace as she was known then—had never wanted to hurt anyone. The woman she was now, the wife and mother, wouldn't hesitate to wipe someone off the earth if they threatened her family.

Chapter 33

EMMA

Emma lay on a lumpy bed, brain whirling and weaving through everything Jaden had told her the night before. Her eyes stayed stubbornly closed. If only it had all been a horrible, elaborate, and in the end, forgettable dream.

Sometime in the wee hours of the morning, Jaden had fallen asleep on the couch, too tired to drag herself to one of the back bedrooms. Ice pellets rattling against the windows and sputtering fire embers had been a lullaby. Emma had sat in a chair across from her daughter, the smell of warm wood and peppermint tea lingering through layers of the past, each deeper than the last. She expected the shock of the last week to bottom out, but still she kept falling.

Jaden had pushed her, hard, for answers the night before. Using questions like a cudgel, trying to understand.

"There must be something important about the box. Something you're not seeing," Jaden had said.

"That's the same question I've been asking myself since Christmas. I don't have an answer," Emma said. "Honest to God, I wish I'd just tossed that damn thing in the lake as soon as I opened it and forgotten all about it. Then, none of this would have happened."

Though unintentional, Emma knew it sounded like a rebuke. Emma had tried to escape it all. Jaden had been the one to scratch at old wounds and expose the past so thoroughly.

They'd speculated that the visit to the odd antique store in Kensington Market had somehow alerted Ben to Jaden's interest, though Jaden said she couldn't have imagined that the ancient man behind the counter would be involved in all this. Then again, until a few days ago, it was unlikely her daughter would have imagined a different life existing under a person's skin.

"I'm so sorry, Jaden. This is all my fault," Emma said in a voice matching the glow of the fire, trying to take the burden she'd placed on Jaden's shoulders. "Maybe it's my penance for walking away, for not facing my demons. That box is my own telltale heart."

Silence wrapped the room as Emma felt tears seep down her cheeks. She wiped at her face surreptitiously, not wanting to cry in front of her child. Then again, of all the things she didn't want for Jaden, perhaps a mother's tears were the least harmful.

"So, what happened the night Konrad died?" Jaden said.

"I wish I knew. I wasn't there. Clara and I had talked about it, but she never would have done it on her own, I don't think. And Konrad should never have been there. He refused to have anything to do with it."

No matter how many scenarios she ran through her head, Emma couldn't imagine one that put Konrad in the trajectory of the explosive.

"I tried to see her in prison, to find out. That's where I went. Down to the prison. I thought if I could learn the truth about what actually happened that night, I'd understand why Ben sent me the music box, why he's trying to dig up the past."

"Do you think Clara's release has something to do with it?"

Emma thought about Clara, her youth draining away in prison while Emma went on with her life. The police had never come knocking at Emma's door; no charges were ever threatened. If Clara had tried to drag Emma with her, it hadn't worked. And Emma closed her eyes to anything else. A single death in a foolish accident didn't get much national press coverage, and the internet wasn't as much of a thing in those days. They weren't all able to ferret out details of each other's lives, especially in White Falls. If Clara had pointed the finger at others, that information never became public and no one had come knocking.

"I don't know," Emma said. "Besides, Clara wouldn't have known anything about the music box. Ben knew about it, but I can't imagine he told her the significance of it. Unless—"

Hiding your past was a little like living on the edge of a spider's web. You could get through the days stepping around the sticky trap, though real contentment was always stolen away by the ever-present fear of tugging on an unseen thread. This type of existence prevented you from stepping back and seeing the patterns in the spider's lair and the perils that lay beyond the edges of the web.

"Did Ben say anything else to you? Or say something that you couldn't quite connect?" Emma said.

"He said the music box came from an ex-boyfriend of yours," Jaden said. "He also said that I had no idea what was really going on."

"He what?"

The faded path of memory cleared, and Emma's mind slipped to the night after Konrad had brought over the music box. She closed her eyes and once again was sitting in her crappy little off-campus apartment, with its cracked ceiling and closet-size bedroom.

The knock was tentative, cautious. Konrad stood in the doorway when she opened, either unable or unwilling to come in even though she'd invited him.

"I like the music box," Emma had said. "It's beautiful."

It was her apology of sorts. In truth, she'd found it fussy and a little too ornamental for her taste. In her mind, the abandoned gift, along with the smooshed box of éclairs, sat on the coffee table like a bright stain on a fractious memory.

Konrad's slip of a smile carried nothing but sadness to his eyes. "It was Ben's idea, but I picked the song," he said.

They stayed like that, each wrapped in thoughts of an inevitability that neither wanted to introduce.

"Walk?" Konrad said finally, doing what Emma knew she'd never have been able to do.

When she returned hours later, wrapped in the relief and grief that come from a breakup, her apartment was unlocked. Kicking herself for failing to lock the door, she was crushed to find the music box gone.

Wishes and hope had a strange way of altering memories, shaping them until they better fit into your chosen view of the past. How stupid Emma had been. All these years, she'd assumed that some lucky thief had happened to hit her apartment on the one night she had anything of value in the place. Even when it turned up on her doorstep on Christmas Day, she hadn't put the pieces together.

Hindsight, Emma thought, was a wasted insight; it came like a coveted present long after you'd outgrown the desire for it. Years of therapy and constantly revisiting the mistakes of her past gave her no absolution, only clarity. All these years later, it was easy to put the pieces together, to see the naked drive and ambition in a young Clara. To understand Emma's own need for acceptance and family and how it had driven her into the clutches of a one-sided, if exciting, friendship. Narcissists were skilled at that, manipulating those around them into thinking right was wrong and wrong was right. The shame Emma felt at her own folly ran so deep that it had colored every relationship, every decision, every thought since that time.

Pain has a way of finding a mark among those we love more than those we hate. Emma had hated herself for launching the idea that had brought about Konrad's death, and she'd hated Clara for making it happen, but the feelings she'd had for Ben were twisted in the roots of a friendship that had initially saved her from herself. She'd been unable to forgive Ben for bringing Clara into their lives, for whatever role he might have played in events, and most of all, for failing her.

Ben, who had always listened from the margins, who had been infatuated with Clara, who was probably the smartest person Emma had ever known. Emma hadn't talked to him since that long-ago day when they'd learned about Konrad's death. He'd tried to call, even came to her apartment, but she'd shut him out, turned him into a ghost in her life.

Emma had no doubt that Clara held a grudge, would be more than capable of stirring up trouble if she chose, but Clara was in prison, had been for over twenty years. Emma had assumed that Konrad's death had irreparably fractured all connections, scattering the four of them into a blistering wind. But what if she'd been wrong? What if Clara's influence lived on, outside the prison walls through a relationship with Ben?

If Clara had a long-standing grudge against Emma, then who better than Ben to help her. He had, after all, been her puppet back then. What if he still was?

Chapter 34

Jaden

A blade of sunlight nudged Jaden awake. A duvet had been tucked around her and a glass of water placed on the coffee table. She let her senses slip back, felt a sofa button dig into her arm, smelled old smoke, and heard nothing. The cabin was quiet. Her mom, usually the first one up, wasn't clanging around the kitchen. Behind half-closed eyes, Jaden called out. Her voice bounced in the empty room.

A ripple of panic pushed her to her feet.

"Mom! You awake," she said, rushing toward the back bedroom where her parents usually slept.

Her mother's form lay under a pile of mismatched blankets, Winnie stretched out beside her. Cold relief flooded Jaden's lungs, followed closely by the sickening realization that this kind of fear would follow her for the rest of her life. She didn't want to digest the meaning in that just yet.

Back in the main room, Jaden looked out the front picture window to see a cerulean sky over a sculpted white world. Ice formations dripped from bending branches, and crystallized snow caught sunlight, reflecting millions of points of light. She opened the front door and thought of Lucy stepping through the wardrobe into Narnia.

Her socked foot skated forward on the ice-coated porch. Not enough to bowl her over but a reminder of the treachery in beauty. Ice covered every surface—the porch, the cars, the trees—they all wore a quarter-inch shell courtesy of last night's ice storm.

At least Ben Chalmers won't be getting through this, Jaden thought.

Coffee, and lots of it, would be needed to deal with the day.

Jaden checked her phone. No bars. The text to her dad from the night before had failed to send. She hoped it was just the usual spotty coverage and not a crumbled cell tower from the storm. They needed to find a way to reach him. And the police.

By the time her mom came into the kitchen, Jaden had already reignited the fire and a coffee pot burbled on the stove. From the food her mom had brought, Jaden pulled out a fresh multigrain loaf and ripe avocados. *Figures,* she thought as she glanced at her own stash of Frosted Flakes and instant noodles.

"Breakfast?" Jaden said.

"Ya, that'd be great." Her mother's voice rasped from too little sleep and, Jaden suspected, too much worry.

They were sitting down to eat when they heard a warble from her mom's hastily purchased flip phone. It sat on the coffee table across the room; both eyed it cautiously as if it were a scurrying mouse. Jaden's relief that the cell towers were working, albeit sporadically, was dashed when she looked over at her mom, whose firm mouth and wide eyes told a still-unfolding story.

Looking directly at Jaden, her mom put an index finger to her lips as she moved to pick up the phone, a plea and a warning. She let it ring one more time, stealing a breath before answering. The phone stayed in her palm, an offering.

"Hello," her mom said.

"Grace, is that you?" The voice from the phone speaker had the scratch of middle age but the pitch of a schoolgirl.

"Hello, Clara," her mom said.

Jaden stepped back instinctively. Her eyes locked on her mom's face; blotches of color smeared her cheeks, but her eyes were steel.

"Imagine my surprise when I was told you, of all people, wanted to speak with little old me," Clara said. The words were innocuous but with a sharp whip of sarcasm at the end.

"I think we can dispense with the niceties, don't you?" her mom said.

The subsequent pause was louder than any words might have been.

"Very well. What do you want, Grace?" The sickly charm dropped instantaneously.

"Was it you?"

"You'll have to be a little more specific? We haven't spoken to each other in over twenty years. A lot has happened in that time. Well, for you more than for me, I suppose."

Clara's tone was like delicate nails on a chalkboard, so incongruous that Jaden didn't know whether to laugh or be afraid.

"The music box. Did you send it to me?"

"And how exactly am I supposed to have done something like that from behind prison walls?"

"I don't know, Clara. Why don't you tell me?"

"Twenty years, and you're still getting everything wrong. I almost feel sorry for you, Grace."

"So, you didn't send me a message?" her mom tried again, her voice rising an octave, whether with strain or hope, Jaden couldn't tell. "A threat."

"No, Grace, I did not."

Her mom closed her eyes, and both shoulders dropped, as if a wish had been let out of her. Realization came hard and thunderous in that moment. Her mom had been hoping that Clara was the one responsible for sending the music box, not Ben.

"What happened the night Konrad died?" her mom said, rushing through the sentence.

"Didn't you read the papers? He blew up."

A creeping chill rode on the back of the girlish giggle that followed.

"You won't get absolution from me, Grace, if that's what you're looking for. I didn't tell him about our plans. It wasn't me who sent him to die."

Our plans? The words were simple, but the screech of them echoed in Jaden's mind. Had her mom known about the details? She claimed not to know, but had she actually been involved? The question flew through the silence. The entreaty in her mom's eyes gave her the answer.

Her mother's body crumpled to the floor, head bowed and hands resting open on her knees like a discarded doll. The phone stayed loosely in her open palm, still spewing Clara's voice.

"You know," Clara continued, satisfaction dripping off the edges. "For a long time, I wondered whether you sent him there by mistake or to teach him a lesson? But I've had a lot of time to think about it since that day, and I've come to the conclusion, you didn't have it in you. You never really understood what was happening."

"I didn't send him." Her mom wrung out the words, a wounded animal gasping for breath.

"Well, why don't you ask your little smitten shadow, Ben, about who exactly sent Konrad out that night? I bet he'd have a story to tell. I mean, with Konrad out of the way, Ben was clearly first in line for your affections. Maybe you should ask him about the music box."

The phone went dead.

Jaden's muscles refused to obey. She knew she should reach out, offer comfort or support, but what did you do when the person who held you up had fallen? She didn't know what to say, what to do. The phone call had been a minute, maybe two, yet her thoughts were drowning in the insinuations and implications in a handful of words.

Finally, after what seemed an eternity, Jaden knelt in front of her mom. She took the phone out of her hand, heard the faint *click* as she folded it back up.

Her mom looked up at her, no tears, just despair etched into every line of her face.

"I'm sorry," her mom said. "I am so, so sorry."

Jaden couldn't deal with that now. One thought bellowed intrusively above all others.

"She didn't ask 'What music box?'" Jaden said.

Her mom looked past Jaden, thoughts whirling by on her face as she tried to follow what Jaden was saying. She squinted, tilted her head.

"Clara. You called her out of the blue, after twenty years, to ask about some music box, and she didn't ask what music box. It doesn't make sense."

Before either of them could work through the implications of Jaden's observation, a loud creak thundered through the cabin. A second creak confirmed their worst fears.

Someone was outside, on the porch.

Her mom's body language shifted, like a mama-bear switch had been pulled. Her jaw tightened, eyes narrowed, listening for the fallout. Without a word, her mom went to the front door and silently slid across the small latch, more useful for keeping out critters than humans.

"Get down," her mother whispered, as she gestured at Jaden to crouch beneath the front windows.

Jaden obeyed the command but looked with dismay at the fire puffing smoke out the chimney and their abandoned breakfast on the table. It was unlikely they could pretend no one was home. Jaden's brain scrambled and lodged itself on a single idea: How had a car arrived without either one of them hearing?

Still in a crouch, Jaden peeked out the front window. Only two cars—hers and her mom's—were parked in front of the cottage. Whoever was here had arrived on foot. Why would anyone in their right mind traipse through the aftermath of an ice storm? Unless they had a reason for not wanting to be noticed.

They heard another footfall. Her mother pointed toward the fireplace side of the cabin.

Behind there, she mouthed.

It was the only wall without windows; there was no way to see that side of the porch or the woods beyond without going outside. The footsteps went silent.

Jaden duck walked over to the kitchen table and, as quietly as she could, reached for her phone. One bar. Shit. She tried dialing 911, but the call wouldn't go through. She wrote out a text and hit send.

The footsteps started up again—slow, methodical—along the porch toward the front of the cabin. Her mom gestured wildly for Jaden to move toward the bedrooms.

Just as Jaden started to crawl, a shadow passed over the gossamer-curtained front window.

Hunched over, Jaden moved toward the hallway, grabbing her backpack and the music box as she passed. With the brightness beyond the window, the hall would be in complete shadow and invisible to anyone looking in.

The door rattled as the figure knocked.

"I know you're in there." A man's voice, not harsh but not friendly either. Jaden thought it might be the same man from the diner, but it was hard to tell over her pounding heart. "I just want to talk." He pulled at the locked door again.

"Grace. Come on now. This doesn't have to be difficult. It's already gotten way out of hand, but we can fix it. Let's work this out. Let Jaden get back to school. All I want is for us to get on with our lives."

Jaden watched in horror as her mother stood.

"Really, Ben?" she said through the door. "Just give you what you want and we all live happily ever after?"

"You can't win here, Grace. How do you think I found this cabin? All it took was a property-registry search and Google Maps. The storm and your daughter's fancy driving slowed me a bit, but I was right behind your girl the whole time."

That stopped her mom. She looked back at Jaden, squinting to see into the gloom of the hallway. Their eyes met. Jaden read a thousand bedtime stories, bear hugs, and home-cooked meals in her mother's face before a flash of cold anger.

"Get out," her mother said in a whisper. Her head motioned toward the hallway, while her hand mimed going down.

Jaden understood: the cellar door. She inched farther along the hallway and quietly lifted the panel.

"You can't ignore me this time, Grace," Ben said.

"Why not? It's worked for me so far."

Jaden hopped down onto the hard-packed earth, head and shoulders remaining above the floor. She would have to crawl to make it to the rear cellar door, but she'd done it hundreds of times in the past. She turned back toward her mother, expecting that she would follow and they'd escape into the woods. Instead, her mother waved her away, giving Jaden a reassuring smile before opening the front door.

In her hand, Jaden saw the oil-black shape of a handgun.

Chapter 35

Emma

"It's Emma now. And you're not getting in here, Ben," Emma said, hands on her hips, blocking the path to her daughter. Winnie stood beside her, eyes watchful but body calm. Whatever happened next, clearly the friendly golden retriever was unlikely to help.

Emma needed to give Jaden time.

She didn't know what was about to happen, nor did she know the version of the man who stood in front of her now. She was, however, certain that she would do anything needed to protect her daughter. If Ben's eye was trained on Emma, Jaden had a chance to get beyond his clutches. Jaden knew the terrain, had spent entire summers exploring these woods. She could get to the main road and safety. Emma prayed it would work.

Ben Chalmers, looking older and a little wider, stepped backward off the porch when Emma opened the door. For just a breath, Emma was assaulted by nostalgia, remembering the cute little dork who had followed her around campus all those years ago.

"Emma, then," Ben said. His voice hadn't changed. There was still that little uptake of breath before he spoke in a flat tenor. "There's no need for me to come in. Let's work this out."

Behind him was a winter wonderland of snow and ice, resplendent in morning sunshine. *There's a quality to the light at this time of year,* Emma thought absurdly, under the circumstances. She knew it had something to do with the position of the sun and the reflection of rays off the snow, but winter light had a different character than its paler spring cousin. It reminded her of glass, and it carried a heavier weight.

Emma smiled at the thought and stepped out, closing the door behind her.

Chapter 36

Ben

Ben was cold. He'd arrived on foot, and the temperature was still below freezing. His wool coat and unlined leather boots did nothing to cut a blistering wind.

Waiting for a tow truck to pull his car out of the ditch had delayed him, but he'd managed to get within spitting distance of the Meadows cottage by car before meeting a police barricade. The guts of the ice storm had hit hard in this area, leaving downed tree branches and a couple of live power lines on the ground ahead. The road was impassable to cars while crews repaired the damage.

A bored-looking OPP officer had shrugged when Ben had asked how long road clearing would take.

"It'll happen when it happens," he said with an attempt at a sage nod. "Where you headed?"

Ben debated withholding that information, but what would be the point. He'd come all this way to settle his past. He couldn't stop now.

He gave the address.

"Oh, the Meadowses' place. You could walk along the road for about an hour and a half." The officer looked Ben up and down. "Or, if you're game, you could walk the snowmobile trail. Get you there in forty-five minutes or so," he said with a smirk.

After getting directions and a crude hand-drawn map from the officer, Ben stepped onto a path that crossed the road and headed into the woods. He'd hiked his argyle socks up over his pant legs and accepted the offer of a pink hunting-style cap from the officer, along with a heavy pair of snowmobile gloves. He felt ridiculous, a feeling reinforced when the officer chuckled behind him.

"Check in when you get there, will ya?" the officer said between sputters of laughter. "Wouldn't want to lose another city mouse out here."

Ben had never seen anything like the crystallized world that awaited him once he found his way to the trailhead. He'd stepped into a fantastical neverland out of a child's imagination. Icicle-dressed poplar and oak trees gave way to open clearings smooth as fresh canvases. The trail undulated over uneven terrain, rising and cresting like walking over storm waves. Though the trail was reasonably packed down from the weight of machines, he still moved slower than expected through the bog-like snow. Ten minutes in, his heart thumped in his chest and his breath came short and shallow.

The cold slunk deeper into his skin as he walked. His leather boots darkened with snowmelt, finding its way through the pores. With every footstep, he crunched through ice, sinking a few inches and losing momentum. By the time he was within sight of the cabin, his chest felt like he'd run a marathon, his feet were numb, and a vise had started to wind its way around his head.

The glare off ice-encrusted snow was worse than the cold, stabbing into his already-pounding head. He might as well have been watching the world through a looking glass pointed into the sun. He stepped off the trail, and his leg sank to mid-calf, nearly toppling him face first into the snow.

Smoke fluttered up from the chimney of the red-roofed cottage. The image promised warmth but, like so many times in his life, not for him. The cabin had a lived-in look, even from a distance. For once, luck was on his side: There were no windows on this side of the building. Whoever was inside wouldn't know he was there, not until he wanted them to.

He heard a scramble from inside as soon as he set foot on the porch. No voices. Just the skitter of feet on warped floorboards. Jaden wasn't alone. He moved slowly toward the front door, gratified to see the RAV4 Jaden had been driving parked in the driveway. There was a second car he didn't recognize, but the Ontario plates gave him a hint.

He called to her, the name unfamiliar on his lips after all these years.

"Why not? It's worked for me so far," Grace Hobbes said.

The front door flew open, and Ben was blown off the porch by a gust from the past.

She stood in front of him on a cold, blue morning in the middle of nowhere. His heart caught at the sight of her. Age hadn't withered her. She still had the monstrous beauty that had drawn him into her orbit. The snow had stolen away sounds, but her voice was crystal clear and sharp. Belatedly, he noticed a golden retriever standing contentedly beside her, its gaze curious.

"You got old, Ben," Grace, now Emma, said.

"Wish I could say the same about you." Ben took a step farther back and glanced at the corners of the cottage. The only other living thing was the dog at Emma's side.

"Still trying to charm me, I see?"

"That depends. Is it working?"

There was no sign of Jaden or anyone else. Though he couldn't be sure, Ben suspected that the girl was hiding in the cottage while her mother ran interference.

"What are you going to do now, Ben? Kill me too?" Emma said.

Her words stung. Despite what she might think, Ben had not been involved in Konrad's death. He hadn't learned the truth about what happened until the funeral.

On the day Konrad was buried, light raindrops hovered in the air, still deciding whether to fall. The funeral home loomed out of a copse of trees. An ornate iron rail along the gabled roof left Gothic traces of a time long past on the building. Impossibly fresh leaves clung to branches as nature continued its relentless path, no matter the horrors and grief visited upon the living. The mansion had once been a family estate, complete with stables and an English garden; now it housed the dead.

As he approached, Ben could see a small collection of mourners, their faces undulating through leaded glass. Clara stood by the massive oak doors that led inside. At the sight of her, relief and trepidation galloped through him, wild little creatures looking for a home. They hadn't spoken since before the accident that killed Konrad. She hadn't responded to any of his messages, and the room she rented near campus was empty.

With a flick of her head, she signaled for Ben to join her around the side of the building. He hadn't wanted to follow. A hard pellet of fear needled at his gut. Inside, Konrad's friends and family were saying their final goodbyes. Clara, dressed in a bright-red raincoat and glitter-coated Mary Janes, was beckoning him away. Something was off.

He spied Grace through the window, pale and beautiful. Though she stood with a small group, she was facing the window. He caught her eye. And was met with an expression of pure loathing.

Ben dropped his head and followed Clara.

"What the hell happened, Clara?" he said when they were beyond the window's sight line.

"No hello? I think I deserve at least a hello. Don't you, Ben?" Her voice was calm, but the hard line of her mouth and the scowl in her eyes were piercing.

"Deserve?" Ben said. "You've been AWOL for the last week. No one's seen or heard from you. I think Konrad's death and being dragged into the dean's office to talk to police puts us way past hellos."

Tiny droplets of rain beaded on Clara's golden hair and dark jacket. Behind her, an old English garden was tucked away; early shoots jittered on a light breeze, challenging the rain for dominance.

Clara offered an impermeable smile. "They wanted an explosion, and I supplied it," she said.

Ben's life tilted on an axis. Even at the time, he knew that his future would be defined by the before and after of her words. It was Clara's casual and relaxed smile, he would later decide, that had marked the threshold splitting his life in two. Until then, he could pretend that Konrad's death had been a horrible, tragic accident, born of ill chance or fate. After, there was no more pretending. Whether it had been deliberate or misfortune was irrelevant; a man's death had been no more than a game to Clara.

Ben opened his mouth. Words jammed in his throat. Clara didn't need to say more. In an instant, the black-and-white world that he'd been living in shattered into lurid color. The truth was in the shrug of her shoulders. Konrad had been a pawn.

Ben felt a fiery blade sink into his stomach.

Clara had lied to him. Had probably always been lying to him.

The week before, Ben had finally confronted Clara. Direct talk had died down at the Militant Animal meetings, but rumors continued, snippets of what-ifs and why-nots circulated in hushed conversations. Clara often at the center of discussion, Grace on the edges. He'd worried about the plans that Clara had printed out. What if they fell into more radical hands?

"Clara, this is getting nuts," he'd said in a lowered voice, sitting across from her in some no-name diner. "They can't be serious about getting violent. It's too much."

She'd held his hand, told him things would never go that far.

"Ben, you worry too much," she'd said. "It's just talk, a way to rile up some passions and reenergize a little purpose in this group. Nothing's going to come of it. I mean, you don't actually think that I would make an explosive, do you? That Grace would? You know us better than that."

But he hadn't. Ben had so badly wanted to believe Clara's words that he'd swallowed them whole, like cotton candy at a summer fair, sweet and sticky and full of nothing.

It was hard to think as Clara's haughty gaze swept over him now, Konrad's friends and family only a few feet away, mourning a loss they would never be able to comprehend. The accident details hadn't yet been released to the public, but they would be, and someone would have to pay.

"Tell me you're joking. Tell me you didn't actually do this," Ben said, ashamed of the plea in his voice.

"Oh, I didn't do this," Clara said, smiling at her little joke. "We did it."

She giggled, as if a man hadn't been blown up and the police weren't looking for the people responsible.

"Don't you remember, Ben?" Clara said, the lightness in her tone so jarring, Ben started to wonder whether her mind was all there. "You said I would make a far better president of Militant Animals than Konrad. That it was someone else's turn."

Once again, Ben struggled for words. He had said that, encouraged her to chase her potential. But that had been months ago, when they were new and lost in the delicacies of a budding relationship. Talk of violence had still been a long way off and not even a consideration at the time.

"You should see your face right now. The fake gawk is really not attractive," Clara said.

Of course, he'd also fooled himself into believing that Clara and Grace's plan had been all hypotheticals and hyperbole. But deep down, in the darker part of his soul that he refused to recognize, he knew. He'd always known.

"I didn't know anything about—"

"Did you forget about your little experiment, Ben?" Her voice was casual, but the words were sharpened blades. She held a photo of a crude mechanism sitting on the battered kitchen table of his basement apartment.

Fear and regret bloomed as the possibility of his innocence vanished. Clara knew.

Too smart for his own good, his mother used to tell him with a playful ruffle of his hair. Oh, how Ben wished she'd been wrong.

After being dismissed from Grace's apartment like a child, Ben had wanted to impress Clara, to have her look at him as an equal in mind and strength. So, he'd found the plans she and Grace had been slavering over and gathered the materials. They'd been readily available at the hardware store and one of the university chemistry labs, visited late at night.

Ben then set about making a bomb in his kitchen as easily as following a recipe.

When it was done, he'd stepped back to admire it, and just like Dr. Frankenstein, he was horrified by what he'd created. The implications doubled him over as he realized the line he'd crossed. The next day after classes, he'd dismantled it into pieces and disposed of the remains. Clara must have stopped by his apartment while he was out.

Ben was smart enough to know he had played the fool. He might not have known the details, but he knew something was happening, and he had wanted to be a part of it. In that need, he'd delivered his own doom to her, a quiet acceptance of what was to come.

"Aren't you going to ask me why I went through with it?" Clara said, a ringing shot in the quiet yard.

Ben stared at her, unable to decipher this new game. He couldn't catch up. He felt a burn in his chest, like the slow crawl of fire along his windpipe. All he could do was mimic her.

"Why?" he croaked out.

"Your precious Grace."

Ben's confusion was real, but underlying it, he was beginning to understand. He looked past Clara to the funeral home. Bodies moved on the other side of the wall so close and so far away from where he was.

"I didn't think she'd go along with it at first," she said. "I really didn't. She liked to talk a big game, but when it came down to it, I never thought she'd actually agree to it. I just liked stirring the pot a little."

Ben looked up to the dull gray sky. Though there wasn't a stitch of a breeze on the ground, high above, the clouds tore through the air, escaping the tedium of human frailty on a jet stream. With every fiber of his being, he wanted to scream at her, to wrap his hands around her lily-thin neck and squeeze until all the lies eked out of her like pus out of a wound. But he couldn't.

"It really was just a bit of harmless speculation. At first. And then she and Konrad broke up. And, well, you know what they say about a woman scorned, don't you? Grace wanted to get back at Konrad."

Every word Clara spoke was like a fresh stab wound. It took everything Ben had to stand upright, to face her.

Clara took a breath, turning her gaze to the budding garden.

"If it makes you feel better, I didn't know Konrad would be there. I really didn't. It's a regret. Maybe she was the one who told him about it?"

The *she* came out of her mouth like a dagger.

"Then again," she said softly, "I didn't know I'd find an expensive music box in your apartment either."

The music box? What did that have to do with any of this? Ben searched her face. He felt like he was trapped in a waking nightmare, poised for the next random neuron firing to send him spinning wildly off course. His stomach flamed.

"The funny thing is, I was so touched when I found it, sitting on your desk, plain as day. I thought it was a gift for me. But it wasn't, was it?" Clara stood like a statue, only her eyes moving as she watched the trees sway behind Ben. "It was for her. And that was not part of the equation."

"What equation?" Ben said.

"There's always an equation, Ben. And you changed the variables."

"Clara," Ben said, hearing the desperation in his own voice. "You have this totally wrong. I was holding that for Konrad."

The desperation clawed at his throat. He was in a maze of words, knew there was a way out, but couldn't find an opening.

"Save it." The wild-animal snarl in her voice terrified him. "You can't help anyone with more lies."

"Clara, this is insane. You have to turn yourself in to the police. I'll help you. We'll tell them it was an accident. You didn't mean for anyone to get hurt."

"God, you're an idiot." Clara gave a cruelty-laced laugh. "If I go down, your precious Grace comes with me. She might not have been there when it happened, but she's as much a part of this as I am."

Ben watched a bead of rain pool at Clara's temple and slip across her face. For the first time in his life, he understood the overwhelming desire to physically harm another person.

He looked to the building beside him, where Grace, along with others, was mourning, and held his tongue.

"Nothing to say, huh?" Clara said, her lip curling upward. "You'll take me to the police but not her. It's always been about her, hasn't it? I thought I could change things. I really did." The conversational tone was jarring. "But I see my mistake now. I couldn't compete with the hold that she has on you."

For just a moment, Ben saw the depths of anger in her eyes. Her fists had curled into tight little balls, while her whole body challenged him to deny it.

He couldn't.

Clara turned away from him and walked up the driveway toward whatever fate awaited her.

Ben watched her go, at a loss for what to do next. Only one thought had settled in his mind, clear and smooth as water—if he had to decide between saving Clara or saving Grace and himself, it wasn't even a contest.

Twenty years later, Ben stood facing Grace Hobbes, as if history were repeating itself in a twisted caricature. He still hadn't found the right words to excuse his actions back then, even though he'd spent a lifetime trying to make up for them.

Though he'd tried to deny it at the time, the core of his conscience had known that Clara had been pulling them all into something ugly, and he'd welcomed it. His sin was that he'd chosen to look away and let it play out.

"I didn't hurt Konrad, Emma. And you know that," Ben said, looking up at Emma Meadows. His feet sank deeper into the softening snow. "You were my friends. You and Konrad."

The name Emma felt foreign and uncomfortable on his tongue. She would always be Grace to him.

"I know you always thought I was stupid, Ben, but did you really think I was that naive?"

Emma's voice had deepened with age. He heard the years, along with her own lifetime of regret. He also felt an unsteady vibration, like the low warning rumble of distant thunder. Emma tilted her head, her eyes narrowing as if studying the shape of him. She straightened her shoulders, coming to her full height, and didn't so much smile as bare her teeth.

He noticed the golden retriever beside her tense, its tail dropping and its eyes trained on Ben.

"Did you think I wouldn't find out the truth?" Emma said.

A sickening confusion kicked at his gut. The truth about what? Ben might have looked away, but Emma had been the one to let herself be pulled into Clara's demented web, had been right there with Clara ogling the plans for a homemade explosive like it was a new cake recipe. And she had been the one to go behind her own boyfriend's back when she couldn't convince him that a more drastic protest was needed.

All Ben had ever tried to do was protect her. He reached into the pocket of his coat for his roll of antacids.

"Whoa there, big boy," Emma said, raising her voice.

Just then, a trio of small brown birds spilled over the top of the cabin, trailing a cacophony of trills and whistles. They swooped from the roofline, pulling up when it was clear the yard was not a safe place to land. Instead, they darted and banked toward the trees.

When Ben looked back at Emma, a gun was trained on him.

"Are you fucking kidding me?" he said. Bewilderment and anger melded into a hard ball in his chest. "What do you think is going to happen here?"

"I actually don't know, but I'm guessing not exactly what you thought." Emma's words were ice. "Just tell me why, Ben? Why did you send Konrad to the car that night? You knew what would happen."

Ben's thoughts congealed in his head. It was like having your memory dragged out of you and run through a meat grinder. He looked up at Emma, who let out a dry laugh.

"You can't hide it anymore. I might have been the one to light the fuse by trusting Clara," Emma said. "But you sent Konrad to die."

Ben flitted through his exposed memories, trying to filter and process conversations and plans from years ago. It was like looking through frosted glass: Some images were clear, but time had blurred the details.

"You can stop with the innocent act now. I talked to Clara. She told me. All these years, I've racked my brain. Who could have sent him down there? We both know that if Konrad had found out she was trying to set an explosive, he'd never have let it happen. Now I know the truth. You're the one who told him. And Konrad being Konrad, he must have tried to sto—"

Her bravado faltered, and the arm holding the gun dropped. She pulled in a shaky breath, and the steel gaze she'd had on him earlier weakened. She looked away from Ben, toward the sky, blinking against the brightness she found there.

"He died," she continued. "I don't know if Clara was right and you meant for it to happen or if it was just stupidity on your part. The end result was the same. You're as responsible for Konrad's death as Clara."

Emma stared down at Ben from the porch like a queen surveying her domain. He didn't have words to respond. How could she be so clever and so wrong?

"Now, a lifetime later, you suddenly need to dredge all this up again. So desperate that you stalked a twenty-one-year-old kid all the way into the wilderness. What could possibly be so damn important now, Ben?"

Ben took a step toward Emma.

"Just stay where you are," she said, lifting the gun back up.

"You started this," Ben growled. "Not me. You're the one who concocted some ridiculous plan with Clara, like a couple of schoolgirls playing grown-up. You forget, I was there, Emma. I heard you. Clara might have made it happen, but you plotted right along with her, right up until the end. Clara told me. You wanted to get back at Konrad after the breakup. And then you send me this stupid video of that damn music box. You knew I'd recognize it. What for? Revenge now that Clara's getting out of prison?"

The dog tensed. Ben had almost forgotten it was there. Emma placed her free hand on its head, but the retriever's demeanor didn't change.

"What are you talking about?" she said.

Ben had to hand it to Emma, the look of surprise seemed genuine, but he knew better now. She was a liar, just like Clara. They were one and the same. Jaden hadn't told him outright, but it was obvious that the music box had been in the Meadowses' home. Jaden had seen it.

Ben took a step closer. A wrath he'd buried for over twenty years came hurdling back, landing in his gut so hard he expected to hear a crash. Whatever Clara had done, at least she was paying for it. How dare Emma stand over him now in judgment.

"I didn't send you or anyone a video. That box just showed up at my house. It was you, Ben. Gaslighting me now won't do you any good." Emma raised the gun higher. Her hands shook.

Ben wasn't buying it. Grace was the only one who could have sent that video. It was her music box. He didn't know why she was lying now, and he didn't care.

He kept his eye on the barrel.

Fear and anger were a toxic mix. Both lived in a primitive side of the brain, unleashing epinephrine and cortisol that smothered reason. Misunderstandings and miscommunications thrived in that space, gorging on confusion until all you could hear was the sound of your own voice. Ben didn't hear Emma's words. He didn't care about her confusion or explanations or excuses. She might have a gun now, but she'd been holding a blade over his life for twenty years.

Grace and Clara had forced him down a lifelong path of redemption for a death he'd failed to stop. And now, Grace had sent him a reminder through the music box, to what end? Or did she lure him into the woods to shoot him? Kill him in this desolate wilderness?

No, Ben thought. *This ends here.* He lunged for the gun.

Chapter 37

Jaden

Jaden recognized the gun. It had belonged to her grandfather.

Grandad had kept a pistol at the cabin, mostly to scare away any bears that might wander too close. It was kept locked in a safe in the back bedroom, the same one her mom had slept in the night before.

When Jaden was younger, Grandad had hauled out the gun one cloudy afternoon and given her a firearm lesson. They'd shot at soup cans lined up along the back of the property. Jaden had missed every single one. Predictably, her mom had been furious when she found out. Into what had been a quiet summer afternoon, she'd reamed off statistics on gun-related deaths. When she gave the number of children killed every year by guns, the enormity had burned itself into Jaden's memory. At eleven years old, she considered the idea that children could be killed a foreign language.

Watching her mom step out into blinding sunlight with a gun in her hand, Jaden felt the same surreal flush as her eleven-year-old self. Another thought, dark and twisted, burbled up from a new understanding of her family: Jaden might have known that Emma Meadows would never touch a gun, but she had no idea about Grace Hobbes.

Jaden heard her mother tell Ben he wasn't getting in the cabin just as she eased the trapdoor closed over her head, muffling the voices. She waited, letting her eyes adjust in the dimness. It was dark, but pricks of light came in between the floorboards and through the cracked wooden door. Even without that, Jaden could have made her way to the rear door without difficulty. She just hoped it wasn't padlocked.

Her backpack, with her phone and the music box inside, was slung over her shoulders as she picked her way over the uneven dirt floor. She paused long enough to snag a pair of snowshoes. Her plan was to circle around to the road by trekking through the woods. The cell signal was usually stronger about five hundred meters up the road. If her mom could keep Ben busy for long enough, Jaden could call the police and end this.

The rear cellar door loomed in front of her. She shoved. Nothing.

The door didn't give.

Panic washed over her as she ran her hands along the jamb, looking for a latch. Her fingers found nothing. She thought about kicking at it but worried the noise would warn Ben. Above her own labored breath, she caught snippets of raised voices, too muffled to make out any words.

When she heard the gunshot, all thoughts of caution fled. She rammed her shoulder into the door and felt the ice give on the other side. A rush of brittle air filled her struggling lungs.

She scrambled up the cellar stairs, jammed her feet into snowshoes, and ran.

Jaden bolted for the trees. The snowshoes made her steps awkward, but it was better than postholing through the calf-deep snow. She felt metal punch through the icy crust. She tried to listen as she ran, but panic obliterated all sound other than her heaving breaths. Her mind skittered until one thought landed like a wallop—Ben Chalmers was here to kill them, and she needed to get help.

Her pace slowed at the tree line. The forest was thick behind the cottage. She knew the hazards that lived in a winter wood—deep snow wells around trees capable of swallowing you whole or saplings that punched through the snow like snares. She needed to move carefully. When she finally stopped to catch her breath, it was silent. Too silent.

As her heart slowed, Jaden realized she was wrong. It wasn't quiet at all. Life continued around her, scarcely aware of her or the drama that was unfolding: Sparrows chattered from the trees, dry leaves rustled on the wind, a crow sounded off as it passed overhead.

Jaden had no idea what the gunshot meant. Had it been a warning, or had one of them been hit? She silently pleaded that her mom was OK. Ben Chalmers stood between her and the car. Even if she had the keys, there would have been no way for her to get to it without him seeing. She had to get to the top of the road and call 911. There was no other choice.

Her only option was to make a big arc through the woods. Going northeast would take her near the snowmobile trail, somewhere among the trees. She guessed that was the direction Ben had come from, since he'd approached from the side of the cottage. She couldn't risk crossing his path. That only left southeast, toward the lake. If she could follow the shoreline, she knew of a deer path through the woods. It would be a hike up steep terrain to get to the road, but better than trying to bushwhack through dense forest. At the road, she should be able to get a strong-enough signal on her phone.

Her mind had a plan, but her body had other ideas. She willed herself to move. There was no response. Fear had shut down the synapses between her brain and legs.

What happened to fight or flight, she thought, unable to convince her body to do either.

Suddenly, a bang echoed off the trees, as wood slammed against wood. Someone, probably Chalmers, had just smashed open the front door of the cabin.

There it is, thought Jaden as her legs jumped and propelled her body toward the lake.

Chapter 38

Emma

Emma lay on cold ground, felt only pain where a bullet had torn through flesh. She heard, rather than felt, the short, rapid breaths that were causing her chest to rabbit up and down. Winnie was barking, the sound harsh against the soft blue sky. She could see the cabin but couldn't decipher the orientation—the stairs off kilter, the red roof perpendicular to the sky, the door hanging the wrong way—until she realized she was on her side, looking up at the world.

With effort, she managed to right herself. Emma was sitting in a pool of pink melted snow, wondering where the color had come from, until she noticed the blood dripping between her fingers. She'd been shot. Emma remembered Ben lunging toward her, his face twisted in anger and pain, Winnie barking and jumping against her, and then the pain of a thousand suns slicing through her.

She looked around to an empty yard. Ben wasn't in her sight line.

Jaden was still in the cabin.

Emma tried to stand, but her legs wouldn't obey. She was present enough to know that she was probably in shock but had no capacity to overcome it.

She'd failed her daughter just as she'd failed so many others. The thought was an agony.

It hadn't taken Ben long to find the trapdoor. The cottage was small, and with the rear door left wide open, cold air and light would have poured in through the cellar and up through the floorboards. Emma watched him march out of the cottage, circle around the porch toward the back, where she guessed tracks would have led across the back field, and into the woods.

"Damn it," Ben yelled, the sound echoing against the sky.

He strode back to the front of the cabin, stood on the porch, and stared down at her, frustration, anger, and something indecipherable lingering in his eyes. He turned away from her as he pulled a cell phone from his coat pocket. She wanted to hear, but her ears were filled with the sound of her own heartbeat and the gasps she couldn't get under control. She felt Winnie at her side, her warm coat welcome but not enough, never enough.

Was Ben calling Clara? Bringing her here to watch the end of a tragedy that had started twenty years before.

The cabin blurred, darkness edging the image. She was falling. There was no hiding this time. She felt the blackness, welcomed it. It was her due.

The last thing she saw was Ben coming toward her, the gun still in his hand.

And then nothing.

Chapter 39

Ben

Grace Hobbes lay at his feet. A bullet had gone through her shoulder and lodged in a tree twenty feet behind her. He could see the sharp jab of her chest as she clawed for air and her enlarged pupils that blocked out the chocolate of her eyes. He tried to take her pulse, but the dog lay beside Grace, watching Ben's movements and growling if he got too close.

Blood seeped into the snow.

Jaden had left the cabin through a cellar door at the back. He'd seen her snowshoe tracks and knew he couldn't follow. The snow was too deep. Still, he had to stop her from doing something stupid and couldn't let Emma get in the way.

He made a call.

Ben scanned the horizon. He didn't understand the terrain, but his job had taught him how to read people. The land dropped sharply behind the cabin into the woods. He'd trudged through the forests getting here and knew the trees were thick and unyielding, even with snowshoes. Jaden would want to get to easier terrain and make her way to the road. Maybe with the hopes of getting to a neighbor's or flagging down a car.

His eyes fell on the lake, frozen, barren, and wide open.

It was a gamble, but one he was willing to take.

Chapter 40

Jaden

"Shit," Jaden whispered as a branch whipped past her. She touched her neck, saw a thin line of blood on her finger.

She veered right, heading deeper into the forest and farther away from the road. From him. She heard labored breaths behind her ear. Spun around. Only to learn it was her own breathing she'd heard, echoed against the panic in her chest.

She had no doubt Chalmers would follow her tracks, but her options were few. Take off the snowshoes and lose precious seconds or keep going. Without snowshoes, his going would be slower, losing ground with every step as he sank into almost knee-deep snow. She weaved again, cutting closer than she should beside trees. Her feet created a wild-goose chase in the snow. If she drew him in far enough, she could double back and cut across the lake farther along. Maybe the trail would confuse him enough to buy the time she needed to get to the road.

Twice, she tripped, landing awkwardly, and scrabbled to get enough purchase to stand back up. Each step uphill slid back maddeningly. Her legs screamed for release. The sun careening off the snow blinded her, forcing her to squint every time she looked to the horizon. Still, she ran.

Finally, when she felt like she'd pulled in her last possible breath, she saw the lake's edge between the trees. She slowed, moving cautiously as the forest thinned. She took a few tentative steps out of the cover of the trees. Listened. The ice was silent beneath her. She felt the lure of the lake. How much easier would it be to cut across open ground?

"Jaden." His voice was close. Too close.

She spun around and almost laughed. Ben wore a neon-pink hunter's cap and canary yellow gloves. He looked like a poorly controlled marionette as he stumbled down the bank toward a small moon-shaped beach skirting the property.

She turned to run.

"Stop," he yelled. The sound echoed against ice and the endless blue. Thinking of the gun, she froze.

There were swaths of red against his cheek, and a cut bled from his eye. Wet snow clung to his dark wool coat. He clambered down the hill toward her, duck stepping and almost tripping before he closed the gap between them.

"Where's my mother?" Jaden said.

"She's OK," Chalmers said, his voice surprisingly calm, given his appearance. "But she's hurt, Jaden. If we don't help her soon, she's going to die."

Jaden took a step backward, Chalmers one forward. He was almost to the edge of the lake.

"I don't believe you."

"That's not my concern right now, Jaden. You're just a kid. This whole thing is bigger than you. And that's OK. I understand. You didn't know what you were getting into. You might not believe me, but I never meant for anyone to get hurt."

Once Chalmers stepped onto the lake, some of her advantage would be gone. Winter winds always thinned the snow on the ice, making snowshoes more hinderance than help on the slick surface. He'd be able to step more easily than in the woods. The sun beamed down.

Jaden could feel it on her face. It had warmed up over the course of the morning. Looking behind Chalmers, Jaden saw that the forest had begun to shed its layers of ice.

As if Mother Nature had heard her thoughts, an icicle dislodged from a tall birch tree and fell plumb straight toward Chalmers. Jaden started running before it landed.

Chapter 41

Ben

Pain like a gunshot ripped through his shoulder and sent Ben crashing to his knees.

He didn't understand what had happened at first. He looked around frantically. Had Emma followed him? Could she have another gun? There was no one there. All he saw was a chunk of ice on the ground beside him about the size of his fist. When he looked back up, Jaden was sprinting across the lake.

His head pounded, and his gut felt like it might explode, but he had to catch her. He ran. It was easier to run across the ice. He didn't have the right footwear, but the snowshoes seemed to be slowing Jaden down as well. He had almost caught up to her. He might have been an old man compared to her, but the hours on the treadmill had to be good for something. He thought about lunging for her, but his hands were numb with cold. He didn't trust his extremities to obey.

Suddenly, she jumped left, darting like a rabbit away from his grasp.

"Jaden," he roared. "That's enough!"

His voice echoed across the lake. She stopped about twenty feet away from him, near the shore of the cottage's small bay. He could see the red roof, smoke still drifting from the chimney. There was no sign of Emma. He didn't need her interfering now.

"It's over," Ben said with a rasp.

Jaden stood staring at him like a caged bird, her eyes wide with fear. She snuck a glance behind herself. When she looked back at Ben, he saw realization dawn in her eyes. Her mother might be wounded. She couldn't outrun him. There was no way out of this.

Chapter 42

Jaden

Jaden allowed herself to fully look at the man who had been stalking her. He was easily over six feet tall and had a savage curl to his lips as he sucked in air. The ridiculous hat and oversize clown-like gloves did nothing to hide the hard line of his jaw and the nostrils flaring in shuddered breaths.

Years ago, Jaden had come across a bear in this same spot, a hungry juvenile drawn by the scent of an easy meal in the garbage bins by the road. Her body had reacted in the same way it was now—heart skipping beats, muscles clenched, every instinct telling her to run even though her mind knew that she needed to stand her ground and look stronger than she was.

"I know what you think," Chalmers said, his words truncated by deep inhales. "Emma's told you I'm the bad guy. That I had something to do with Konrad Sharma's death. It was never like that."

"To hell it wasn't," Jaden said.

Her mother's name on his lips ignited her anger. She took a step back. Jaden needed to keep him talking, keep him distracted.

"You're a murderer," she said with as much venom as she could muster.

Chalmers dropped his head. He was quiet for so long Jaden wondered if the blow from the ice chunk had been to his head. She snuck a look at the ice beneath their feet. There. Just under a snow-free patch. The shoreline took a sudden drop here, affecting the water flow. It wasn't a strong current, but enough to make the ice weaker.

When Chalmers finally spoke and took a step toward her, there was menace in his voice.

"What the hell do you know? You're twenty-one years old. I am so sick of stupid self-righteousness. Every idiot thinks they're making the world a better place by marching or writing in pathetic little student newspapers. You really don't get it, do you? Konrad was the problem. Your mother was the problem. All of you people thinking you're doing good but leaving nothing but harm in your wake. Telling yourselves the end justifies the means. Do you honestly think your mother was just a flower child? Maybe she didn't plant that device, but she made all of us vulnerable to it. She left him out there like a lamb in a wolf's den. And now she's dredging it all up to drag us back there. Why? I don't know, maybe she thinks she's doing what's right, but she's not. She never was. And this whole thing needs to end, one way or another."

Jaden felt tears, unbidden, start to fall. Within his anger and vitriol, she could see that this man truly believed her mother was dangerous, and menace lay in the flare of his nostrils and the cold fury in his voice. In the face of her tears, his anger lost some of its momentum; the edges of it softened, but stony notes remained.

"Hey, no, no, no. Don't cry, Jaden. It's going to be OK. I really don't want to hurt you or Emma. Look, I've called an ambulance for your mom. Help's on the way. They should be here in the next ten minutes. All I want is for this to go away."

"Why? Why is this fucking box so important?"

Jaden was crying in earnest now, sloppy, wet tears, and her nose dripped. She wiped at the snot with her sleeve, feeling like a child lost in the woods.

"The God's honest truth, I don't know," Chalmers said, his shoulders dropping. "I didn't start this. This whole mess was started by Clara Morel over twenty years ago. I was just young and stupid enough to go along for a while. And I thought I had put an end to it. I'm the one who turned Clara in to the police. I told them what happened. I'm the reason she went to jail."

"Bullshit," Jaden said, the word burbling up from her chest like bile. "I did the research. Your name never came up."

Chalmers dropped his head, and she heard a soft scoff.

"I was nineteen. Younger than you are now. My parents didn't want me testifying in open court. All the cops needed was a signed affidavit that they could enter as witness testimony. I was never called at the trial."

The earnestness in his voice was disarming. His body, previously coiled, loosened as he spoke, his arms flapping at his side, like a little boy frustrated by the answers.

"Why are you here? You knew my mom decades ago. Why now, after all this time? Why didn't you just leave us alone?"

Jaden's words were stuttered and childlike, forced out between shaky inhales.

"I would have, but your mom sent me a video of that music box just before Christmas," he said. There was an ache in his voice that Jaden was starting to believe.

Jaden wiped at her face with a sleeve.

"You have to believe me," he said, his voice sliding into a plea. "I was just a dumb kid. I knew Clara was stirring up talk, but she told me it was all a game. I should have stopped it, talked her out of it or called the police. I know that now. I saw the signs, but I ignored them. I didn't want to believe. And I've built a whole life trying to make up for that one mistake."

He told her a truth but held back the parts of himself that he'd tried so desperately to bury. What good would come from this child knowing the insignificant, if cowardly, role he'd played in Konrad's death and the aftermath. Konrad's death was one of the reasons he'd joined CSIS. He thought a career with the good guys could make up for some of the damage he'd help cause.

"It might not seem like it to you," he said, "but I'm a by the book kind of guy. I've helped track down terrorists and pedophiles. None of it can make up for Konrad's death, but I've tried my best to live the life he would have expected."

His anger had quieted. Ben's hands rested at his side, palms out. His breathing was slow and labored. The snarl in his lips had smoothed out, and he squinted against the sun that had now fully cleared the trees.

"I've been good at my job," he said. "Methodical, committed, fair. I've built a life, a happy life, despite everything. I have a wife, two beautiful kids. I just want to live it. The records were sealed because I was so young. If it all came out now, and if the internet got a hold of it, I could be skewered as the jilted boyfriend. I could lose everything. My job, my family, my life, all because of one stupid, childish mistake."

Jaden didn't know what to think. Maybe he was right. She thought about all the lies her mother had told her, the life she'd hidden away for years. Maybe it was better to end this now? She wanted to believe him.

As her panic subsided, thoughts came to her like bubbles trapped in the ice.

The phone call from Clara, her mom's face when she saw the music box on Christmas Day, the whole twisted history of Militant Animals. The pieces added up but awkwardly, like a large center was still missing. Clara was serving time for the explosion, but someone had sent Konrad there that night. Jaden was trapped in a triangle of lies between three people, and it was impossible to decipher the truth.

Ben had said he'd received the video the week before Christmas. It didn't add up, she thought, looking at his blanched face, his lips starting to show signs of blue from the cold. Could he be lying still? After all, he'd lied to his family, his employer, probably even to his friends about his past. Just like her mother.

Uncertainty and fear battered against her.

With her eyes trained on Ben, Jaden slipped the backpack straps off her shoulder and gently set it on the ice.

"You want this thing so badly," she said. "You can have it."

She slowly opened the bag. Inside, her phone and the music box lay side by side. There were no bars on the phone. Worse, a red exclamation point made it clear the text she'd typed out earlier hadn't been delivered. There was no signal. She hadn't gotten close enough.

The next thoughts galloped over Jaden, sending her stomach plummeting. If there was no signal, how could Ben have called an ambulance for her mom like he said? And if he had, there was no way the ambulance could only be ten minutes away. The nearest emergency unit was a forty-five-minute drive. He was lying.

She looked up toward where Ben stood just in time to see his hand slip into the pocket of his coat. Through the material, she could see him wrap his fingers around something. An image of the gun in her mom's hand flashed through her mind, the memory of the earth-rattling gunshot from earlier flooding her ears.

"Jaden. We have to go," Ben said. "Your mom needs help."

Jaden lifted the music box from the bag. It caught the sun, and a sliver of a rainbow danced on a patch of snow. Carefully, she took a couple of steps forward and set the box down. With the snowshoes, her weight was evenly distributed, but you never could be sure with unstable ice.

She stepped away, taking advantage of Ben's focus on the box to move closer to the shore.

"You want this stupid box. Here it is," Jaden said.

She watched the ice beneath his feet. They were about twenty feet away from the shoreline. She knew what could happen if they both weren't careful. He stepped forward. The ice held.

"It's not about the music box. I just wanted to talk to your mom," he said. He crouched to pick it up. Jaden saw his hand, still in his coat pocket, begin to slide out. In her mind's eye, she saw the tip of the gun's grip against dark wool.

Jaden ran.

"Wait," Ben called and started to follow her, but it was too late. He'd moved too sharply.

Jaden heard the crack, like thunder against the quiet morning.

And then a splash. Without looking back, she knew that the ice had broken open under Ben's feet and he had gone through. She ran until she reached the shore and then turned around.

He was scrambling, his hands clawlike against the ice. His face was white. By his thrashing, she could tell he was trying to find purchase to hoist himself up, but the drop there was too deep.

A guttural scream rose from him, echoing itself over the lake until her heart matched the rhythm. She moved closer, stepping carefully onto the ice. If she didn't help him, he was going to drown.

His movements became more wooden and grotesque. Jaden thought of an infant, its limbs moving randomly and gawkily as it explored the range of its body. She couldn't look away. She threw off her snowshoes and dropped to her belly, inching over the ice. When she got close enough, his hand—as cold as the water but still viselike—clamped onto her wrist and started to pull her forward. She tried to scrabble back, but had no leverage on the ice, her feet slid uselessly.

Panic rose in her. Ben's mouth tried to form words, but nothing came out. A roar filled her ears as his arm tried to haul his body up, using her as a faulty anchor. She lurched forward, hands sinking into water cold as death.

Her eyes met his, and in them, she saw a fear and desperation that obliterated all meaning in the world. In that moment, she knew he would drag her down to save himself. And that told her everything.

She rolled, twisting her arm loose from his wet and slackening grip. She continued to roll until trees appeared in her sight line and she knew she'd found hard land again. On her back, the sky gazed down on her, impossibly blue.

She lay panting, willing her body to get up and run, but panic had hold of her now. It lay in every muscle of her body, like sludge as her lungs begged for more air. When she could finally move, she rolled onto her hands and knees, unwilling to risk standing up in case she'd misjudged and was still on ice. She saw Chalmers then, his hands scrabbling on the ice, causing deeper fissures, expanding the black hole around him. She opened her mouth to yell at him to take off the wool coat that had absorbed too much water, to wriggle onto his belly like a seal and drag himself over the ice. But then she remembered the cold, steellike grip of his hands as he had tried to drag her down to save himself.

His head went under once. He broke the surface again with a look of terror as he gasped for life-giving air. She met his pleading eyes, held them for a breath, and then looked up to that painfully clear blue sky.

When she looked back, realization spread across his face like a stain. He was dying, and Jaden could do nothing about it. She may have imagined it. Trauma can, after all, create wishful thinking. But for a moment, just before he went under for the last time, Jaden thought she saw him smile.

In the silence that followed, Jaden pushed herself to her knees, sobbing. She grabbed at lungfuls of air as if she were the one drowning.

In the distance, she heard the faint wail of a siren.

Chapter 43

Ben

Ben was still trying to understand the source of a loud crackling noise when the world dropped out from beneath him.

He fell. His entire body gasped, allowing water to slide through his lips and scorch his windpipe with cold. He managed to keep his head above water, but the pain came next. His nerves announcing their presence as if the water itself had jagged teeth gnawing at his skin. Breath was short and sharp. The edges of his vision started to darken, not yet a pinprick but moving that way.

He willed himself to stop the fight long enough to take in his surroundings. He'd heard of cold shock and knew it was the panic that most often killed you.

After he had nearly pulled her in, the girl had rolled out of reach, her head touching earth, while her feet remained on the ice. She lay on her back, unmoving. He could see the rise and fall of her chest. He timed his breathing to hers, letting it slow as he regained control.

When breath was no longer debilitating, he clawed at the ice to pull himself up, kicking his legs and using the ice for ballast. The sickening crack came again, and this time, he knew what to expect. He felt his body flail for a heartbeat and then plunge as if hooks were pulling him down. He submerged. Water seeped into his mouth, searing his windpipe with cold.

He kicked harder and resurfaced. Water stung his eyes and nose. He hadn't inhaled, but still it found its way in, seeking to choke the life out of him.

He grabbed again at the ice, but his hands no longer obeyed his will. His kicks were growing weaker, each one taking more out of him than he had left to give. His teeth chattered so hard, he thought they might crack.

Time neither sped up nor froze. The very concept of it fled his mind. Whether he had been in the water for seconds or minutes, he couldn't have said.

Ben met the girl's eyes then. She'd rolled onto her hands and knees and was staring back at him, his own fear and desperation mirrored in the face of a child. Shame and anger slammed into him harder than the cold. He knew. She could do nothing to help him.

Jaden sat back and turned her gaze to the painfully blue sky.

Her body shuddered convulsively, and he heard the faintest murmurs of *I'm sorry* above his own thrashing and wild heartbeat. He strained to hear, silencing his body, and was relieved that his teeth had stopped their rattling.

It was true what they said, epiphanies speak louder when facing death. Ben understood now. How could he not. Years ago, he had sacrificed a woman who thought she loved him to save himself. He had lived within the embrace of the lie that he'd done it for Grace, but he knew better now. Watching the girl disintegrate in front of him, he understood that he would have dragged her to hell if it would have saved his own skin.

A reluctant peace came without admission. A recognition of who he was—who he'd always been—even though he tried to deny it. He didn't know whether Clara or Grace had sent the music box and the threat, but it didn't matter. Justice had come for him. And he was willing to submit.

He allowed himself a deep breath, felt it spread through his body like golden honey. Warmth filled him then. A burning that grew from his chest until ice and snow were forgotten, and his mind's eye saw a sand-soaked beach under a setting sun. He saw them then.

His family.

His wife, burying her toes in the sand. The kids running in and out of the waves, laughing. The sun caressed his face. Mary turned to him, her smile filling his eyes, and beckoned him over to her.

He smiled back.

And let go.

Chapter 44

Jaden

Jaden dove back onto the ice. She crawled toward the gaping hole, spreading her weight and praying for a miracle. Her mind screamed it was too late, but despairing hope drove her forward. She reached the edge of the scarred ice, looked down, and saw only black, unforgiving water. Ben Chalmers was gone.

She couldn't have said how long she knelt in the snow, shivering and holding vigil over the man who had terrorized her for the last few days. When the paramedics found her, she was voiceless with shock and her clothes sodden. They carried her out of the woods on a stretcher, but her mind remained on the side of the lake, fixated on Ben's smile just before the water swallowed him.

Her mother was conscious and OK, a paramedic told her as they slid Jaden's stretcher into a waiting ambulance. She kept her eyes fixed on the tops of the trees, which shed ice shards, sparkling like confetti on the waiting snow. No need to worry, the bullet had passed cleanly through, they said. Jaden would see her mom at the hospital.

The next few hours passed in flashed images, as if she were looking through an old View-Master with its carousel of pictures: wheeling into the Sault Ste. Marie hospital on a stretcher, the smell of exhaust from the ambulance bay, an emergency room nurse arranging to call Jaden's dad.

The relentless cacophony of the hospital—erratic pulses of nearby monitors, chattering voices, the clatter of doors and equipment—hammered at the back of Jaden's skull. After hours in the hush of the woods, her body was overloaded by sound and the sickening smells of disinfectant and disease.

Eventually, she was wheeled into a private room where her mom lay beneath a stiff white sheet, arm wrapped tightly against her chest in a sling. The bullet had passed through her shoulder, ripping cartilage and flesh and leaving behind a crimson pool on the snow.

A survivable wound, the doctor had called it. Jaden wasn't sure what survival meant anymore.

When an OPP officer came by to meet with them, her mother did most of the talking. Jaden filled in the blanks about her encounter with Chalmers down by the lake. Emma Meadows told most of the truth. She left out the parts about her connection to a man who'd died over twenty years earlier and the music box that had started it all.

Ben Chalmers, she said, was a lonely man whose pathological obsession with a long-lost crush had ruined him. He had been stalking her daughter and tracked Jaden to the family cottage in the hopes of getting to Emma. The gun had belonged to her father-in-law, her mom said, and she only meant to scare Ben with it. It went off accidently when he lunged for her. The family dog had jumped up in the melee, causing them both to lose their balance and the gun to go off.

"Seems Winnie is smarter than all of us," her mom said. The dog was being held by local animal control but had come through the confrontation unhurt.

The officer nodded ambiguously, taking down more details and warning them that follow-up would be likely, but for now, they could rest.

Local police had reached out to the Canadian Security Intelligence Service, but there was no record that Ben Chalmers had been working in an official capacity. As far as his boss knew, he had taken a few personal-leave days. There would be an investigation to see what, if any, protocols had been broken. A team from the Ontario Search and Rescue would drag the lake in the next day or two, but recovery was expected to be difficult. Apparently, there was a current where he'd gone under, and Chalmers's body had been carried off. It was possible they'd need to wait until the ice melted. No one seemed to have a sense of urgency.

When her dad arrived that night, Jaden watched her mom break down in earnest for the first time. She clung to her husband as if her life depended on keeping him beside her. Maybe it did. Jaden didn't really know what to think anymore about her parents' marriage, her mother, or even herself. Every time she closed her eyes, she saw Ben Chalmers's face, the second before he went under, a sad slip of a smile on his lips.

Jaden had been discharged with minor injuries, but the doctor wanted to keep her mom overnight.

"Better to make sure there's no infection while you're still with us," he said, with a tinge of a foreign accent Jaden couldn't place. "Not the best place to spend the remainder of the holidays, I'm afraid, but better than a return trip to the hospital later."

The doctor gave Jaden and her dad a polite little nod before leaving the room.

"I love his accent," her mother said after the doctor was out of earshot. "It's like he's always a little surprised."

Her father chuckled, though Jaden could see worry in the stoop of his shoulders and the deep lines between his eyebrows.

Mark Meadows hadn't had a clue that his wife and daughter were up at the family cabin, nor had he ever heard the name Ben Chalmers before.

Because it was a holiday week, he'd still been in custody waiting for the paperwork to sort itself out when the White Falls detachment had gotten a call from the Sault Ste. Marie hospital. They hadn't been able to reach him by phone so were enlisting the help of the local police to locate him. Jaden would later learn more about why O'Shea had cuffed him. He upended a table in the interview room, a moment of lost control that spoke more to her dad's fears than his character.

Jaden looked at her mother, unable to articulate the emotions that warred inside her. Who was this woman she had known her whole life? A few hours ago, her mom had confronted a man with a gun in her hand, and now, she was joking about the doctor's accent. Jaden dropped into the room's only guest chair and put her head in her hands.

She felt her dad's hand, firm and warm, on her shoulder. It was some comfort. Her family was safe, together again. Still, every time she closed her eyes, Ben's face came back to her along with the wail of sirens.

One troubling thought resurfaced like a stick caught in the eddy of her mind: Ben Chalmers hadn't been lying. He had called an ambulance. Why would he have done that if he wanted Jaden and her mother dead?

Chapter 45

Emma

Emma's heart tore open when she looked at her daughter. Jaden sat on a hard plastic chair beside the hospital bed with her head in her hands, a little girl, lost in a big, bad, terrible world.

"You know," Emma said to Mark after the doctor had left. "I'm actually hungry, but this hospital food is pretty bad. Is there any way you could find something a little more appetizing than green Jell-O for us?"

Mark, who had listened to the story of the last few days with a look of disbelief, jumped at the chance to do something, anything. His habitual disheveled look had been amped up, leaving his unwashed hair to reach newer heights. Emma was pretty sure he hadn't eaten in days. He stood beside the bed, a sentinel watching over the women he had nearly lost.

Emma knew he had questions and his own story to tell about the last few days. She'd heard the broad strokes, including that her car had been photographed in the parking lot of a small cottage resort a little west of White Falls. Emma barely remembered turning in there, but then again, she hadn't remembered much about the strange drive that had taken her away from her life. She'd driven in a sort of trance that day. Her only thought, to remove the danger to her family, even if that danger was because of her.

The next day, Mark had also turned in to the same parking lot while out looking for her. It was impossible to calculate the random decisions and coincidences that had to have lined up for both photographs to have been taken. Confirmation bias and a recent break-in at one of the resort's cottages had done the rest. Blood found on the kitchen counter had also amped up suspicion. In the end, the blood was linked to whoever had broken in a rear window, cutting themselves in the process. The police were satisfied that neither Mark nor Emma had been inside the cabin.

"Say no more," Mark said as he grabbed for his coat. He squeezed Emma's shoulder and gave Jaden a kiss on the head as he passed. He was out the door before Emma could blink.

"Your father. Forty-six years old and still can't stop moving to save his life."

Jaden gawped at her.

"Sorry. Poor choice of words," Emma said.

A nurse came in humming. She checked Emma's vitals and flitted about the room on squeaky rubber soles before writing in the chart. Emma glared at her, waiting for a chance to talk to her daughter alone. When the door finally closed behind the nurse, Emma breathed in the smell of antiseptic and suffering and began down a path that had no end.

"I owe you an explanation," Emma said.

"No, not an explanation. The truth." Jaden's words were brittle and cutting.

If only the truth existed, thought Emma.

It was simpler when you were twenty-one and life was easily divided into right and wrong. There was no truth in any of this. Only points of view. Emma looked toward the window and saw her pale, distorted reflection against a darkening world outside.

"I was partially responsible for Konrad's death. Clara and I both had been pushing for more impactful protests," Emma said. She owed her child at least this much. "I thought we were being overlooked. The media had found us cute at first, but you know what they say about today's sweetheart. We'd been putting in all this effort, but nothing was changing. I believed we could do more."

Jaden, elbows propped on her knees and eyes downcast, looked like a dimming light fading in an incoming storm. If only Emma could still protect her daughter, like she'd protected her from the monsters in her closet when she was little. But this wasn't make-believe anymore. Jaden needed to understand that monsters could come from without and within and that protecting those you loved sometimes meant protecting them from yourself and your bad decisions.

"Konrad was charming and charismatic," Emma said. "People were drawn to him instantly. He could command a room. All things I wasn't. I so badly wanted him to change with me. I thought we needed him. People looked up to Konrad; they listened to his words. It's the way of the world, isn't it?"

Emma felt a crippling sadness flow through her veins, thick and slow, like syrup. She thought of Konrad, of the world that her daughter would face, of all the mistakes she'd made that had ruined lives.

"So, I pushed. But I never wanted violence. Clara, Ben, and I got stoned one night and cooked up a plan for a small explosive. It was all a hypothetical, a game, but Clara took it seriously. I wanted to harness her energy, channel it toward constructive projects. I was so wrong. By the time I figured it out, it was too late. I knew Clara Morel wanted more. I thought I could tone her down, manage the worst impulses, but I didn't have any control over her. I never did."

After Konrad died, Emma's guilt had been crippling. She blamed herself. For everything. When she'd left Toronto, it hadn't been to save herself but to keep others safe from her. She also wasn't sure who she could trust. Clara had been unpredictable, and Ben had been her lackey. She looked for a quiet life, at arm's length from the world, where she could protect herself and bury the impulses that had led to Konrad's death.

"I don't know how Konrad was there that night. I had no idea Clara was going through with it. I couldn't have told him where to go. Still, he loved me, and I betrayed that. And not a day has gone by since that I don't try to make better choices, to put others first, and to remember Konrad by being a better person than I was back then."

For the first time since Ben Chalmers had arrived at the cabin, Emma saw something beyond hurt in Jaden's body language. It was too hopeful to call it forgiveness, but perhaps, if Emma was lucky, there was some room for understanding.

"Then I met your father. A good person. Kind, caring, and incapable of falling into the world I'd left behind," Emma said. She smiled at the thought of Mark, the handsome goof who'd given her love when she'd thought that would never be possible for someone like her. Sharing the truth of who she'd been risked losing him. So, she disappeared into a new person and tried to forget the past. "In time, I came to an agreement with myself. And then you came along, and I realized that my greatest power was to raise you to be good and empathetic and engaged, just like your dad."

Jaden looked up at Emma then. A tsunami of pain racked her daughter's whole body, flooding her eyes with a regret Emma wasn't sure either of them would be able to survive.

"What about Ben? Was he a good person?" Jaden said.

How did you teach someone to move forward when they were responsible for a death, however justified? It marked you, like an invisible brand that cleaved the person who had existed before from who you were after. Emma wanted to tell her daughter that Ben Chalmers was a monster, that his actions were dangerous and ruinous. That he had been responsible for sending the music box, for putting Konrad in harm's way. That Jaden was right to let him die.

The truth would mark Jaden and collapse whatever bridges still existed between mother and daughter. Ben had stalked her little girl, followed her to the edge of civilization, and arrived by stealth to the cottage. How could she not see that as a threat?

Then again, Emma had been the one to bring the gun. Emma had been aggressive and threatening. She hadn't wanted to hurt him. All she wanted was to draw his attention to her, long enough for Jaden to get away and get help. But then Ben had lunged at her and managed to wrestle the gun out of her hands. Winnie had jumped on him, and the gun went off, a bullet catching Emma in the shoulder.

"I don't know," Emma said. She had no idea what had happened after she'd passed out. All she knew was that she and Jaden were alive, Ben was dead, and emergency services working nearby because of the ice storm had been called to her location. One thought kept twisting in her mind—Ben was the only one who could have called 911.

And it had probably saved her life.

There was no black and white in life. Gray was the permanent color of our days, but if we were lucky, we could fill the space with bright splashes of love and family and friendship.

In the end, all we could do was strive to walk with the better angels.

"But," Emma said and saw Jaden look to her with an entreaty. "I believe with everything I have that Ben Chalmers was not going to let us leave there alive." The lie was a wound to her soul, one she would live with to protect her daughter.

Perhaps it could be possible for Jaden to find her own path to forgiveness.

Jaden's face crumpled at the words. She collapsed onto herself like a rag doll abandoned by a careless child. In a flash, Emma saw every single person Jaden had been: the giggly infant reaching for her hand, the ambling toddler with sticky fingers and endless questions, the contrary teen with big dreams and an easy laugh, and finally, the brave, terrified, and brilliant young woman in front of her now who strove to be the person Emma saw every single day.

Emma opened her arms wide. "Come here, honey," she said.

Jaden stumbled into her mother's arms. Both women clung fiercely to each other in a world that had the potential to tear them apart. Beyond, Emma heard the noises of a small hospital—quiet conversations, restrained laughter, the rattle of a cart on linoleum—as the world continued on its slow, relentless pace forward.

"It's OK," Emma said, smoothing her daughter's hair and breathing in the familiar smell of her. "Everything's going to be OK. I've got you."

Finale

Vengeance was more bitter tasting than she'd expected. Or perhaps it was just the oversteeped tea she'd been sipping for the last hour while she read and reread the news articles online.

Clara Morel sat within the boiled-cabbage smell of her tumbledown Toronto apartment, a tablet propped up in front of her like a shrine. The tea had long gone cold, but she stayed, savoring the column inches devoted to ruin and retribution.

"CSIS agent dies in personal obsession." She whispered the words, letting their sweetness wash away the bitter tea.

The national coverage of the incident was disappointingly fleeting. Only a single day's worth before the twenty-four-hour news cycle took over. Canadians were more obsessed with other prosaic concerns, like the launch of a women's professional hockey league or ongoing wars in Ukraine and the Middle East. Clara didn't care. She hadn't wanted the world to know about her revenge, only those who mattered.

Twenty years Clara had sat in prison, thanks to those ungrateful traitors. Sure, the original eight years had stretched out, courtesy of some sideline activities that had been uncovered, but she would have never been in jail in the first place if Ben Chalmers hadn't made a statement to the police, gaining his freedom by eliminating hers. He hadn't appeared at the trial, but she'd seen his affidavit through discovery. He'd admitted that a version of the explosive device had been kept at his apartment but that Clara, and only Clara, had been responsible for building an explosive device and placing the car outside the laboratory.

Instantly, her leverage and credibility were obliterated. Not once did he mention his precious Grace.

It didn't go exactly as anticipated, but then again, nothing ever does in life. Prison had taught her that. She'd wanted them to suffer, of course, wanted them to destroy each other in fits of fear and paranoia. But Clara hadn't expected them to extinguish each other so completely. She couldn't decide whether this was a pleasure or a regret.

It had been tedious, but not difficult, to find them again. She'd had some access to the internet during her day paroles over the last year, and the information was laid out like golden pebbles on a gravel path. Grace had changed her name, perhaps unaware that every name change in the province was published in The Ontario Gazette. *Clara had gone day by day through the legislative notices until the name Grace Hobbes popped up along with the location and date of the change. Once she knew it was in White Falls, social media had done the rest. Not that Grace had any social media presence, but there were always threads. Ben had been easier. He'd spoken at intelligence conferences, and his wife had an active social media profile, with photos of him and the kids splashed across her page.*

Clara hadn't understood the taste of true satisfaction until she'd learned that Ben had drowned. She lay on the bed in her tiny wallpaper-peeling bedroom and imagined what it must have felt like to slip under the surface of the frigid water, dark cold pressing down on your limbs and chest, saturated clothing pulling and clawing at your body, stiffening muscles and robbing you of air, until death grinned down on you like a tormented lover.

It had taken months for Clara to get her hands on the police-report details and fully understand the wheels she'd set in motion. A little late-night hacking when she was finally released and she had the complete report. The music box Clara had sent to Grace had been a linchpin. Once Clara had shoved it into place, Ben and Grace had been pulled into its orbit.

According to the report, Emma told the police that Ben had sent her the music box as a threat and then stalked her daughter to settle old scores. She never mentioned Clara or her past role with Militant Animals—other than as a reference to their time together as students and the events around Konrad's death.

No one figured out that the box had been dropped off at the Meadows house by a former inmate of the Cedar Ridge Women's Correctional Facility who had been a roommate of Clara's for a number of years. They all assumed Ben had been the mystery postman. It was enough to make Clara laugh out loud.

There was some disappointment. Clara hadn't been there to watch them self-destruct. She liked to imagine what it must have been like, both of them blaming the other for Konrad's death, for the music box, neither sure whether they could trust their own thoughts. She doubted they would have worked out who had actually been responsible for sending Konrad out that night.

Clara had found Konrad where he always was, in the law-library reading room, sitting at the far end of a long table, while a black-night window rose beside him. He spent his evenings hiding in work. She'd approached gingerly, not wanting to pierce the quiet of the space and startle him.

He hadn't been around much since the breakup with Grace. None of the Militant Animal members noticed. Konrad had been slipping away for months, his absence at meetings the norm, but still he refused to relinquish leadership. Clara was surprised by the shadow of a thickening beard on his face and the doughy sluff of his features. He looked less like a leader and more like every other frazzled law student, a flock of birds on an electric wire.

She'd prepared herself for this meeting. Slipping into the bathroom, she'd stared unblinking into the mirror until her eyes shone and tears bloomed down her cheeks. She took shallow breaths, tricking her body into believing that danger was near. By the time she was standing beside Konrad, she had almost convinced herself something was terribly wrong.

"Konrad." She let her voice weaken.

He looked up, and she watched a parade across his face: confusion, recognition, concern, and finally alarm.

"Clara? What is it? What's happened?"

It was like telling a tale to a child. He lapped it up without question.

"Grace," she said, pleased with her shaky whisper. "I think she's in trouble."

She told Konrad a semblance of the truth. The details were accurate; only the characters had changed. A car, a lab, and a device meant to get attention.

"I think she and Ben went ahead with it. The stupid, silly plan. The explosive that we talked about a few weeks ago when we were stoned. Jesus, Konrad," she said. "I think it's happening tonight."

His mahogany features blanched. He was standing now, staring down at her, questions on his lips.

"Where?"

"I'll show you," Clara said. "We have to stop them."

The Toronto heat clung to Clara's skin as they approached VitaCore Laboratories. Not even the leaves on the stumpy trees rustled. The parking lot was largely empty, though the car didn't look out of place on the industrial street lined with large boxlike buildings. She knew it was impossible; still Clara heard a sound like a ticking as of clock.

Ticktock, ticktock.

"There, it's that one," Clara said, pointing to the old junker she'd bought off a newspaper ad for 250 bucks. It had barely made it the ten kilometers to this spot; she doubted it would ever leave again.

In truth, it had never been Clara's intention to hurt anyone. She just needed to show Konrad and the Militant Animals members what real leadership looked like. She'd done the calculations. Change required sacrifice and real risk. Konrad would never bring them to the place they needed to be, and she needed this group to get noticed if it was going to serve her own ambitions.

Konrad told her to stand back. He opened the driver's side door slowly. Clara wasn't scared. She needed to make it look real, but she was sure the affixed timer wouldn't go off. She'd studied the plans, set the equation.

She'd already called the cops, warning them that Konrad Sharma had planted a bomb in front of VitaCore. She'd be gone by the time they arrived, of course, and Konrad would be found here, his prints on the car and device. She'd be a hero, Konrad would fall, and she'd take her rightful place.

And then it all went wrong.

The next thing Clara knew, she had the taste of metal and burnt flesh in her mouth, and cold, hard concrete kissing her cheek.

The cops came for her a week after Konrad's funeral.

Clara looked to where a trickle of sunlight muscled its way through the grime-smeared window of the rooming house kitchen.

As far as the internet knew, Emma and Jaden Meadows went back to the dreary lives they'd had before Ben Chalmers had plowed into them. Clara felt a smile pull at her lips. Improbably, she shivered with a frisson of pride at the backwoods wasteland that Emma had withered away in all these years. It wasn't exactly a prison, but it was pretty close.

She rose from the table, leaving behind the cold tea and cheerless kitchen.

The sun was shining outside. And a chapter had finally closed.

Clara opened the front door. Stepping into an autumn morning. Sunlight fell on her skin. She heard the chatter of unseen chickadees. Smelled freshly mowed grass. She walked down the rickety steps of the split-up Victorian that had served as her temporary home and never once looked back.

Epilogue

Jaden stared out the window of the squat four-story building, perplexed by the horizon. Her eyes were greeted by a smooth field of green as far as she could see, bleeding upward into a cloud-scattered sky. There were no skyscrapers blocking the ends of the earth, no snarled traffic below, no gray, spiky skyline. The University of Manitoba campus sat along a snaking curve of the Red River at the southern end of Winnipeg, beyond which lay nothing but open prairie.

She hadn't gone back to Toronto in the new year. She couldn't. Nightmares clung to her even in the waking hours—a black nothing swallowing her whole and Ben Chalmers's sad smile just before he slipped under. Counseling helped, but she still woke in the middle of the night sweating with cold and wandering the house for hours. How did you move forward when you caused a death? Justified or not, Jaden had been responsible for a man's end. She would have to find a way to live with that.

The OPP had been quick to close the case of Ben Chalmers. Jaden suspected it had a little to do with the blue wall of silence and an unwillingness to cause more pain than needed to the family of a law enforcement brother. She couldn't imagine the hurt his wife and children were enduring. Even with everything that had happened, Jaden still walked away with her family intact. Ben's family lost a husband, a father. Even the memory of the man they'd known had been ripped away with the story her mom had told the police. Jaden didn't blame her mother, not entirely, but she needed space.

She'd expected an argument from her mom when she told her parents she wanted to transfer to an out-of-province school in September, but things had changed. Her mom, usually overbearing and protective, had nodded and squeezed Jaden's shoulder, an unspoken understanding passing between them.

Her dad, however, had been fiercely opposed. His failure to learn about his wife's past, to protect his little girl, to protect his family, haunted him. Every time Jaden left the house, he needed to know where she was going, who she was seeing, when she'd be home. And if she was late, the texts were endless. Jaden understood why and tried to honor his concerns, but it was like being an adult trapped in the life of a twelve-year-old. A little distance was needed to reset before patterns became entrenched and the future they all desperately needed was too far removed from who they'd become.

The compromise had been Winnipeg, her mother's hometown. Still only a long day's drive from White Falls but far enough to give Jaden the space she needed. The prairie city, with its low buildings and wide-open sky, gave her room to breathe. She spent most evenings on the balcony of her apartment watching the sun crawl toward day's end, until it lit up the horizon like lava. The locals called it prairie fire; Jaden liked the word and wrapped it around her mind like a balm. It wasn't home, and she didn't think it ever would be, but it was a place for her, for now.

In between classes and a part-time job at a mom-and-pop diner, Jaden thought about the endless circle of a single life. Her mom had traveled into the northern Ontario woods to break out of the orbit she'd found herself in, only to be drawn back in through her daughter. Jaden, unwittingly, had done the same, leaving behind what she'd always known to find a place beyond the revolutions she'd been unwittingly handed. Was it possible to break out of the trajectory you'd inherited? To live a life you claimed as your own?

She didn't think so, and meeting Max had confirmed that for her.

Max started as the friendly guy she'd sat beside in one of her seminar classes. He was kind and smart and just goofy enough to be interesting. He'd spoken to her heart in a way she didn't think was possible again. When Jaden learned that his mother had gone to high school with her mom, she'd laughed hysterically at the universe's sick sense of humor.

Max's mom was Jessica Lee, and she had stories about a woman named Grace Hobbes. Jaden had spent an evening in her home, tears of laughter streaming from her eyes as story after story spooled out about her mom's younger life. Snow races on cafeteria trays, midnight skinny-dipping at cottages, even a road trip across the border to North Dakota—all things that would have horrified Emma Meadows.

"Before her parents died, your mother was fearless," Jessica said one night over after-dinner tea and a stack of old yearbooks and photos. "See, look at this one. Voted most likely to change the world or die trying."

On the table in front of them was a photo of a too-young version of her mom, long hair flying behind her and an irrepressible mischievous grin aimed at the camera. She stood at the top of a snowy hill, launching what looked like a human logroll race, bodies poised before the descent.

"Believe it or not, your mom accidently rolled under a running car that day. Scared the hell out of me," Jessica said, her eyes smiling into a past that Jaden could never fathom.

Jaden gathered these glimpses of her mother like shells off an endless beach. Each one was precious, yet only a small part of the ocean. She collected them, listening until the echo of the roiling past hummed softly in her ear. Maybe some day, she'd ask her mom about them.

Jaden didn't know whether she would fully reconcile with her mother. Much depended, she supposed, on her own healing and her capacity to forgive. She would try, though. The biggest lesson she'd taken away from all of this was that denying yourself forgiveness could lead down an irredeemable and vicious path. She had no desire to gift the same to her own children. No matter the circumstances, she vowed that the people in her life would know everything about her own past. The truth, she realized, was a legacy unto itself. Those we love deserved to know what shaped us and how to navigate the darker corners of our histories.

Jaden hadn't found happiness. Not yet. She had a long way to go before she arrived at that moment. But she could say she'd found contentment. And for now, that would have to be enough.

Acknowledgments

Any acknowledgments must be anchored with my undying gratitude to my incredible agent, Lori Galvin, at Aevitas Creative Management. Her gentle and thoughtful guidance has saved me from my worst impulses and made every aspect of the publishing experience better.

This book only exists because of the talented and dynamic team at Thomas & Mercer. My senior editor, Liz Pearsons, has believed in me from the beginning, and I am eternally grateful for her unending patience. My development editor, Charlotte Herscher, is a wonder. Her thoughtful and unbelievably spot-on suggestions and edits have made this book so much more. The copyediting team—Liz Gluck, Alicia Lea, and Jenna Justice. I have no idea how they do it. Their talents are undeniable. And last, though never least, the graphic designer, Lisa Amoroso, who took my vague thoughts and turned them into magic.

I have the true privilege to call several unbelievable writers who I admire my friends. The list is long, but some of you helped shape this book or helped once again save me from myself: Suha Mardelli, Alexis MacIsaac, Jennifer Chevalier, and Lisa MacDonald, your insights, talent, and always-firm support have been indescribably perfect.

Writing, though a lone activity, is not a solo sport. I am eternally grateful for the love and support of friends whose empathy and constant humor are indelible and irreplaceable. A few of you have suffered through two books with me now. Jan Heneberry, Lauren Humpreys, Amy Plint, and Laura Pitcairn, you have held me up, pushed me gently forward, and been a shoulder whenever I needed it. Your mark is not only on this book but on my life, and I am forever grateful.

To those friends not explicitly named, don't take the absence of special mention as an absence of you in my heart. You know who you are, and you are all freaking amazing. My life would be poorer without each and every one of you.

My parents, Pat and Barry Miller; my brothers, Brahm and Tristan Miller; in so many ways I would not be the writer I am without you. My fantabulous nieces, Sadie, Rowyn, Briella, and Rémi, you astound me. You push me to be better just by being you.

To my in-law clan, Obaachan, Ojiichan, Kenji, Aya, Miya, Martin, Miyo, Kai, and Mika, thank you for letting me be part of your lives and for never once questioning this weird idea I had to become a writer.

My ThrillerFest queens—Kathleen Gwozdz, Pamela Guggina, and Liz Stroud—you are awesome. You gave me the boost I needed at the perfect time to make this book happen. Love you all and can't wait for next year and to follow your writer journeys.

To the extent that writers have muses, there are two that drive most of my writing: a fascination with the beautiful, messy, complicated, and serene bonds that connect family and an admiration of the breathtaking landscapes along with the complicated history and culture of Canada. Much of my writing is an ode to the strength, drama, and resilience of this strange, beautiful, flawed but astounding land. Times are tough right now, and some would seek to tear us down, but our strength is undeniable.

And last but the most important: Kohji, Kiyomi, and Ren—you are everything and always will be.

About the Author

Photo © 2023 Derrick Rice, Union Eleven Photographers

Born in Winnipeg, Manitoba, Tamara L. Miller earned her PhD in Canadian history before embarking on a career working for the federal government. Starting out as a doe-eyed policy analyst, she eventually moved into an executive role with the Government of Canada. She later left public service, older and perhaps a little wiser, to become a writer. Her debut novel, *Into the Fall*, was published in 2025. Tamara is a past president of Ottawa Independent Writers and has written several articles published online by the likes of the Canadian Broadcasting Corporation (CBC) and *Ottawa Life Magazine*.

Over the years, the author has called many Canadian cities home but now lives in Ottawa with her family and two long-suffering cats. She's always been fascinated by the raw beauty of the wilder places in the world and escapes to them whenever possible.